Bloodstone Island

Bloodstone Island

A Caper

William Jordan

Library of Congress Control Number: 2014919560
ISBN: Hardcover 978-1-5035-1110-1
Softcover 978-1-5035-1111-8
eBook 978-1-5035-1112-5

This is a work of fiction. Names, characters, places and incidents either are the product of the author's imagination or are used fictitiously, and any resemblance to any actual persons, living or dead, events, or locales is entirely coincidental.

This book was printed in the United States of America.

Rev. date: 10/30/2014

To order additional copies of this book, contact:
Xlibris
1-888-795-4274
www.Xlibris.com
Orders@Xlibris.com
671715

Contents

For my wife
Wendy
and
Our three children
Douglas, Caryn, and Brian.

1948

Chapter 1

"The Envelope, Please"

Life at Brookside Country Club had almost returned to normal. The same held true for the small resort town of Livermore Falls in upstate New York as the community and the club resolved their severe differences. Old chums Sydney Wadsworth and Toby Worthington could once again savor their favorite pastime, golf. Returning to their home course, victorious over their last misadventure, they basked in the early afternoon sun on the greensward near the club pond. Like two old bulls put out to pasture, they rested contentedly in their Adirondack chairs, while muttering about recent events and how, after some scratches and bruises, their recuperative powers were not what they used to be. Because of their heroic efforts, the august Brookside Country Club had been saved for at least another generation, and now a measure of peace and stability prevailed throughout the club.

The club manager, Sandy Cummings, knew that tranquility at Brookside would be short-lived. In less than two weeks, Governor Dewey would be arriving at the club for an important election speech in his campaign for the presidency. Ostensibly, the venue was arranged to recognize Sydney and Toby as citizen crime fighters.

The *Livermore Falls Journal* reported that:

> *Having broken up a major crime syndicate that spirited criminals in and out of Canada, Governor Thomas E. Dewey*

ordered a special commemorative medal struck to mark their recent accomplishment.

Following the governor's appearance at the start of play for the Wadsworth Cup at Brookside CC, he will present the medals personally in a ceremony on Saturday the twenty-third at 1:30 p.m. on the Livermore Falls village green. Following the ceremony, the governor will give a speech on how citizens and government can work together in fighting crime.

In the past, Sydney featured himself as something more than a financial supporter of the governor and welcomed his visit to the club, whereas Toby felt the drop-in was an intrusion on his privacy. Toby resented the fact that the governor invited himself to shoot his ceremonial cannon to start play for the Wadsworth Cup. Perched atop the clubhouse, everyone knew that only Toby fired it on special occasions. Governor Dewey had wisely timed his arrival with the start of the state's foremost amateur golf tournament. Up until now, Toby had never granted the privilege of firing his cannon to anyone, not even to those of celebrity status. Soon, a trust between Toby and his cannon would be violated, and the thought irked him to no end.

Daydreaming, Toby's thoughts were interrupted by the vision of a young lady descending the stairs from the club veranda. When she reached the bottom, she turned in his direction to cross the lawn. Even from the distance of a full 9-iron shot, he recognized the evocative stride of Simone, Baron Louis d'Chard's former ward and personal assistant. French, she walked as if all her supple moving parts were summoned upon simultaneously. Several wives in the club objected to Simone being hired for a new position at the club's front desk, no doubt because of her youthful and suggestive mannerisms. The male-chaired House Committee was not sympathetic to their objections other than agreeing to provide her with a larger-sized skirt and blazer.

Bending down, Simone delivered a note to Toby that Harriet Bartholomew had left an urgent call for him. From the comfort of his chair, Toby glanced over at Sydney and noticed that he seemed to be busy at one of his favorite pastimes, dozing. He decided not to disturb Sydney in the event he might have to disclose the nature of why he was about to leave, remembering that anytime the subject of Harriet came up, there was sure to be a row.

Physically, he still ached from his recent experience surrounding the death of Harriet's third husband, Jeffrey. With the help of his 7-iron to lean on and a tug from Simone, Toby rose from his chair and followed her back to the clubhouse, doing his best to keep up. He wondered, *What in the devil does the old trout want now? Good grief, maybe she's discovered Jeffrey's loot in the steamer trunk. No, she'd keep that a secret. Only Sydney, the chaplain, and I know he wanted it to go into a caddie fund. God, help us if she's bartered the trunk and Jeffrey's belongings to some junk dealer.*

At the front desk, Toby caught his breath and dialed Harriet's number.

"Hello," chirped Harriet, sweetly as a songbird, expecting it to be Toby. "To whom do I have the pleasure of speaking?"

"It's me, Toby Worthington. You called?"

"Oh, Toby, you dear boy. How good it is to hear your voice again. We've been through so much together recently, with Jeffrey's death and all. We should talk soon, don't you agree? I wondered if I could impose on your good nature to come to tea this afternoon."

"There's nothing terribly urgent on my calendar, but there is one problem. My Oldsmobile is in an upstate repair shop, so I'm afraid you'll have to collect me from here."

"Oh, I'm so sorry for you, Toby. And I can't help either. My beautiful Lincoln's been impounded by Bebee, that idiotic police chief of ours. Hit and run, he claimed, when it's entirely his fault for parking too close to me at the club."

"Beebe can be impossible, but don't worry, Harriet. I'll have a staff member drop me off and take me home later. Did you say four-ish?"

"No, but your suggestion is perfect! It's almost that time now, so why don't you come along as soon as you can? Ta-ta."

Toby asked Simone to fetch the club's station wagon, affectionately called Woody, and drive him to Harriet's. While waiting to be picked up, he contemplated his meeting with Harriet and the consequences of leaving Sydney out of the loop. Still, by taking action on his own, he found that he was rather pleased with himself; even though this could be another one of Harriet's well-conceived traps. He thought, *Maybe I have a weakness for traps, but no worries, this old fox is not going to be trumped by the likes of her. At least not again, not this time, old girl. Sydney will just have to sit this episode out until I find out what's what.*

* * *

Toby rang the door chimes at Harriet's and was greeted once again with the same familiar strains of Danny Boy. Simone, acknowledging Toby's wave of dismissal, drove back to Brookside. He was not prepared for his first sight of Harriet, who answered the door in a fluffy peignoir replete with a pink-feathered collar. Rhinestone slippers completed her ensemble. She pushed her tousled hair back with one hand and with the other swung the door wide to reveal her full form.

"Oh, Toby, you got here so quickly I didn't have time to change. Come right in. This is Madeline's day off, so you'll have to excuse the wretched mess everything's in."

"Of course, Harriet, no need to explain." With a little trepidation, he reluctantly stepped over the threshold. He observed that her manner was more common than usual and that her less-than-genuine smile belied the stress of her husband's violent death only days earlier. As he parked his companion golf club into the umbrella stand, he noticed that all of Jeffrey's belonging sent from the Stoney Creek Fish and Game Club remained piled in the foyer. The steamer trunk immediately caught his eye, and he wondered what possible form of deception he could use to separate her from it. Again, he pondered if she had even opened it. *Not very likely*, he thought.

Harriet took notice of his interest and decided to distract Toby rather than follow up on his curiosity with the old steamer. "If you don't mind, Toby, I'd rather skip the tea. I was going to suggest a scotch instead when you arrived."

"By all means, Harriet. Just a pinch now, lots of ice."

"Follow me, Toby dear," she purred, her steps resounded with the scuff of her slippers, leading him down the long tile hallway to the conservatory. Harriet's flimsy attire gave way to her Rubenesque figure, and once her buttocks were set in motion, it conjured up in Toby's mind the vision of two bear cubs scuffling in a gunnysack.

Toby stopped at the entrance to the conservatory, while Harriet detoured to an alcove with its built-in bar. He decided to take the initiative by inquiring, "Tell me, Harriet, there must be something quite troubling for you to ring me up?"

"Oh yes, Toby." At the bar sink, she hesitated a moment and poured an extra splash of scotch in his glass. "You're probably the only person I know that can help me now, the only one I can really trust. And, dear Toby, that includes an army of inadequate so-called attorneys and estate planners."

Toby shot back, "I appreciate your vote of confidence, but I'm not sure why you think I have the expertise you need. Beyond crossword puzzles, I'm afraid I'm quite useless."

"Nonsense. You can't fool me," Harriet scolded. Her hands were trembling, and the ice rattled against the two glasses of scotch she brought into the conservatory. She placed them on a glass coffee table in front of a cushion-laden wicker sofa and scrunched down into the far end like one who intended to stay for a while. Placing an overstuffed pillow in her lap, she patted it lightly with one hand and said, "Won't you come over here now and sit down, Toby?"

Toby selected the far end of the sofa from Harriet and reached for his glass of scotch. The first burning sip that reached the back of his throat seemed to put him at ease. "Now then, Harriet, what is it that has you so worried?"

She clutched at her glass-bead necklace and twisted it nervously back and forth. "I don't suppose you ever met my second husband Terry Hadley? Terrance Dudley Hadley. You might have known him as a member of the club years ago. He had a very painful illness and wasn't able to get out to the club very often."

"Yes, I do seem to recall Terry. A stomach ailment, I believe the paper said. Never really found out what was the cause? Strange, he being a doctor, as it were."

"Good, Toby, I see you do remember. Duckie was a fine surgeon in his day, but he would never consult another doctor to remedy anything. Pride, I suppose, who knows? Of course, back then, he was of such an age he could have died from a bad chill. Sounds cold of me, but it's true. Of course, there was big a difference in our ages, but that didn't seem to matter at the time. He needed someone young and strong like myself, someone attractive that reminded him of his first wife who could fix his pillows and make him laugh." Reaching for her glass, she changed course and said, "Well, look at you. With all my carrying on, you've finished your scotch." Harriet got up and took both their glasses to the bar. "Let me fix you another?"

"Now, just make it a short one, Harriet," pleaded Toby, raising his voice to reach her in the alcove. He winced at how blunt she was when speaking of her former husband. Longing to light his pipe, he remembered how she ranted about his smoking in the club boardroom. He thought, *Perhaps if I just held the pipe in my hand, she wouldn't mind, and I would feel more comfortable in her presence.* He called out to her again, "It's not too much to assume that my visit is linked somehow to Terry, is it?"

"You're so right, and I hope you're still interested in helping me. Yes?" She feigned a laugh. "I'd up and die if you weren't going to. While you're sitting there with nothing to do, why don't you open the large manila envelope on the coffee table? The one on top. The source of my predicament is inside."

Toby fumbled with the plain yellow envelope. Unsealed, he bent the metal clasp back and removed the contents. "I've got it, Harriet. Hmmm . . . bunch of legal documents. No problem if your need my signature on something, is that it?"

"Oh, Toby, if it were only that simple," said Harriet, returning to her spot on the sofa. "The papers on top are copies of a deed to a property in Maine. Duckie owned it before we were married. By the way, everyone called him Duckie. Of course, the island is rightfully mine by virtue of his will. Unfortunately, it's been held in trust ever since my *sweetie pie* passed away. Let's see, that was '38. We'd only been married three years. Oh, how he loved to call me his little *cupcake*." She whipped a tissue out of her housecoat pocket and dabbed her eyes.

Quickly regaining her composure and back on message again, she said, "And according to the trust, would you believe I have to meet certain conditions in order to inherit? I've had ten years to comply, and now I'm at the end of my tether, so to speak."

"How extraordinary," said Toby, taking her hand. "Try not to upset yourself, Harriet. Surely things will work out. Still, I can't imagine how I could possibly fit into the picture."

Pulling herself together and taking a healthy swallow of scotch, she continued. "It's really quite simple, and I'll explain everything, I promise. And why don't you light your pipe before you strangle that poor thing to death?"

"That's kind of you, Harriet, and I must say you have my full attention." He thought, *If she allows me to smoke, the old bird has either gone daffy or she'll do or say anything to sway me. I don't know what it is, but there's a dark side to her. Oh hell, it couldn't hurt to find out what kind of help she really wants.* "Could you start by filling me in on the property?"

"I suppose that's as good a place as any." Harriet cleared her throat with another sip of scotch. "The property is an island off the coast of Maine. Part of an archipelago, actually. It's been in Duckie's family for an age. A few hundred acres, I believe. Woods and rocks mostly. I think it was about 1890 when his father built an enormous summer home overlooking one of the sheltered coves on the west side of the island. Twenty rooms, I think, and almost as many fireplaces."

She turned from Toby to gaze deep into the bottom of her glass as if she were seeking an image in a crystal ball. "On a good day, you could make out every house on the coastline. Of course, our island could only be reached by boat back then. I recall there was a short dock on piling stretching out from a sandy beach. On one side, a float moved up and down with the tide. It had to be hauled out for the winter. Heavy seas, as you can imagine. But of course, you understand all these things."

Harriet gently withdrew her hand from Toby's and rose to her feet. She began pacing back and forth, with an occasional off-course weave through the tall fichus trees and plantings in the conservatory. In front of Toby, she stopped to stare at the ceiling, looking as though she was trying to encapsulate her thoughts or finding just the right word. Toby's eyes followed her every movement, noting that her demeanor seemed much too theatrical for his liking.

Suddenly, Harriet plunged down next to Toby, smiling as if she had remembered her lines in a play. "Now where was I? Oh yes, the Portland Packet still runs up and down the coast, calling on villages and island people. And then there's the mail boat if they still do that sort of thing. If the old dock is still in repair, I suppose one of those funny-looking floatplanes could tie up there.

"The trust has money for fixing the docks and routine maintenance. They evidently pay the taxes, utility bills, and a healthy sum to some lackey administrator who probably never went out to the island, Humphrey somebody. Oh, Toby, now you've hardly touched your scotch. I do hope this isn't boring you."

"Indeed not, Harriet, quite fascinating actually." He hoisted his glass, draining its contents, and scrubbed his mustache with his never-to-be-used handkerchief. "Do continue."

"Well, Duckie's guests would arrive by boat for a weekend or even weeks at a time. I remember it took a staff of eight to run the place, and they lived in cabins up behind the residence. Duckie had a full-time caretaker, Walt somebody—as I recall, a real nutcase—a widower with a young son. When we closed the place up for the winter, there would only be the two of them left on the island. I have no idea what happened to them after Duckie died and the house was boarded up.

Anyway, after he inherited the island from his father, he retired early and spent several summers there with his two great loves, partying and fishing. One of the guests told me that he loved to run back and forth to the coast in his "launch" for provisions. That, or for any other excuse, he could dream up. It was quite seaworthy with a wide beam and long open deck aft ideal for fishing parties. Our house cook always had tons of fresh fish on-hand, which included a lot of repulsive species too ugly to describe. Thank God our Cookie fed most of it to the gulls. Walt's side job was to scrub all the fish stink off the deck. Enough of that."

She tucked her hand just behind Toby's his right ear. Her tone turned serious. "Long before I entered the picture, an incredible tragedy occurred when his wife Marsha accidentally drowned, swimming off shore. The paper reported that she and her husband were out on their boat, drifting with the tide, when it happened. In calm seas, he had gone below for a nap, and when he returned topside, she was gone, a book lay open on her deck chair. As I said, that happened before I met Duckie, and one of his closest friends told me that he'd become reclusive ever since she died." Harriet paused then in a whisper said, "Most everyone thought his withdrawal was the result of blaming himself for the accident. A few, I'm told, who knew his wife Marsha to be a strong swimmer, weren't quite so generous with their assessment, if you take my meaning."

Harriet's mood flitted back and forth as it was in her nature to turn easily from one subject to another; from being serious to being flighty. "You know when I first met Duckie on the island, he was still nurturing the same old boat. He specialized in internal medicine. Guess what he christened it? The *Blood Vessel*."

Toby chuckled politely. He discretely checked the time and looked for an opening to take his leave before he got in over his waders. "A man of good humor, I take it."

"Early on perhaps, but he was rather reticent during our short time together. He had a long illness, and it sapped his strength. As you may recall, we spent his last two years at Brookside and never set foot on the *Blood Vessel* again or return to our island Shangri-La." Harriet walked her fingers down from behind Toby's ear across his lapel and onto his knee where her hand came to rest.

Toby pretended not to notice her flirtation. "Excuse me for interrupting, Harriet." Toby tapped his pipe against the glass ashtray on the coffee table. "I'm curious. All very interesting, don't you know, but since we're discussing names, what in the devil did you call this island of yours?"

"Well, the meat of the coconut is that when explorers discovered this chain of six islands, they considered them to be gems, but not prized enough in the sense of diamonds and rubies. So they were named after semiprecious stones. For no particular reason, Duckie's father purchased the one called Bloodstone Island. I can't imagine why, but people on the coast just call it Blood Island."

The name of the island sent a momentary chill up Toby's nape, and if his feet could speak, they would have urged him to leave. "Toby, aren't you at least curious what's in the other envelope? I think you should be."

"Of course, I am, Harriet. Now that I know the lay of the 'island,' so to speak." His attempt at a witticism went unnoticed.

"Well, as I started to tell you, Toby dear, there are conditions to my inheritance, and this is where I hope I can count on you. By now you must suspect that I have to travel to the island, and I couldn't possibly attempt it on my own, and you are the only man I can turn to." Her lips trembled. "You will take me, won't you?"

In the wake of appealing to his manhood, Toby was suddenly caught off guard for a plausible rebuff. "Well, well, I don't know . . . well."

Harriet deftly removed her hand from Toby's knee and pressed a finger against his lips. "Shush . . . now. Before you come to a hasty decision you may regret, I want you to think for a moment. This teensy weensy trip to Maine isn't just about me. I know you have a gentleman's sense of duty to women and to me as a member of the club, but you might think about yourself for once."

Quite taken aback, Toby said, "Whatever do you mean, Harriet?"

"I mean that you just might just enjoy yourself on a little adventure with me. When was the last time you were out of Sydney's clutches? Not that Sydney isn't your dear friend. You could use a little time in your life to call your own, even if it's only a couple of days. Yes?"

Toby stared across the room, trying to recall when he had last indulged himself. Drawing a blank, he sighed and reached for the envelope. "Now what all's in here?" He dumped the contents on the coffee table.

"Everything you need to know. First of all, Toby, we have to get to Bloodstone Island and back without the whole club knowing what we're doing."

"Exactly," he replied. "And I assume you have a scheme for keeping everything hush-hush?"

Having once again captured Toby's curiosity, she said, "You won't tell? No, of course, you wouldn't. We'll drive over to Port Henry on the coast. Then we'll catch the Portland Packet steamer to Bloodstone Island. Look here, I had the time tables sent to me."

"Harriet, in case you've forgotten, neither of us at the moment has a car to drive anywhere."

"Be patient with me, Toby. Let's pretend we're leaving before dawn tomorrow, after you've packed your bags, of course. Chief Bebee's got my Lincoln impounded on the vacant lot behind Field's grocery store, but, ha-ha, I have another set of keys." She seemed pleased with herself and continued to titter as she unfolded a mischievous plan. "I'll sneak into the lot, pick you up, and we'll drive out of town. That oaf Bebee will never miss it. After we return, I'll put my car back in the lot, and no one's bound to be the wiser. Such fun."

Toby mused at the thought of conning "Two Bullets" Bebee. Still, he imagined it only as a cut above a stunt by high school kids.

Harriet picked up one of the documents and pressed ahead with her plan by paraphrasing the contents. "One of the conditions in Terrance Hadley's will is that I shall have remarried. Another condition is that I have to prove to the trust that my husband and I actually went to Bloodstone Island and stayed there for at least twenty-four hours. What a silly wicked man my husband could be at times. Loved to fancy himself as a trickster." Her tone turned facetious. "Duckie, in one brief moment of generosity, gave me ten years to meet the terms or else."

"Or else what, Harriet?"

"Or else the island will be deeded over to his deranged son, which is highly unlikely. The next in line is the state of Maine."

Toby's tenor turned sympathetic. "How strange. What could have been his motive? I doubt if the state would want it. They would probably just auction it off to some local land baron." Befuddled, he inquired, "Why didn't you go there with Jeffrey when you had the chance to? I believe you were married to Jeffrey eight years before his—how shall we put it—his fishing accident a few days ago. If you'd gone with him during your married years, the property would be yours today."

Harriet's shoulders slumped, but only momentarily before she drew in a deep breath. "Because he refused, time after time. Jealous of Duckie? I don't know. I've learned, much too late, that not all men are like you, Toby."

Toby blushed.

Dabbing her eyes with a tissue, still moist with earlier tears, she said, "If Jeffrey hadn't died suddenly, this property would have slipped right through my fingers. Must be worth three or four million now." She sipped the last of her scotch, the ice bumping against the end of her nose. "I guess its value would be sufficient to shelter a widow like me."

"Indeed," said Toby. Shocked, his eyes blinked like a malfunctioning traffic signal. "But you need a husband before you set foot on Blood Island. Of course, I'm out of the running!"

"Now calm down, Toby. Don't get worked up. Under the circumstances, who else can I possibly turn to? At least you can hear me out." Harriet got up from the sofa and stood in front of Toby as if to block any sudden attempt of his to flee, a move she seemed to have anticipated. "Try to relax, Toby. Our marriage would only last three to four days at most." She paused to exclaim, "That's something of a record for me."

"I must say you astound me, Harriet. Well, go on."

As if to collect her thoughts, she traipsed around Toby, circling him like a cat about to pounce on its prey. She stopped behind Toby and leaned on the back of the sofa before she spoke to him over his shoulder. "There's a justice of the peace in Port Henry. I hope you don't think I'm presumptuous, but I've filled out the paperwork and made all the arrangements for our marriage. As soon as the knot's tied, we'll embark on the Portland Packet. Three or four days later, we'll be divorced, and you can be playing golf with Sydney again as if nothing happened."

"All very neat, Harriet. Suppose I do agree to go along with this caper, don't you think we should have some sort of written agreement?"

Harriet flinched. Her lips puckered up tight before she could answer Toby's unexpected question. "What did you have in mind?"

Toby stared straight ahead, cleared his throat, and announced, "For instance, I hope you don't expect me to carry you over a threshold or consummate the marriage for that matter."

"Certainly not." Harriet managed to stifle a guffaw and returned to the sofa. "I can't imagine you being anything but a perfect gentleman. Is that the extent of our agreement?"

"Yes, thank you, Harriet, except that I want a clear understanding that our marriage is annulled four days after we get our wedding license." Toby couldn't believe what he had just uttered. He pondered, *How in hell did I get hornswaggled into this misadventure? Sydney's bound to have a fit. What kind of explanation can I palm off on him? Only the truth about my stupid gullibility will do. Well, I can't go back on my word now.*

"We're agreed then," said Harriet. "Let's have a drink on it. We can work out the details later." Toby smiled weakly and nodded his head in agreement.

Harriet's demeanor definitely changed. She was perky now, and her steps were years livelier. But on her return trip from the bar, her slippers didn't keep pace with her feet, and she tripped on a raised tile. For a brief moment, Harriet was airborne before landing headfirst in Toby's lap, preceded by two tumblers of scotch. Toby muffled an obscenity, although Harriet managed to let one fly.

They both struggled to their feet, slipping on the wet tiles and ice cubes. Like two beginning skaters, they hung on to each other until they regained their balance.

"Oh, Toby, I'm so sorry. How clumsy of me."

Toby chose not to respond. He was wet from his knees up to his waist and tried to dry off by scrubbing himself with a throw pillow from the couch.

"Come now, Toby, you've got to get out of your pants. You can take them off in my bedroom. It's just down the hall."

"You can't be serious, Harriet."

"Of course, I am. You can hand your pants to me through the door, and I'll get them dried off for you." With some trepidation, they dripped their way, arm in arm to her bedroom.

Harriet opened the door and led Toby in until they were standing in front of her chaise lounge that was titivated by her scanty nightwear slung over the back. Toby's eyes fell on the overstuffed paisley upholstery. Behind him was Harriet's turned-down bed with its satin sheets and embroidered pillows scattered about. Dizzy, his head felt like the inside of a cocktail blender as he contemplated the consequences of either falling forward onto the chaise or backward onto the bed.

"Now, Toby, you hold still while I slip your jacket off. Don't you say a word. I'll hang it right over there on the back of my vanity chair." Concluding her short round trip, Harriet resumed undressing Toby. "You poor dear, Toby. Now after I get your vest off, I'll help you unbutton your braces. After all, I know how to do these things."

"Yes, yes, Harriet, thank you, but I think I can take over now."

"Are you sure? Do you think you can get your wet pants off over your shoes? They're soaked."

"Come to think of it, no. This is all so irregular. Perhaps it's best if I drop my pants to half-mast and sit on your bed, then you'll be able to pull my shoes off. If you don't mind, Harriet, I think it would be best if you closed your eyes before I drop my pants."

"What? Oh, of course, Toby. I should have guessed." Getting down on her knees, she said, "Before you drop your drawers, let me undo your laces while it's still OK for me to look."

"Thank you, Harriet. You're such a good sport. I'm sorry this little undertaking of ours is getting off to such a rocky start. Something to laugh about later, don't you know?"

"I don't think so, Toby." Her words were suddenly chiseled in ice. "I hoped you'd think of me as more than a good sport." When he dropped his pants down, Toby fell back on the bed without stopping at the sitting position. He lay there on his back, flapping his arms as if he were making a snow angel.

Grasping the side of the chaise, she rose up and heaved a sigh. "Now I'll leave you to your own devices, Toby. You're on your own." She scooted to her wardrobe room where she kicked off her wet bedroom slippers against the far wall. Donning a fresh pair, she returned, saying, "I'll be back in a couple of minutes to pick up your pants." Harriet trundled out of the room fuming, her peignoir clinging to wet spots. She slammed the door and headed for the laundry room to set up the ironing board and plug in the iron. Slipping on the wet tiles again, she cursed for having been so clumsy earlier.

Reclaiming her composure, she knocked on the bedroom door and elevated her voice, "Ready?" Toby opened the door just sufficiently enough to slide his trousers through on a hangar he found in her wardrobe closet. Forcing the door farther ajar, she peeked inside. "Thank you, Toby. And if we're to be married, you'll have to keep your garters on straight, if you take my meaning."

Right after she collected his pants, the front door chimed. "Toby's driver must be back and getting impatient," she groused. Answering the door, she was too startled to speak, and her first impulse was to slam the door shut and start over. "Why, Sydney, whatever brings you here?"

"Toby, of course. Simone at the club told me he might be here. By the way, Harriet, aren't those Toby's pants you're holding?"

Caught out, she stuttered, "Why, why, yes they are. You see, Toby got them wet, and I was going to dry them out when you arrived."

"I see," said Sydney, "and you, Harriet, appear to be a little damp yourself. Apparently, I've come at a bad time."

"Well, yes, and Toby is rather indisposed right now. Shall I have him call?"

"No, that won't be necessary, Harriet. I'll be on my way."

Chapter 2

A Wrong Turn

Sydney, dazed by his encounter with Harriet, could think about little else. He thought Toby had definitely crossed the line this time. Years of camaraderie through thick and thin, better than twenty, he recalled. On the drive back to the club, he muttered, "I never thought our friendship could be shattered by some gold-digging floozy like Harriet." For Sydney, the split in their friendship couldn't come at a worse time. The governor was showing up, especially to award them a medal. "How shall I explain it to the Gov that Toby was indisposed and had a previous engagement? Well, I guess this dices it. He's beyond any help I can give him now, even if I wanted to, and frankly I don't."

He brought the borrowed Brookside station wagon to a screeching stop under the club portico, got out, slammed the door, and marched into the foyer. Passing the front desk, he tossed the ignition keys on the unattended reception desk and reminded himself to make a dignified entrance into the main dining room.

I don't suppose anyone will be inviting me to join their table, Sydney thought. *No one does lately. Afraid most of my old mates have crossed the bar.* Still stunned from his encounter with Harriet, he reverted to one of his old habits before going down the long gallery to the dining room. He dropped his 7-iron into the umbrella stand and made a quick right turn into the men's restroom to freshen up.

Engrossed in thought, he failed to recognize that the interior had undergone significant changes, including the new dead-giveaway floral wallpaper and lace curtains. In search of the urinals, he circled around behind a mirrored wall with its white marble wainscot. Suddenly, he remembered that after the fire, the club directors decided to convert one of the three restrooms on the main floor into one for the ladies. In silence, Sydney sighed and stood motionless for a moment to reflect on his original design for the clubhouse, *Good God, how could I predict in 1926 that women would be taking over the restrooms at Brookside?* In disgust, he threw his hands straight up in the air and exclaimed, “That, along with everything else.”

The utter silence was shattered again when a flood of blathering females burst through the restroom door. Panicked, he could neither escape nor retrace his steps. Sydney realized immediately that to be discovered in the ladies restroom would be disastrous. The board would have no choice but to drum him out of the club he founded. *Holy jehosophat,* he thought, *they'll skewer me on the code of conduct, and I'm the one who wrote it?*

Not wishing to fall on his sword, Sydney fled into the far-end toilet stall and latched the door. He dropped the toilet seat and, with the alacrity of an arthritic house cat, crawled on top of the toilet lid so his pants and shoes could not be observed from the adjacent stall. His leather-soled wing tips skated frenetically on the lid until he secured a handgrip on top of the stall partition. Turning around carefully, he sat on top of the toilet tank and resolved to crouch there for however long it took until the ladies cleared out and he could manage a discrete escape.

He assumed that the afternoon ladies bridge club had decided to call it a day and converged in mass on the new women's restroom. Sydney had no affection for this card-playing wine-sipping group that was growing in popularity. Besides, he hated tattletales, and this group was the main conduit of club gossip. For some of their members, gossiping was more popular than competitive bridge. On his newfound perch, he assumed a relaxed posture suggestive of Rodan's Thinker, and although his first impulse was to plug his ears with toilet tissue, he decided instead to eavesdrop. Snooping of any kind was against his nature and a practice that he found repulsive, especially in others. However, the combination of curiosity, opportunity, and predicament temporarily overwhelmed his code of ethics.

Sydney discovered years ago that he had acquired the rare ability known as selective hearing. Perhaps in his younger years, as a practicing attorney, it proved advantageous to tune-in to all the conversations within earshot and choose the ones most pertinent to his interest at the time, not an easy task to master. To his way of thinking, he did not consider it eavesdropping, but that whatever he overheard was deemed analogous to a public information announcement on the radio. Although his hearing acumen had degenerated in recent years, he had no trouble overhearing a voice he recognized as Dr. Sanders's wife, Lucille.

"They've done a nice job decorating in here, haven't they, Margaret?" observed Lucille above the hubbub.

Margaret, recently seated in the stall next to Sydney, replied, "Oh yes, Lucy. I love these little purse shelves they've put in the stalls, don't you?"

"Yes, but isn't it nice that the men on the board finally got the message that we wanted a restroom on this floor? When that old poop, Wadsworth, built this place, I bet it never crossed that pea-sized brain of his to put a ladies room on the first floor."

Georgia giggled at Lucy's observation. "It didn't have to cross his mind. Sydney's a bachelor. He never had to negotiate in a bedroom. Not to brag, darling, but some of us are better at it than others." A knowing titter ran through the room that rushed to Sydney's burning ears.

"Now, Georgia, be nice," rebutted Phyllis. "You can't take all the credit just because your husband's on the board. So's mine."

Sydney curled up into a ball and thought, *So that's it, a god damn conspiracy.* Cringing, he bit his lip. Choking to catch his breath, Sydney unraveled his bow tie and draped it over the coat hook on the stall door.

"As ridiculous as it might seem," Phyllis continued, "that old poop Sydney and his pal Toby happen to be heroes or so it says in the paper, and Dewey thinks so too."

"Oh, p-u-l-e-a-s-e."

"Yes, but don't forget they stood up for the club when certain people I know were rushing to sell their memberships."

The sniping quelled, and as the bevy of bridge enthusiasts thinned out, Phyllis asked the remaining few, "By the way, where's

Harriett today? She said she'd come, even though it's only a few days after Jeffrey's—well, who would believe—an accident."

Margaret, still in her stall, quipped, "Well, it's her third husband, after all. I suppose she's developed some sort of immunity when it comes to grieving over their odd departures." Margaret flushed the tank.

Sydney flinched at the sound. Disgusted, he thought that Margaret's timing of the flush was intended to put a point on her remark, a metaphor for ridding oneself of miscreant husbands. After slamming her compartment door shut, Sydney could hear Margaret's heels clicking away from his location, apparently headed toward her friends that were still queued up at the sinks. Once there, she continued her diatribe against Harriet.

Straining to listen, Sydney heard her reveal, "I think Harriet's already onto her next paramour. According to my sources, she's been seeing something of Sydney's buddy-buddy, Toby Worthington. I wouldn't be surprised if they're together this afternoon, and I doubt if they're playing bridge." Another chortle roiled through the ladies room. "And I don't think he's up to rising for the occasion." Sydney bit his tongue to keep from lashing out in anger. Phyllis didn't like where the chatter was leading and shot back so everyone could hear, "Be careful now, Maggie dear. The walls have ears." She could be heard taking her leave, and shortly thereafter, a clatter of heels revealed that the remaining few had followed suit.

Several minutes passed before the restroom found the silence it had lost. But not until he was certain of his seclusion did he lower his cramped-up legs to the floor, one of which had gone to sleep and collapsed under him. Wobbly, he decided to take a whiz since it both seemed appropriate under the circumstances; and after all, it was the purpose of entering what used to be a gentleman's restroom.

Steadied now, he opened the compartment door a crack for a look-about. The exhaust fan drew a myriad of heavily perfumed odors past him along with those of disinfectants and cleaning agents, the combination of which was so repulsive that Sydney was about to become ill if he didn't escape to fresh air immediately. His sight lines clear, he tiptoed to the entrance door and put his ear to it. *Good*, he thought. *No voices in the hall, no footsteps. I might not get a better chance.* Sydney slipped out into the hall and recovered his golf club with the air of a composed gentleman. "Excellent," he sighed. *Simone must be away from the front desk. What luck. I could have run into diners. The early crowd should show up any time now.*

His pulse returning to normal, Sydney confidently strode off toward the dining room. Before entering, he made a customary stop at the mirror in the dining room foyer to adjust his tie. His jaw fell slack at the image staring back at him. "Merciful God Almighty!" he exclaimed.

"Something the matter, Mr. Wadsworth?" asked the hostess.

"Oh no. I just remembered something." Sydney struggled to pull his wits together. "I seem to have suddenly lost my appetite and won't be joining you tonight." He turned back toward the gallery and parted with, "Besides, I'm without a tie, and I wouldn't dream of asking you to break the dress code on my behalf."

He thought about how stupid he was to leave his tie in the ladies restroom. *There's no going back in there. Perhaps it'll get tossed out or at worst end up in lost and found. Whoever finds it probably won't even know what it is. Stop worrying. Get back to your quarters.*

Sydney spotted Simone still at work, busy tidying up the front desk to leave. He deftly approached, asking, "Simone, would you have a moment to take me up to the village and drop me off at my hotel?"

"Certainly, Mr. Wadsworth, if you don't mind my driving. I'm still a little clumsy learning how to shift the *Woody*."

"Nonsense, I would be much obliged. I hope it's not taking you from your duties."

"Not at all, monsieur," she responded with her lovely French accent. She took the keys from the reception desk drawer and proceeded toward the driveway, with Sydney in her wake. Simone slipped behind the wheel and pushed the seat back to accommodate her tall athletic frame. She reached seductively into the breast pocket of her club blazer and oozed, "Oh, Mr. Wadsworth, you may be pleased to know that I found a tie, and I thought it might belong to you, since I noticed you're not wearing one now. Isn't it the kind you wear, like the one you had on earlier today?" She turned the engine over and ground the station wagon into low gear. It stayed in first gear until she made a right turn out of the club onto Lookout Drive toward the village, whereupon she crunched "Woody" into second gear. "Well, what do you think?"

"About your driving or the tie? You're driving is fine, and the tie seems to be the right kind." Sydney feigned to inspect it and struggled for words as his brain went numb with the fear of not knowing where this conversation was going. "Of course, it could belong to one of the staff—busboys, waiters, janitors."

"Pardón, I don't think so. They wear those little—how you say—clippy ties?"

"Quite right, I, if anyone, should know." Sydney's skin began to crawl, knowing that somehow she believed the tie was his. *Maybe Simone spotted me coming out of the restroom,* he thought. *Relax. After all, it's her word against mine.*

He handed the tie back to Simone. "Of course, I have so many ties. I've given dozens away over the years, left them in hotel rooms, all over. It's hard to say where. I suggest you leave it in the club's Lost and Found and see what results."

"Very well, but aren't you at least interested to know where I found it?"

"Not really, absolutely nothing would surprise me these days."

Simone, nonplused, drove in silence until she had pulled the "Woody" up to a stop in front of the 1876 House. "Have a pleasant evening, Mr. Wadsworth, and sleep well." She smiled wryly.

"Thank you for the lift, Simone. Have a pleasant evening, and I do plan to sleep well." Gabriel, the doorman, greeted Sydney with his usual bright smile and snappy salute. On this occasion, Gabriel, noticing how drawn and pale Sydney looked, escorted him to the entrance and opened the heavy brass door.

Passing the front desk, Oscar, the oncoming night clerk, hailed Sydney. "Mr. Wadsworth, sir. There's an important message here for you."

"Well then, bring it here." Oscar circled from behind the counter to deliver a small plain envelope. A hastily handwritten *Sydney W.* was scrawled on the scented stationery.

"Thank you, Oscar. My apologies if I seem surly. Tisn't my nature, don't you know. This has been a trying day that doesn't want to end." Anxious for a bit of good news, he stepped into the parlor to tear the envelope open and read the note on the spot.

Sydney,

I'm sorry I walked off on you this morning, and you must believe that what you saw of Harriet and me this afternoon isn't what you think. I want you to know, even though I'm sworn to secrecy, except you of course, Harriet and I are on our way to Port Henry, Maine, tomorrow morning. There, we'll be married, but it's only a temporary arrangement for a couple of days. You can trust me on that score. From Port Henry, we'll leave right away on the Portland Packet to Bloodstone Island. She desperately needs my help to secure her rightful ownership of the island. It's the least I could do for her old number 2 husband, Terry Hadley. Do you remember him in the senior member matches? No matter, I don't, but I think he would have expected or at least wanted a member, someone like me, to help Harriet out of a tight spot.

Don't worry. I'll be back in plenty of time to pitch in on the governor's reception. Remember, everything has to be hush-hush.

As ever,
Toby

Sydney went to the closest armchair and slumped into it. Clutching the letter to his chest, he closed his eyes. "What to do . . . what to do?" *Perhaps a scotch and a good hot tub will help sort things out.* The crumpled envelope fell to the floor from his outstretched hand.

Chapter 3

A Trip down Maine

Toby had already returned to his lodgings at the Maple Leaf Inn before Sydney read the note he had his driver drop off at the 1876 House. Toby unwittingly anticipated that Sydney would not receive it until the following day, long after he and Harriet skipped off to Maine. Ordinarily, he would have had a quiet dinner at Brookside with Sydney this evening, except they were on the outs with each other.

Being aware of his slightly inebriated state, he decided to approach his rooms on the second floor by sneaking up the back stairs, thus sparing himself of any potential embarrassment by a chance encounter with the proprietor or other guests. Reaching the top, his 7-iron golf club slipped from his grip and tumbled end over end to the landing below followed by Toby's farewell, "Good night, old friend. I'll collect you in the morning."

In his rooms, he collapsed into an overstuffed armchair and concluded that a hot bath would help him gather his thoughts about the following day's activities. The plumbing at the Maple Leaf was not only cranky and stingy on the second floor, but controlling the water temperature also required the kind of constant observation that Toby was unable to provide at the time, that along with the amount of water required.

Satisfied that he'd properly prepared the tub, Toby placed his robe on a side table overflowing with prewar *National Geographics*, a tumbler of scotch, and a box of wheat thins for dinner. With the tub filled to its overflow drain, he climbed over the edge and slipped backward to the bottom of the tub, which not only turned Toby red as a cooked lobster but also scalded his tallywacker as well. A tsunami-like wave spilled over the edge of the tub on its way to the ceiling of the living room floor below. Gradually adjusting to the water temperature, he sunk back with a sigh and thought, *Now let me see if I can figure out what in hell really happened at Harriet's. I don't mind helping out the old trout, but getting married is nasty business for someone in my shoes. She might have thought about polishing off Jeffrey, but of course, she didn't. Still she may have done her first husband in and Duckie also, both with stomach ailments. Hummph. Too late to stir up old suspicions now . . . besides, I might enjoy myself on the coast . . . if I close my eyes really tight, I might imagine Harriet as attractive as . . . as she might have been a few years ago.* His mind wondering off, he failed to notice a less-than-polite knock on his chamber door.

* * *

Both Sydney and Toby had sought out the solace and comfort of a session in a hot bath where they could to think more clearly and be revitalized. Even Sydney had expounded to Toby some years ago that world peace could be achieved if everyone on the planet stopped whatever they were warring about and soak in a good hot tub.

Harriet also must have been a proponent of this or a similar theory. Alone and now ensconced in her tub overflowing with lavender-scented bubble bath, the details of her elaborate plan for the days ahead began to fade from her grasp. The hot water soothed her wounded psyche, and she scolded herself for leaving Toby with an awful impression. She had long admitted to herself that she was no Emily Post, but she couldn't come up with a good excuse for her clumsy behavior. Worried that Toby might renege on his promise when he came to his senses in the morning, she considered ringing him to apologize, but under the circumstances, most of her immediate thoughts were only fleeting ones. And when the embarrassing encounter with Sydney tripped its way into her awareness, she winced and poured more hot water into the tub. *Thank heaven I'm marrying Toby and not that ogre Sydney*, she thought. *Toby's not a bad catch tho. Another day, another time, he might have been a keeper, probably worth a bundle. Why did Toby decide to help me? I wouldn't if I were him. I've got to get my hands on that damn island, but he must want or expect something too. I'll have to worry about that later. At least Sydney won't be sniffing around.*

Her thoughts became more and more random, a dreamlike search for reflections that would amuse and delight. She drifted far back into school-day crushes when she teased boys and exchanged impish valentines. Her fleeting recollections were mingled with dates at the drive-in theater with players on the high school football team. Remembrances of conquests, although loveless, drew a faint smile of self-satisfaction. A hiked skirt in the front row of her college American history class delivered a short-lived affair with its handsome impressionable young professor. It conjured up another pleasant memory of gratified desire, but little else. Flashes of past romances recalled memories of how she could use her attractive looks, stylish attire, and feminine wiles, which often led to seductions that for her had a low degree of difficulty. She drew in a deep breath before blowing away the bubbles that had accumulated on her arm and hand. Pensively, Harriet watched them float away to pop and die as all dreams inevitably do.

After an hour-long bath, she slipped into her pajamas, conventional slippers, and satin housecoat. She trundled off to the kitchen. For a late supper, she snacked on leftover items she didn't want to have spoiled while she was gone. Dessert consisted of a Bromo-Seltzer to settle a turbulent tummy. Pausing before leaving the kitchen, she scribbled a to-do note for her housemaid, Mrs. T, explaining that she would be away for a few days.

To organize her thoughts, she headed back to her bedroom. Hoping to itemize what essentials must be done to begin the long journey to Bloodstone Island, she grabbed a notepad on her dressing table and retreated to the chaise where she stretched out. Her eyes closed involuntarily like a child's Kewpie Doll put down for a nap. As she drifted off to sleep, the notepad fell from her hand to the floor. It was empty except for the three words she scrawled earlier, "envelopes, bullets, bicycle."

* * *

When her alarm rang, it was 4:00 a.m. Head splitting, she struggled into an outfit she had laid out on the far end of the bed the afternoon before. Braced with a leftover cup of tepid coffee, she ventured out of the house into the dew-laden darkness. It was only a few steps across the driveway to the barn where she and Jeffrey had kept their cars and bicycles.

Harriet was not pleased to see the condition of the bikes. She lifted hers off the wall, and when it dropped to the floor, it sounded like a spilled box of bedsprings. Mice had eaten away at the seat cushion. The headlamp was useless, and battery acid had leaked on the frame. Looking down at the pedals, she observed that the chain sprockets were thick with the accumulated grease of years past. Almost a decade of rust and neglect on the old Schwinn had worked its will. Ignoring the fact that the bike had not been cared for during its Rip van Winkle years sleeping on the garage wall, Harriet nonetheless heaped a stream of blue epithets directed at the manufacturer.

Kicking the stand back and mounting the bike, she heard both tires wheeze and go flat. To find the air pump and needle would take much too long, and dawn's early light was not far off. Panic set in.

"My kingdom for a goddamn horse!" she bellowed, knowing full well that her beloved horse, *Bluebell*, was far from her reach at the Stanford farm where her precious Morgan was boarded.

Unfortunately, a rusty bike does not respond to the crack of a whip. Now she was in a praying mood rather than a swearing one. "Lord Jesus, I just need to get to the village. That's not too much to ask, is it? I can take from there."

It's a dark stretch of road from her house to the village, and with the tires folding around the rims, she had to walk the bike part way. Fortunately for Harriet, no vehicles were on the road to witness her at that predawn time of night.

The far corner of the parking lot behind Field's General Store is where Chief Bebee kept impounded vehicles. One of them was Harriet's car, wrapped up in yellow tape like a birthday present. Like the others, large numbers and letters were written in soap on the doors and windows. Spotting her precious V-12, she muttered. "Don't worry, baby. Harriet's come to rescue you."

She crept along the back perimeter of the lot and pushed her bike into a hedgerow of blackberry bushes where surely no one would discover it until winter. With a final shove into the blackberries, she thanked the Lord and cursed Schwinn, all in the same breath.

Suddenly, she remembered that her long-range plan included returning the car to the lot without Bebee discovering it was missing. "Damn, what am I going to do with this tape all over my car? A plague on you, Bebee."

After sliding into the soft leather seat behind the wheel, she turned the ignition key on and gave a sigh of relief as the Lincoln's engine responded dutifully and began to purr like an overfed cat. With the headlights off, Harriet squinted around and between the soap lettering on the windshield and eased out onto Main Street, trailing yellow tape. All that remained was a quick stop at home to gather her luggage. In her driveway, she left the driver-side door open and engine running while she tossed her bags in the trunk. *There's no time now to clean up the car*, she thought. After slamming the house door shut and locking it, she swept behind the wheel and stuffed two envelopes into the map pocket on the back of the passenger's seat. Now it was off to gather up Toby.

The journey to Bloodstone Island had begun.

Chapter 4
Lunch in the Berkshires

Morning's first soft light cast long shadowy fingers across the village. Sunlight splayed on the dew in front of the Maple Leaf Inn, and the lawn sparkled like a field of diamonds where Toby stood tapping the marble flag sidewalk with his 7-iron. Nervously, he stroked his bushy white mustache.

While he thought he understood Harriet's' motives, he was not so sure of his own. *There must be more to Bloodstone Island than a pile of rock in the Atlantic,* he pondered. *How did I ever let that woman trap me into this? Well, I guess I'm going to find out. Dammit, I have better things to do. Maybe I don't. I'm just an old sot.*

He stoked up his pipe, knowing it might be his last opportunity for a smoke since Harriet despised the habit and didn't mind letting him know. Savoring his *Three Nuns* tobacco, his pipe sent a Vatican-like coil of white smoke into the cloudless sky. True to his word, Toby was well prepared to join Harriet on this expedition to an island off the coast of Maine. He had prepared his luggage for just about any eventuality. After all, Harriet had suggested that he might even have an enjoyable time on their trip together. Besides a collection of matching leather valises and satchels of various sizes, he included a collection of tennis and badminton racquets and his travel set of golf clubs. Still, concerned that he could be in for a spot of trouble and based on his recent experience when he last ventured forth from Brookside Country Club, he decided to bring his old service pistol and plenty of cash, known to him and Sydney as the "ready."

A lone car wound its way erratically up the West Road. *That must be Harriet,* he surmised. On closer inspection, he was astonished at the ominous sight of a large green Lincoln streaming yellow ribbons like a kid's car at a football rally.

Harriet cozied the big cabriolet up to the curb, rolled down the window, and said, "Oh, Toby, I was so frightened that you might have changed your mind. You're such a dear."

"Really, Harriet, you did have my word. Other than that, I don't know what to say, except that your car looks like a float in a May Day parade!"

"Don't make fun." She forced a smile. "I think it looks more like someone that just got married."

"Now you're frightening me again," replied Toby. "Where shall I put my things?"

"In the backseat if there isn't enough room in the trunk." She looked at his stack of baggage and remarked, "We're not going on an ocean cruise, you know." Harriet spun the rearview mirror around to examine her makeup and refresh her lipstick. "In any case, we won't be putting the top down. According to the radio, we're heading into a big storm brewing off the coast of Maine."

"Weather's nice enough here, but it stands to reason there's always something to spoil a trip, don't you know?" Grumbling and wheezing, Toby made several attempts to stuff and arrange his luggage in a logical order. Finished, he started tearing away at dozens of yellow ribbons stuck, snagged, or hooked on the Lincoln.

"Come along, Toby. No time for that now. We've got to get a move on." With Toby on board, Harriet tossed a New England road map into Toby's lap, an unspoken suggestion that he navigate their trip and keep his mind on the road instead of her mission. She stayed behind the wheel and shunned Toby's offer to drive. Ostensibly, she informed him that she insisted on driving so that Toby could become familiar with the car and get a feel for it. The sense of urgency on her face told a different story, however, that the further they were from Livermore Falls, the less the chance Toby would change his mind and insist on turning back. She didn't waste time in getting as far out of town as possible. Harriet loved everything fast, and fast cars were no exception.

After settling into the cushy front seat, Toby accepted his duty reluctantly. His Aqua Velva aftershave was no match for the pine-scented air freshener dangling from the mirror. And Harriet's lavender-fragranced toilet water could not compete with Toby's smoke-laden blazer. Neither was in a talkative mood beyond the usual small snippets that precede a long trip over hill and dale roads. Yesterday's imbibing activities still had a lingering effect on either one's ability to think clearly.

Half an hour after they reached the Vermont state border in midmorning, she eased off the gas to enter the small community of Bennington. "I've been here several times before," Toby pointed out. "It's a cozy little don't-do-much town on the way east to New Hampshire. The town does get in the way of Route 7 from Montreal to points south. It splits Bennington in two about ten miles from Massachusetts. Route 7 runs smack into Route 9 we're on. Just no getting around it." Toby chuckled.

Harriet nodded but failed to see the humor. She slowed down to a crawl and reached into her gaping purse sitting on the floorboards. She plucked out a package of peppermint Life Savers and offered them to Toby. Surmising that he failed Harriet's breath test, Toby nonetheless declined with quick wave of his hand. Instead, he reached into his breast pocket behind his never-to-be-used-handkerchief for a packet of Sen-Sen breath fresheners.

Harriet returned to her upright position behind the wheel and glanced again in the rearview mirror, confirming that a car had been following them for the last several miles. The expression on her face resembled something more than a grimace, like someone concerned for her life. As Harriet stuck the mints back into her purse, she fumbled through a collection of costume jewelry, key chains, compacts, coin purses, and an old romance paperback to make sure that she had remembered to bring her little Derringer pistol. Her search was rewarded, but it didn't change her expression or seem to provide any real comfort.

"What's the matter, Harriet?" Toby asked. "Seen a ghost?" He looked up from the map. "You've suddenly got a death grip on the wheel. Why don't you let me take over for a while?"

"I'm all right, Toby. It's just that I think there's been a car following us for the last hour."

"Well then, perhaps we should find out, give 'em the slip, so to speak. Recently, Sydney and I have picked up some practical experience when it comes to that." Toby motioned to a filling station. "Pull in there. We can gas up and change drivers. I know this area."

The clear skies in New York had turned to overcast in Vermont, and a light drizzle started when Harriet pulled up to the pumps. Bubbles began to form from the soap lettering on the car windows. Tiny rivulets of milky streaks flowed down the windshield that made visibility next to impossible. Harriet switched on the windshield wipers, which only exacerbated the problem by whipping the soap into mounds of suds.

The station owner, witnessing their arrival, came out to watch. He yelled through the window on Toby's side, "Is this some kind of new-fangled window washer you got there? Don't know what they'll think of next. We clean windshields here, but I'll have to charge ya for cleaning up this mess, less you're up to it yerself."

Toby, looking sheepish, got out and said, "I rather think it's just be some bratty kid's doing, wouldn't you agree? Of course, I'd thank you to do the cleanup and top off the tank."

Harriet, in a snit, had made a beeline for the restroom. Returning, she joined Toby in the station office where he'd spread out his map on the glass countertop. Initially, Toby felt a mild rush now that he was in the driver's seat, charting their course to Port Henry. "We'll continue east," he said, pointing with his fountain pen like a field marshal, "until we come to the intersection of Route 7 and Route 9 in town, then we'll turn south. It may be quicker anyway to slip down into Massachusetts, then we'll continue easterly on the Mohawk Trail. I'll be very surprised if we don't shake whoever's following us."

"Whatever you say, Toby." Her hands trembled. "Don't look now, but I think the car that's been following us is parked across the street and down two blocks. It's an old faded blue Coupe."

"All right, Harriet, but now I want you to settle down and act nonchalant going to the car. Oh, and I'll drive."

Finished cleaning up the Lincoln, the owner shouted, "How about all the yellow ribbons?"

Pocketing his wallet, Toby replied, "Sorry, no time for that now. Train to catch in North Adams, don't you know?"

* * *

The trip south onto the Mohawk Trail was uneventful. Periodically, they took turns looking in the rearview mirror for a light blue Coupe but came up empty. Both felt calmer and more secure as they progressed.

Toby decided to open a conversation. "I wouldn't mind if you told me who you think it is following us. If I don't find out, I've half a mind to turn around and head back for Livermore Falls."

"Oh, please, Toby, you wouldn't do that?" Harriet pleaded. "Listen to me. I have no idea who might be following us. It could be absolutely nothing. I'm just a little jumpy. A lot has happened in the last few days, after my Jeffrey's death and all."

"I realize that, Harriet." His tone was sympathetic. "It must be a lot to take in, but are you sure you've told me everything, like what's at stake in making this trip?"

"Almost everything, Toby." Her eyelashes began to flutter, and she turned away. "There are a couple of things that recently came to light."

Toby swallowed hard. "I should have known!" He struck the wheel hard with the palm of his hand. "And why couldn't you have told me earlier?"

"Because I was afraid you wouldn't come."

"Agreeing to marry you, Harriet, makes me feel like I've already put my life at risk. What should I know that could possibly be more dire than that?"

"Now you're angry, Toby. And you're driving too fast."

Toby breathed in deeply. "I'm not driving too fast, but I'm certainly going in the wrong direction."

"Now, Toby, don't talk like that. I'm not used to it. Be your old sweet self and let me explain." Harriet turned and reached behind her seat to remove the envelopes from the map pocket. "I was going through Jeffrey's things a couple of days ago, and I found two opened letters that were hidden in his desk drawer. Toby, he never shared the contents with me, I swear."

"Well, go on then. Out with it. I might as well know now."

"Please, Toby, there's no need to raise your voice. I even brought the letters with me so that you could read them for yourself. But I don't think you're in the right frame of mind right now."

Harriet dropped the letters into her cavernous purse. "I'm hungry, Toby dear, and it's almost lunchtime. Why don't you look for a nice roadside inn, and we can read the letters together without being cross to each other?"

"Good idea, Harriet. Sorry my boiler blew up, but I do hate surprises."

The next several miles drifted by quietly, as if they had taken an oath of silence. Hardly a glance was given to the occasional roadside eatery advertising home cooking. An hour had passed before they encountered a road sign advertising the Crooked Chimney Inn, three miles ahead. A follow-up sign publicized its continental cuisine, "one mile ahead on your left." Finally, they encountered a large sign for the inn, which indicated the entrance and their hours of operation. Toby slowed down at the entry. The presence of several late model cars confirmed to his satisfaction that this establishment probably had a reputable restaurant. Harriet agreed; they drove in and parked the car within easy eyesight from the inn.

The inn consisted of a three-story converted mansion, which captured Toby's interest. As they approached, he expounded to Harriet how this mansion probably originated around the turn of the century. The first floor was located a half story above grade, with a broad screened-in porch virtually the full length of the front façade, except for the main entrance, which was located at the northeast corner by a wood-shingled round tower. "Well, Harriet, it looks like we've had a stroke of luck, if the fare is as good as the architecture."

Harriet was mystified by Toby's sudden preoccupation with the inn's design features. Granted, she was always impressed with his good taste but befuddled by his current ramblings. Simply put, she mused that if it weren't freshly painted all white, the inn would make the perfect setting for a Halloween horror movie.

Toby stopped in the entrance walkway between the American and Massachusetts State flagpoles. To impress her further with his knowledge on the inn's architectural merits, he held forth. "Harriet, notice how the ornate porch provides a unifying design element for the jumble of odd-sized dormers? It's the asymmetrical motif of what's known as the Carpenter Gothic period. This inn is a remarkable example." Pointing upward with his golf club, he said, "If it weren't for the invention of the band saw, we wouldn't have all this beautiful scrollwork on the eaves. Remarkable, isn't it, how they've emulated in wood the stone work of masons in Europe's great cathedrals?"

"In case you haven't noticed, Toby, it's still drizzling, and my hair can't stand much more of it." Harriet, disinterested by now, also pointed to the roof. "Look, Toby, there's the crooked chimney. Now can we move along? It looks like a spiral staircase to nowhere."

In the foyer, a young hostess greeted them and asked if they preferred dining inside or on the porch. In spite of the dampish weather, they elected the latter where they could oversee the parking lot. The hostess gently removed Toby's golf club from underarm, placed it in the umbrella stand, and led them to a quiet table at the far end of the porch. They were pleasantly relieved to find such a refined establishment out in the sticks, as Toby would put it.

A neat young waiter wearing white bucks, obviously on summer break from school, approached with napkins, an abundance of silverware, and a pitcher of ice water. Completing his task setting their table, he introduced himself, handed them a menu, and asked if they would like an aperitif.

"I would," said Harriet. "Would you please order for me, Toby?"

"Certainly. Thank you, waiter. We'll both have a Dubonnet."

"Toby, did you notice that every piece of china and silverware has its own embroidered doily? Brookside could use a little ambiance like this."

"If you say so," replied Toby, perusing the menu. "I think I'll start with the tomato aspic."

Harriet, seated alongside Toby, nudged him under the table with her knee. "If you'd take your face out of the menu for a moment, you'd see a trooper walking around my car."

"Oh good Lord, he's taking down your license plate. We may be in for it, Harriet."

The trooper, writing notes, methodically stalked the Lincoln for a few minutes like he would a wounded animal. Instead of returning to his patrol car, he headed for his trapped prey in the Crooked Chimney Inn.

Chapter 5
A Slight Detour

The state trooper removed his Smokey-the-Bear-like hat when he entered the foyer. The hostess approached him immediately then inquired, "Good afternoon. Are you here for lunch or can I be of service someway?"

"Yes, Miss, can you show me where the owner of the Lincoln in the parking lot is seated?" Anxiously, he shifted his weight from one side to the other and twirled his hat.

"I noticed them drive up," she replied. "Shall I let them know you are here?"

"That won't be necessary. I'll introduce myself. Would you mind pointing them out to me?"

"Not at all, but there isn't going to be any trouble, is there?" she asked. She thought, *Good gravy, the last thing we need is a scene with the law.* Her ingrained composure was rapidly disappearing, and her feet were ready to scamper in the direction of the kitchen where her father was attending to his duties as chef.

"Trust me, Miss, this is a routine matter."

Several of the diners on the porch turned to witness the trooper's conversation with the hostess at the front desk. A collection of whispers grew into a discernable murmur that swept its way down the length of the porch until it reached Toby and Harriet who stared blankly at the approaching trooper.

Harriet bit the corner of her lip. "Here he comes, Toby. He looks like a young Gary Cooper, doesn't he? My God, will he ever get here?"

"Let me handle this, Harriet. We don't know how much he knows, if anything. We'll just tell the truth."

The trooper approached slowly and walked with a swagger, one hand above his service pistol while cradling his hat on the opposite side. Stopping at their table, he politely introduced himself, "Good afternoon. I'm Trooper Wyatt." He smiled broadly and then asked, "May I inquire which of you owns a green Lincoln out in the parking lot?"

"She does," replied Toby, pointing at Harriet.

"Well then, may I see your driver's license, ma'am?"

"Certainly, young man, but must we do whatever you have to do right here?" She turned around to reach for her purse hanging on the back of her chair. "I must protest, and I trust you won't be needing anything further."

"Sorry, folks, but I answer to a cranky sergeant." He looked intently at her license and seemed satisfied that she indeed was who she claimed to be. After returning it to Harriet, he asked, "Do you mind telling me the nature of your traveling today?"

Toby leaned forward to answer for her, "Honestly, officer, I find your inquiry is quite personal and over the top, if I may say so. Harriet Bartholomew and I are to be married, hopefully later today. So perhaps we can get on with any other questions you have for us."

The trooper, taken aback, offered his congratulations and remarked. "Usually, the type of yellow ribbons on your car might indicate some kind of criminal activity. When you passed me a few miles back, it roused my curiosity. I heard some police districts over in your neck of the woods are using ribbons to identify all sorts of things."

Toby feigned a weak smile. "Of course, officer, I see your point now. Allow me to explain. I have a number of friends in law enforcement back in New York." He cleared his throat and swallowed hard. "No doubt they're the chaps who decorated our car as a get-away gesture. Obviously, the rascals thought it would be amusing to call it a crime for a man of my age to run off with this young lady!" He chuckled and turned to Harriet, "Isn't that right, dear?"

"It certainly is and, as you can see officer, the farther we're away from them, the better off we are."

"Yes," the trooper responded, "I understand now how they can be the cause of some mischief." His voice dropped an octave and developed a more serious tone. "Let's step outside to your car. I'd like to check the registration, and, sir, I'd like to see your identification."

Harriet's cheeks flushed right through her rouge. "We haven't even ordered our lunch yet. Say something, Toby."

Toby's face turned crimson because he was too flabbergasted to know what to say to either Harriet or the officer until he whispered, "Sweetie, I think it's best we do as the officer suggests."

"Good," replied the trooper. "Since you haven't ordered, you haven't a bill. If there's no problem, I'm sure the nice folks here would be glad to take your order when you return." His words were soft, but they struck home, just like the unannounced flash of lightning and the following deep roll of thunder that portended a violent storm in their path.

Waiters and waitresses began moving diners to tables inside the inn's dining room away from what certainly would turn into a cold driving rain. Toby and Harriet were no longer a source of conversation as they followed the trooper out to the parking lot. A fork of lightning lit up the roiling sky followed closely by a loud clap of thunder. Wind-driven clouds obeyed the weather god's command by pouring their contents on the Crooked Chimney Inn.

Harriet, drenched, shot in behind the wheel and asked Toby, also soaked, to pass her his ID and the car registration from the glove box. Meanwhile, the trooper detoured to his patrol car to pick up a rain slicker. Returning to Harriet's car, he hunched over next to Harriet's door and tapped on the window. Partially rolling down it down, she held up the car's registration along with Toby's ID. He examined them briefly and said, "Just fine, Mrs. Bartholomew, thank you. You too, Mr. Worthington. But I'm afraid I have to ask you to follow me back to the station house in Middleton Springs. It's only a couple of miles from here, and it shouldn't take you more than a few a minutes out of your way. I have to do some routine checking that I can't do from here. I hope you'll both understand?"

"Not really," Harriet puffed, "but I guess we'll have to do as you ask."

"Thank you, ma'am. Pull in behind me at the highway entrance, and we'll be off."

Harriet, in a fitful state, horsed the Lincoln forward; and it behaved in kind. Throwing wet gravel across the parking lot, the Lincoln behaved as a perfect reflection of its owner's spitfire temperament. The downpour continued as they waited impatiently for the trooper to arrive. The car's defroster had yet to clear the fogged up windows, and like two metronomes, the wipers slowly marked the passage of time.

When the trooper finally arrived and signaled them to follow, Harriet broke the silence. "Please, Toby, don't call me sweetie again." She sighed. "We're not married quite yet, and at this rate, who knows if we'll ever be."

"Sorry, old thing. I'll try not to use any more endearing terms. You know I only said it for the trooper's benefit. Flatter you? Given your present attitude, I can't imagine why I should."

"Don't you go pouting on me, Toby." Harriet saw his wounded expression and realized that she had injured him, but not mortally. "You know me by now. I say things impulsively, and I always regret them later."

"Yes, well—" Toby fumbled for another Sen-Sen.

As they barreled down the road behind the trooper, the wipers had trouble keeping up with the torrential rain as well as the overspray from oncoming cars and trucks. Harriet had difficulty keeping up with the patrol car as it disappeared from time to time into a dip in the road or a sharp turn.

The distance separating the two cars had widened enough that Toby urged Harriet to speed up. "I think you'd better press on a bit. We don't want to end up losing him."

"In this weather," Harriet said, "he could cooperate a little and slow down. If he loses us, it'll be his fault."

Suddenly, a strange look swept across her face as if she were having either an epiphany or a seizure. Usually squinting to focus on the road ahead, her eyes popped open, and her jaw fell slack. Her cheeks flushed, and her fingers squeezed the wheel. The car leapt ahead at her insistence and sought to go airborne over the top of a rise in the road. On the other side, the Lincoln flattened onto the pavement with a thud and plummeted toward a deep swale in the roadway that was flooded at the bottom.

Toby raised his voice, "Harriet, wake up or you'll kill the both of us!"

"Oh no, I have no intention of doing that," she said like someone emerging from a hypnotic trance. "We're going to be just fine."

"Is that so? If I didn't know better, I'd say you were having a stroke. Now slow down before we hit that floodwater at the bottom." Leaning back against the seat, his fingers dug deep into the armrests, Toby's heel instinctively burrowed into the floor carpet as if the brake pedal were on his side of the car.

"It's all right, Toby. Calm down now. I just had a really good idea."

"About time. This car can't skip across water like a rock, don't you know? Damn that trooper. He should have been here waiting for us to catch up. I haven't seen any place where he'd turn off."

Her startled appearance gone, she cautiously forded the shallow stream of water on the roadway. Accelerating the Lincoln up the far side of the swale, she looked in the rearview mirror and observed, "It won't be long before that stream will be impassible. Bad news for anyone still trying to follow us, ehhh, Toby?"

"I suppose," said Toby, relieved to be across. They drove for several minutes before they witnessed a pair of brake lights flashing about a quarter of a mile ahead. But they couldn't tell if it was the trooper's car. To Toby's complete surprise, Harriet spun the wheel, turning to the left; and the Lincoln lunged off the main highway onto a two-lane country road.

Toby, lurching against his door, said, "Harriet, have you gone mad? Now we're really in for it, the hoosegow. Every lawman in the northeast will be looking for us. You'd better turn around while we still can."

"Toby, we've done absolutely nothing wrong." Harriet grinned. "As far as we know, we're still following the trooper. Isn't that so, Toby?"

"No, dammit. And it doesn't matter whether we've done anything wrong or not, as long as the law thinks we have. Now if you don't mind, I strongly suggest that we turn around immediately before it's too late."

"Oh, Toby, let's not argue like some married couple. This is my car, and we're going to get my island. Hell or high water, as you men like to say. And that's that."

"If that's your final answer, then you might as well know we'll have to get rid of this car. And the sooner, the better."

"I suppose you're right, Toby. You're so much more clever than I am at these sort of things."

"Of course, I am. I have to be on my toes all the time looking after Sydney, which is what I should be doing now. Some holiday." The red in his cheeks had risen beyond his nose and reached the furrow in his brow. "Drive on. I'll let you know when to stop."

"Whatever you think," Harriet cooed. "We do complement each other well, if I do say so myself."

Snaking back and forth on a winding road, Toby could only surmise that their general direction was northeast. Jostled about in the car, it was virtually impossible for Toby to read a map while Harriet was busy avoiding water-filled potholes. They avoided one-lane gravel side roads in the belief they would eventually arrive at a crossroads general store, if not a small village.

The downpour continued throughout the afternoon. Steam fog rose from roadside swamps and shallow ponds. Only their anxiety about being lost kept them awake to stare through the mist for a road sign, another passing car, or some indication of life while the steady drumming of the windshield wipers said, *Take a nap, take a nap.* Mile after monotonous mile slipped by as they drove through wooded countryside, occasionally interrupted by a small family farm.

Midafternoon brought a respite from the rain, and the fog lifted like a stage curtain. The clouds were thick and had that dirty gray look about them as if they were just catching their breath before dumping another load of rain on them. Hungry and thirsty, Harriet and Toby welcomed a weathered hand-painted sign that advertised, *Lodgings Ahead, Modern Plumbing and Food.*

"Must be coming to a town," observed Harriet, "thank God. And I do have to go, if you know what I mean."

"Of course, I do."

A large blue building came into view with a misspelled sign that read, "Bob's Collishion." "Look on the right, Harriet. This might be just the place we're looking for. Quick, pull in the drive."

"Toby, I'm starved, and like I said, I have to go-o-o. Couldn't this wait?"

"Not on your life, not if you want your precious island."

Harriet pulled off the road and whipped the Lincoln up the gravel drive, bringing it to a halt in front of a bus-size sliding door. She left the motor running. Leaning over the steering wheel to get a better view, she said, "I haven't a clue why you wanted to stop here for. This place is a little too spooky for me. So why don't we leave now?"

"Nonsense, Harriet. Leave this to me and turn the damn engine off." Toby slipped out of the car with his 7-iron in hand and puddle jumped his way to a handwritten sign posted beside the door. "For service, ring bell." He rang and then tiptoed his way around the upland side of the barn. Rapping on a window with a curtain made of spun spider webs, he hoped to rouse someone inside. With his nose pressed against the glass, he was barely able to make out the shadowy forms of vehicles sleeping under tarpaulin blankets. Pulleys, ropes, chains and block, and tackle hung from overhead beams, waiting to be called upon. Farther down the side of the barn, he rapped on a locked door with the handle of his club, but to no avail.

Toby did not want to give up too easily on his mission or go back to the car knowing that Harriet would be waiting with a legitimate argument to leave. He kept out of sight from the car and continued to investigate the grounds. It was not long before Harriet was playing the horn like an instrument in a preschool musical. Toby muttered, "She can damn well keep her britches on for a few more minutes."

He walked like a stork through a thicket of wet underbrush, waving his golf club back and forth like a scythe until he reached the far side of the barn. As expected, he came upon the remains of Bob's handiwork, which had been either parked or piled up in an open yard. It was comprised mostly of rusted out junks and cannibalized prewar cars. A wobbly barbed wire fence enclosed the area and supposedly protected it from drive by scavengers. It did little to keep out the encroachment of blackberry bushes and nettles.

He glanced up and across a fallow meadow that gradually rose a hundred yards up to an old three-story house reminiscent of the 1880s. In scale, the lower floors suffered from a disproportionate turret that struggled hard to reach a height from which it could look out beyond the boundaries of its own property. With his naked eye, Toby viewed the extensive evidence of rot, broken glass, and collapsed porch stairs. *Perhaps,* he mused, *this vintage house had been abandoned several years earlier, even during construction, since no paint was apparent on the structure.* Its monochromatic hue of weathered gray blended in with the turbulent clouds overhead.

Toby's gaze looked halfway down the meadow from the old house to a rusty metal-clad trailer home that was perched on top of concrete blocks. A modest pea garden framed the south side. Lights were on inside the trailer, and two pickup trucks were parked outside, waiting patiently for an assignment. He had no intention of approaching the trailer home, especially after a dog with an aggressive attitude began to bark and growl ominously as if it were hungry for the leg of an outsider. Still, he rejected the notion of going back to the car, knowing what Harriet had waiting for him. Curious, he continued his trek around the barn being careful to keep out of her sight. Between a tall shrub and the barn, he seized the opportunity to relieve himself.

The distant sound of a deep-throated truck starting up interrupted Toby's slog around the building. He glanced back at the source coming from the driveway in front of the house trailer. The sight of a pickup spinning out of the yard and down the road encouraged him to retrace his steps and greet the driver before he had a chance to encounter Harriet. Loping through the overgrowth, he was wet to his knees before he arrived back at the Lincoln in time to see a rusted out prewar Ford pickup pulling up to the barn with the engine shut off.

While it was still coasting to a stop, a gangly bald man in greasy overalls jumped out of the cab. He saw on Harriet's startled expression staring at him through the windshield and shouted over, "Don't be skeered, lady. Saves on gas and brakes. See, my truck stopped before it hit the door. Done it a million times." His explanation neither comforted Harriet nor persuaded Toby of the driver's skill.

"You must be, Bob," greeted Toby, extending his hand.

Absent his right hand, the man offered his left one to shake with Toby. "Never was a Bob," he said. "Wife and I just thought it was a nice friendly name for the business at least compared with our own. I'm the owner, and you can call me Stump. Friends do. Now what can I do for you nice folks."

Flying out of the car, Harriet interjected, "You can show me where the bathroom is."

"Sure, need anything else?" Stump rolled the garage door back and pointed inside. "It's in the far back, lady, the door next to my calendar collection." He switched the lamps on and remarked how lucky they were that they still had electricity in spite of the horrific storm.

"Actually, Stump, we could use your services," said Toby. Stump looked slightly bewildered as he surveyed the Lincoln. "Look at our front bumper. It's dented and badly scratched."

"Oh, I can see that now. But I'm sure I don't have anything in my bone yard to match it. I'd have to order a new one up, torch off the old one, then bolt or weld on the new one." Stump went on to explain in detail all the difficulties he would have accomplishing this task. Toby listened intently and politely kept nodding his head in agreement. "Sure is a beauty you've got here. Prettier than Cleopatra's barge, I'd say. Never seen it like before 'cept in pictures, of course."

The chilly wind started to pick up again, and Toby jumped into the Lincoln the moment they were inundated with hail. At first it sounded like corn popping on the convertible top and then like a drum corps. A flash of lightning and a clap of thunder chased Stump and the Lincoln inside the barn. Outside, the hail piled up on the ground, while inside the lamps flickered and buzzed as if in their death throes. Seconds later, everyone was plunged into darkness; and that's when Harriet, from the back of the garage, let out a graveyard wail of operatic proportions.

Toby turned on the car headlights so that Harriet could find her way back to the front of the garage. When she arrived, her fear turned to anger. "Toby, there's a man back there in one of the cars. I'm not staying here another minute."

"No need to be skeered, lady. That's my uncle Ned. Comes down here to take a nap in one of the cars every so often, wants to get away from the chatterboxes at home."

"Is that so," said Harriet, "well frankly, Stump, I find you and your calendar collection disgusting. And there's no toilet paper in your bathroom."

"I know. I rarely ever use it myself," replied Stump, "and it's hard to keep an item like that in stock."

"He's trying to be funny with me, Toby. This is a horrid place, and he's a horrid man. Well, say something."

Toby sought to change the subject quickly and asked Harriet to calm down since no personal harm had come to her. He whispered that they would be moving on as soon as the storm let up. Harriet immediately took refuge in the Lincoln, slumped down behind the wheel, and locked the doors. Toby turned to engage Stump in conversation.

"Stump, we're going over on the coast of Maine for a couple of days. It occurred to us that we could leave the Lincoln here while you patch it up, that is, if you had a loaner car for us while we're gone."

"Loaner?"

"Yes, perhaps one of the cars you might have sitting around your shop. Actually, you wouldn't be loaning a car to us. We would be renting it, so to speak. Cash, of course." With a flashlight, Toby glanced around the garage at a number of cars in various stages of disrepair. The only one not under a tarp looked far more ready for his bone yard than a future on the highway.

"Now that's an idea that appeals to me," said Stump on reflection. "If twenty dollars a day isn't a problem, follow me and have a look at this baby. I'll need an extra hand with the tarp." He picked up a flashlight and led Toby to the back of the barn. When they lifted the canvas cover, Toby expressed amazement at a restored 1939 Chevy panel truck. "My son Amos and I have been working on this critter for the last five or six years. Like new, except we had to replace the whole front end—engine, transmission, seats, radiator, the works."

"Perfect," said Toby, "plenty of room for all our luggage." Toby stroked his hand affectionately over the hood and fenders. He marveled at the handsome two-tone chocolate color scheme—milk and dark. "How fast is she?"

"It's fast enough for you two. She'll do eighty." Stump smiled and drew in a deep breath.

"Adequate," replied Toby. "But that doesn't sound all that fast to me."

"That's in second gear. We never dared to open it up in third."

"Well, so you say." Toby was impressed. He continued his inspection and peeked in the cab but felt a twinge of revulsion when he spied a spinner on the steering wheel and a pair of fuzzy dice hanging from the rearview mirror. "Tell me, Stump, how did you acquire this beauty?"

"Well, the short of it is that it was towed in here from a wreck. As you can see on the side panels, it was a local delivery truck. The owner, Fannie Tucker, had no insurance, and the accident was her fault. She went out of business and left me stuck with it."

"To your good fortune, I'd say." Toby waved his flashlight over the hand-painted side panel to read the advertisement. "Since 1932, **Mother Tucker's** Fine Chocolates and Confections Co." "Leaving the signage was a nice touch, Stump. I think we've got ourselves a deal. Let's draw up an agreement."

Returning to the Lincoln, Toby gave a rap on Harriet's window. "Come on, Harriet, unlock the car and get out. We can't dilly-dally here all day. And bring the envelopes with you. From now on, you're known as Mother Tucker, and you're in the chocolate business."

Taking Toby's hand, Harriet got out of her car. In a state of total confusion, she tried to assess the situation and asked Toby what in the devil was going on. He explained that they were going to rent one of the vehicles here for a couple of days while Stump replaced the front bumper on her car.

"Him?" she stammered, pointing at Stump. "You're going to let him work on my car? Really, Toby, you must be out of your senses. And if I'm to be Mother Tucker, I suppose that makes you Father Tucker?"

"Hold on, Harriet, When you look at the vehicle we're renting, you'll understand."

Toby ignored her question and left her to deal with her own befuddlement. He turned his attention to Stump. "Would you mind giving us a hand, Stump? We'd like to move our luggage from the Lincoln to the truck?"

"Hey, Mr. Worthington, remember, I've only got one hand. My wife does most of the heavy lifting around here. Want me to give her a buzz?"

"No need. I can manage." Toby sighed. He walked over to the truck and swung open the pair of rear doors.

Harriet cut in, "Are you sure you know what you're doing, Toby, or should I say what we're doing? Now be careful with my luggage. I think it was a present from my first husband. I can't remember anything right now except I know it wasn't from Jeffrey. He had no taste for such things."

Toby continued to ignore Harriet who rambled on like someone waking up from a deep sleep. Stump stood nearby to kibitz Toby, who traipsed back and forth between the Lincoln and the panel truck. Hungry and tired, he dropped his buttocks on the truck's back bumper in hopes that a short respite would give him new strength. He looked over at Stump and asked him directions for the quickest way from here to the Maine coast.

"Well, let me think," said Stump, pressing a finger to his forehead. "First of all, if I were you, and I ain't, I'd keep goin' in the same direction you were headed. Then I'd go until you get to Luke Hemmingway's barn, red with white winders. Take a right . . . you'll come to Stan's filling station . . . nice older feller . . ."

"This is all very interesting, Stump, but quite frankly, we're in a hurry and could use something more direct in nature."

"Well, I'm coming to that. Just hold your horses. I've got better things to do than stand around here all day givin' you directions." Annoyed, he took off on a different tangent that evidently bothered him. "It's plain to see you're not wed to that woman. No rings. But if you're plannin' on ever marrying that fussbudget you're travelin' with, I don't know if I want to help you get to the altar."

Toby was surprised at Stump's speculation. Searching for a reasonable answer, he replied, "She's really not a bad sort, don't you know? Actually, Harriet's a very sensitive creature, a little spoiled but just out of her element right now." Toby suddenly realized to his own surprise that he found himself apologizing for Harriet's behavior.

"Sorry 'bout that, Mr. Worthington. Show me that map of yours, and I'll get you on your way over to Keene, and you can take it from there."

Chapter 6

A Storm of a Different Nature

After endless miles of twisting and turning through New England back roads, it seemed like days rather than two hours before they arrived in the outskirts of Keene, not too many miles from their destination in Port Henry. The rain had tapered off, but again, it did not have the usual signs of a storm about to quit.

Stripped of their Lincoln, which now hid under a tarp at Stump's place, the bushed pair decided to surrender any outward appearance of their true identity and took on a guise designed to match their newly acquired vehicle, Mother Tucker's Chevy truck. Stopping at a street intersection, Toby shed his Brookside blazer and club tie in favor of a cardigan sweater from his luggage. Harriet followed suit and tossed her jewelry into her cavernous purse and tucked it out of sight behind the driver's seat. Donning a windbreaker from her travel case, she carefully zippered it up over the club logo on her blouse.

In downtown Keene, they pulled up in front of what appeared to be a popular local diner. They surmised that either the fare was good or their customers were simply gathered inside to take shelter.

"Don't forget to bring the envelopes, Harriet. Maybe I'll get a chance to find out what you're so reluctant to tell me."

Harriet replied, "All right, but don't get upset with me when you read them, and promise you won't make a scene?"

Toby ignored her plea and lent his hand to steady Harriet's progress as they dodged puddles leading to the stairs at the far end of the diner. The revamped railroad car from the thirties sported a sheet metal skirt and flower boxes around its foundation. Once inside, Toby, a newcomer to diners, froze in bewilderment. He stared at a long sit-down counter with customers perched on tall spinner stools that faced the kitchen. Harriet, indifferent, marched ahead of him on the narrow aisle. Behind the counter, a short-order cook with a white chevron hat worked his craft under a rattling exhaust fan that sucked up his cigarette smoke along with steam rising from the grille. Light ricocheted everywhere off the quilted stainless steel walls and ceiling, which highlighted the counter and street-side booths.

A raspy female voice called out over the hubbub in the diner, "If you wanta eat here, you'll have to sit down." The waitress working the cash register at the opposite end put out her cigarette, picked up two menus, and pointed toward an open booth facing the street. Toby, jolted back into the present, caught up with Harriet.

From opposite sides of the booth, they slid toward the window, which was obscured by condensation on the inside and rain that beaded up outside. In a childlike impulsive gesture, Harriet drew a heart with an arrow through it on the glass.

Toby quickly wiped it off with a napkin. "Rea-l-l-y, Harriet," he exclaimed, lowering his voice.

Harriet pressed closer to the window. "I thought I saw an old blue coupe go by just now, like the one that was following us."

"Being edgy again, Harriet. It's probably your imagination. Must be more than one blue coupe in New Hampshire." Toby changed the subject. "Look here, doesn't this beat all? It's a coin-operated music machine. Come on, let's see what it has to offer." Toby retrieved his bifocals to examine the selections. "Hmmmm. Three songs for a quarter. 'Ballerina,' 'The Gypsy, Nature Boy.' Crazy stuff they listen to today. Now how about Perry Como's, 'Prisoner of Love'?"

"Save your money, Toby. Here comes our waitress," whispered Harriet. "We have to keep a move on. And if you're going to be my husband, I wish you wouldn't act like a little kid in a candy store. You're beginning to attract attention."

"Humph." Toby sputtered. "Little kid, am I? As if you aren't." Indignant, he reconfirmed his opinion that she's something of a bore.

"Coffee?" asked the waitress, handing them a menu.

"No, thank you," said Harriet. "Water will do." The odor of stale cigarette smoke combined with the smell of the customer's damp wool coats did little to wet her appetite. She preempted Toby's protocol of ordering for her. "Two house specials please."

"Well, Harriet, perhaps now you'll let me read the contents of the envelopes. I think you said it will help me understand what this trip is all about?"

"Well, not quite all, Toby." The usual overbearing tone of her voice suddenly turned defensive. Beneath the table, she slipped off a shoe and gently stroked his calf with her toe. "There are some disturbing contents in the envelopes I think you should know." And then she added a caveat, "Even though they're probably not all that important."

Bewildered by her flirtatious advance at this point in their conversation, he feigned not to notice it and thought, *She should know by now I'm not some seducible old fool.* He replied, "I've already anticipated there might be one or two problems to surface."

"Well," said Harriet, "that's good because it's hard to tell you absolutely everything when we're always on the run." She slid the first envelope across the table. "I found these envelopes in Jeffrey's desk drawer when I was tidying up after the funeral."

Although it was addressed to Harriet, Toby observed that Jeffrey obviously had opened it and kept it concealed from her, going back to right after their marriage some eight years earlier. "Postmarked Philadelphia, I see." Toby knew Jeffrey as a common thief and bounder. He immediately thought that Jeffrey had been scrutinizing her mail beginning from the first day of their marriage. *But,* Toby mused, *why did he choose to hide just these two letters from her? And what purpose did Jeffrey have in not destroying them?*

Unfolding the letter, he read the glued-on cutout letters that wove their way drunkenly across the sheet.

CLAIM BLOODSTONE ISLAND, AND THE ISLAND WILL CLAIM YOUR BLOOD.

"However cryptic, Harriet, it's quite clear that somebody wishes you serious harm. If I may say so, it seems to me that Jeffrey didn't want you to risk your neck over a rock outcropping in the Atlantic, unless you and he found it a matter of some financial urgency."

"Of course, Toby," appearing shocked, "you're right. That must have been the reason why he always had some excuse not to take me there."

Toby paused to consider other motives Jeffrey could have had. "Another thing, he may have kept this letter as a means of dissuading you not to go in case you tried in earnest to prevail upon him. Don't you know, it might have crossed Jeffrey's mind that his own life might be jeopardized?" Toby returned the threatening letter to the envelope and handed it back to Harriet. "It occurs to me that I could find myself in the same spot if I continue on this trip with you."

"What do you mean, if?" She slipped her shoe back on.

"If means just that, if. I didn't bargain for stakes this high. I gave up a perfectly good golf match with Sydney for what I expected would be a couple of games of badminton, a dram or two of scotch, and a simple three-day marriage." Toby removed his glasses momentarily to wipe them off and then chuckled.

"What do you find so amusing, Toby?"

"Well, I was just thinking how out of character it would be for me, a bachelor at my age, to wind up my life as a dead bigamist. In a macabre way, it gives me a tickle even though I can't abide the thought. I've always felt obliged to help out a member of the club with some minor difficulty. But this? Here I am suddenly confronted with this messy business." Looking like a wounded Cape Buffalo, he moaned, "Honestly, Harriet, how could you involve me?"

She turned away from Toby and stared out the window at the street beyond. The waitress arrived to serve their lunch, and this simple act put a period on their conversation. Moments passed before Harriet turned back, choosing to look down at her plate. In silence, she poked her fork aimlessly at the scoop of watery mashed potatoes crowned with a cube of melting butter.

Harriet sighed. "I see that getting you involved in my problem was all wrong from the start. I couldn't think of any other possible solution except my own. Makes me pretty selfish, doesn't it? But you must believe I didn't want any harm to come to you. Besides, I've always thought of you as heroic and in command of any situation. And I do care about your feelings, Toby dear. I really did want you to enjoy our trip." Glancing up, her eyes searched Toby's for some sign of empathy. She licked her empty fork. "We still could, you know?" Her lips implored.

Ignoring her appeal, Toby's thoughts drifted off into that space where only asteroids dwell. It was his turn to sit in silence and ponder what Sydney might think or what he would do if he were here in his shoes. He thought, *Dammit all to pieces. He'd know what to do. Well, I'll give her this. She does have balls.*

She reached into her windbreaker to find a handkerchief. Dabbing her eyes with an unused corner, she said, "I've been all mixed up since Jeffrey's sudden death." She pushed her plate away abruptly, and the sliced tomato perched on top of her ground beef patty slipped off like a burial at sea. "Please listen, Toby. I hope you can forgive me, if not now, perhaps later? I don't want Bloodstone Island to sour our friendship. If you're determined to turn back, I'll understand."

With an ironic smile befitting a sidewalk crack, she said, "It's too late for me to find another husband on such short notice. You must promise, no matter what your decision might cost me, you won't feel guilty about losing my island." She heaved a sigh, took a sip of water, and cleared her throat before delivering a final shot in her latest volley to convince Toby of her sincerity. "I've come to realize that I could never excuse myself if any harm came to you."

"Like dying?" Toby replied. Toby paused to down the remaining peas he piled on his fork. "Don't fret, Harriet. I'm not about to abandon ship. My sails are set. I'll get you to your bloody island and back too. But you'd better not be having me on, even though you probably are." He looked over the rim of his glasses now perched at the far end of his nose. "Although you've expressed a willingness to let me off the hook, so to speak, I find that there are some things I have to do even against my better judgment. And in your case, it seems to be happen with great frequency." He smiled.

"Oh, Toby, you darling man, you won't regret your decision. I'm so terribly grateful, and I could up and kiss you right now."

"Don't be ridiculous, Harriet. I'm doing this in some measure because you're still a member of Brookside. If you're determined to keep going, I'll stand by my commitment, no matter how insignificant the circumstances seemed to me at the time. I've never walked off the course during a match at the club—never quit, I tell you—no matter how poorly I was playing or how badly my opponent was drubbing me."

"Please, Toby, I understand your wish to defend your principles, although I must admit I'm a little mystified by your attachment to Brookside. After all, it's just a clubhouse with a silly old golf course. The club's really important in your life, but I'd like to think you're doing this for me?"

"Well, I suppose you could say that too." Toby flushed. Still, he was irked by Harriet's remark that trivialized Brookside. His old friend Sydney spawned the course and clubhouse masterpiece. It personified a genteel way of life that not only provided Toby with a great deal of satisfaction but also insulated him and Sydney from the rest of the sordid outside world. Deciding against expressing his irritation, he said, "Perhaps I better have a look at what's in the other envelope. By the way, if you don't want your peas, I'll have a go at them."

Harriet slid her plate and the other envelope over to Toby. "I'm afraid you'll find a puzzle inside this envelope too."

"I'm sure, if you say so." Toby noticed the postmark was recent and surmised that the letter arrived only days before Jeffrey took off on his fatal fishing trip to the Canadian border. "This one's postmarked Portland, Maine."

"Yes, but before you go any further, there's a small detail I forgot to tell you about in Duckie's will. I guess I should have told you yesterday afternoon at the house. With all the confusion, it managed to slip right on past me." Harriet cleared her throat again while Toby continued to devour Harriet's peas. "You know, I inherit Bloodstone Island from the trust, but only if I meet the conditions we talked about. If I'm not able to inherit, my stepson becomes heir to the island. Actually, the state of Maine is third in line to acquire the property. I told you my husband was a trickster."

"Now you tell me, not that I'm entirely surprised. Duckie doesn't seem to be the only one with a trick or two." Toby dropped his fork and watched it slip beyond his grasp to the floor. "Duckie's son? Perhaps you better tell me about him."

"Of course, but if you've finished your lunch, don't you think we'd better be on our way? We want to catch the Portland Packet, remember? I can explain everything while we drive. I'll take the wheel, and you point the way."

Toby grumbled but agreed to leave once again against his better judgment, especially since he hadn't opened the second envelope. With his resistance on the wane under her withering barrage of persuasion, flattery, and flirting, there was no turning back now. A hungry Harriet, but with little appetite for the house special, plucked the garnish of parsley from her plate and devoured it as she slid out of the booth while Toby, fumbling for a tip, signaled the waitress to bring their check. The rain had taken a respite, and once outside, they gulped the invigorating fresh rain-washed air.

Behind the wheel, Harriet adapted quickly to the vintage delivery truck once she familiarized herself with the nuances of the clutch. Once on the main drag, she checked the mirrors for any sign of the blue Coupe and satisfied herself that they had given the slip to whoever might be following them. The idea of her new identity as Mother Tucker was no longer repulsive but instead had a certain appeal to her sense of youthful adventure.

Before Toby could ask about Duckie's son or open the other envelope, she said, "We may be in some danger. If we are, I want you to know I can take care of myself. Just in case, I brought along my pistol."

"I don't believe it."

"If you don't, reach in my bag behind your seat."

After sifting through a collection of small objects unfamiliar to Toby's touch, he pulled out a customized .32 caliber Derringer with a jeweled pearl grip, designed no doubt for a lady in distress who might need to protect her honor in a Chicago speakeasy.

"You call this a pistol? Good God, woman, are you sure this isn't a cigarette lighter? It's a damn good thing I brought along my army service revolver."

"I'm so glad you thought ahead, Toby. I guess we're both ready for whatever.

Chapter 7

The Wicked Stepson

Deep in their own thoughts, Toby spread their map out on his lap to count the remaining miles to Port Henry. Satisfied with his calculation, he opened the conversation. "Well, Harriet, perhaps now is as good a time as any to tell me about your stepson."

"Of course, but there's not a whole lot to say about Claude, especially his later years anyway. Everything I know about him came straight from Duckie. I never had to meet Claude, thank God. Actually, neither he nor I know what the other looks like. Would you believe our ages aren't all that far apart? And you don't need to know mine."

"Consider me forewarned, Harriet. I happen to be familiar with the silly taboos women have about their age. You and your stepson, an awkward relationship, I assume?"

"Quite. I completely lost track of him ages ago, and he's never tried to contact me. All the better, I think."

"Really? Sounds like he might be an odd sort of fellow."

"More than odd. Duckie and Marsha never understood their son Claude very well. Even at an early age, they were alarmed, frightened sometimes, by outrageous things he said and did. Something amiss in his belfry, I'd say."

She took a deep breath. "One time, innocently enough, Claude took an interest in digging worms when he was about six. Duckie told me he thought he had been collecting them for fishing. That would be too logical, yes?" She glanced across at Toby to see if he was paying attention. "Claude washed them off, boiled them, and stuck them in his school lunch peanut butter sandwiches. He ate them in front of the class to see if he could make the other kids barf. When some of them did, so did his teacher. Would you believe Duckie thought the whole thing was rather humorous? Probably wished he thought of it when he was a kid."

"Harriet, is this pertinent? It's positively repulsive, and where's it leading?"

"I know it's icky, but you did ask." Harriet paused in her soliloquy to honk at the car ahead that was going too slow to suit her ilk. True to her habit, she bit her tongue, stomped on the throttle, and lunged past a vintage sedan, shouting, "Idiot!"

Harriet picked up where she left off about Claude. "Toby, you remember how little kids used to bury their pets in the backyard, like a goldfish? A good Christian burial in a cigar box with a cross made of twigs and string?"

"Of course I do, quite clearly, as a matter of fact. Along about Claude's age, I found a young robin with a crippled wing and broken leg in my front yard. Flew into a window, I imagine. Two of my buddies and I made a splint for the leg, and we decided to pray together for its recovery."

Toby heaved a sigh. "It trembled and died, probably of fright whenever I think back on it. We put this poor little fellow in a box I brought out from my mother's bedroom. From there we went to the nearby lawn of the parish priest. Holy ground, we believed. There, we dug a humble grave with a couple of spoons Freddy snitched from his parent's kitchen." Toby paused to reflect on the simple ceremony that followed, "I must say, Harriet, it was, without doubt, the most touching funeral service I've attended in all my years."

"Toby, it's easy for me to say that you and Claude have absolutely nothing in common. For one thing, he didn't like birds, animals, or pets, but he did love matches, so he took up cremating dead birds and critters. After a while, he went so far as to look for run-over critters to incinerate. But that was just the beginning. When Marsha's cat, Precious, wouldn't eat the mouse he trapped for it in their cellar, Claude hung her cat from a beam in the garage and blamed it on the cat's lack of appetite. Ha, as he got older, things really got out of hand. By the time he was thirteen, there was one incident that meant no school this side of hell would have him."

"Fine, you might as well get on with it then."

"Yes, Toby, this is the turning point for Claude. At his last school, he torched the headmaster's hencoop, not any old hens, but a rare and prized strain of Patagonian fowl. Caught out, he stood in front of the town magistrate and laughingly referred to his deed as a real chicken 'barbeque.'

"To avoid Claude being sent to a reform school, Duckie didn't have any choice except to find a private institution that would accept him. After he found one up in the Catskills, Marsha and Duckie seldom visited Claude, especially since he threatened to kill them both on sight."

"Criminy, this isn't some ordinary family spat. Why on earth would Duckie want to will Bloodstone Island to him?"

"I really don't know. Maybe he thought Claude's condition would improve with treatment, and he'd grow out of his crazy behavior. Or that Claude could make Bloodstone Island his home? An out-of-the-way retreat." Harriet sighed, "Duckie had his quirks too when it came to knowing right from wrong. When I think back on it, they probably had a lot in common. After what I've just told you, Duckie didn't think he was all that different from other young boys growing."

Harriet continued to stare at the road and oncoming traffic while her recollections continued to surface. She remembered how Duckie finally had his son incarcerated in a facility that specialized in youngsters that required physical restraint. She told Toby that when Claude was fifteen, Duckie had him sent to a psychiatric hospital in Switzerland because his hostile behavior had become worse.

Toby said, "Where do you think Claude is now?"

"I wouldn't know, but soon after Duckie died, Claude apparently lit out of the hospital. He's probably roaming around Europe some place."

"That or following you in a beat-up blue Coupe!" Toby huffed. "Really, Harriet, you must have suspected that Claude may be following you. That tall scruffy fellow that bumped into you leaving the diner, that could have been him. Why would he have asked if you were really Mother Tucker?" Toby's remark startled Harriet, and she shivered.

Toby began to sputter, "The way you've been acting since we left town, well, dammit, it must have crossed your mind that it was Claude that wrote that threat to you." Irritated, Toby's voice became as raspy as a file on a metal railing. "Claude sounds like a perfect candidate to try and pop you off, unless, of course, you're having me on again?"

"To be perfectly honest, Toby, it did cross my mind. But like so many things, I suppose it just kept going right on through." Her self-deprecating clever remark sailed right past Toby.

"There's just too much for me to think about all at once. I wish you'd be more understanding. After all, you are my fiancé." Toby gulped, and before he could respond, Harriet had decided to switch the conversation far away from the subject of Claude. "I think you should read the second letter, and you'll know why I find everything so confusing."

Thoroughly annoyed, Toby ripped the letter out of the envelope and flipped his reading glasses across the bridge of his pudgy nose where they slid down into their customary resting spot. Reading it aloud, he did not expect good news and hence could not be disappointed with the contents.

* * *

Wimbley, Baseheart, and Pierpont, Attorneys at Law
12-36 Old Wharf Street, Suite A
Portland, Maine

September 8, 1948

Mrs. Jeffrey Bartholomew
14 Golf Course Drive
Livermore Falls, New York

Re: Bloodstone Island
Dear Mrs. Bartholomew:

As you know, our firm in a custodial capacity was entrusted with the care and management of Bloodstone Island by the late Terrance D. Hadley of New York City, New York, according to the terms stated in his last will and testament.

It is with deep regret that I must inform you of the following recent circumstances and events that have come to light surrounding Bloodstone Island. Over the last ten years, a Mr. Humphrey Katheter of our firm had been in charge of overseeing and administering the trust. On September 2, Mr. Katheter disappeared, and in spite of reporting him missing to the authorities as a possible fugitive from justice, no evidence has surfaced to suggest his whereabouts.

By launching an internal investigation, we discovered that Mr. Katheter had been derelict not only in his duties but also managed to defraud the trust and drain it of all its monies and assets. Further, he never went to the island on inspection trips but filed reports and billed the trust nonetheless. We also learned that he disbursed trust funds from our affiliate bank, the Portland Guarantee and Trust, to nonexistent companies for repairs and maintenance that went into his personal bank account in Augusta. We have since discovered that his account had recently closed.

Since his disappearance, Mr. Wimbley and I chartered a boat to examine Bloodstone Island first hand. Because of a rough sea, we were not at liberty to conduct as thorough an exploration as the current state of affairs demanded.

Obviously, the elements have taken a heavy toll on the real property over the years. In addition, during our brief time on the island, we noticed disturbing evidence that squatters, trespassers, or persons of a similar or more criminal disposition may inhabit the island. Besides the various types of litter strewn along the shoreline, we encountered several handmade signs that threatened trespassers with bodily harm, some weathered and some of a recent nature in language unsuitable to describe herein.

For the above-stated reason, should you go to Bloodstone Island to comply with the terms of Mr. Hadley's will, we advise extreme caution.

In the meantime, we look forward to your response.

Your obedient servant,

Percy
Persevere Pierpont

* * *

Toby fell silent as he tried to grapple with the contents of the letter. His two hands, grasping the letter, fell slowly to his lap. Harriet, not knowing what to expect, gritted her teeth. The rain picked up again, and the wipers began their annoying journey back and forth across the windshield. Harriet searched the radio for the comfort of another voice, but without the antenna extended, the radio would only yield brief belches of static.

"Turn that thing off, Harriet. I've something to say. I wonder if you've given any consideration as to our accommodations on dear old Bloodstone Island. I've put aside the notion of any recreational activities while we're there, nuptial duties aside, which I've abrogated by contract. I've suddenly become absorbed with the notion of spending the night in a rat-infested dilapidated mansion with a bunch of reprobates or worse lurking outside in the bushes bent on doing us in."

"Now none of that, Toby. I've brought along the keys, including the one to the wine cellar. And Duckie kept his best scotch under lock and key. You forget that I know where everything is that we'll need. I'm sure there's no electricity, but there are oodles of oil lamps everywhere. You can make a nice fire in the master bedroom. I'll find the blankies, fix a light dinner, and we'll cuddle up for the night."

"That's all very comforting, Harriet. But haven't you at least considered backing out of this whole venture? It doesn't seem worth the risk to me. Let Claude have his Blood Island, and if he isn't interested, let the state have it."

"I wish it were that simple. It's all that I have from my marriage to Duckie. And I'm not willing to walk away from it, not without a fight."

"A fight that puts me in the ring? Now that I think of it, I guess I put myself in it. All I know is that when we get there, I'm going to bed with my revolver under the pillow."

"Good," replied Harriet, "and my pistol will be in my front porch if you need it."

"What on earth are you talking about?" replied Toby.

"In my brassiere, silly."

"Well, I must admit you do have an ample front porch for such a purpose."

Harriet giggled.

Chapter 8

Cover Your Bridges

Toby returned to the map spread across his knees and in an attempt to save time searched for alternate routes to Port Henry. A few precious hours had slipped away because of a variety of reasons including an encounter with the New Hampshire State Police. Toby checked his pocket watch and realized it would take a miracle to make it to the justice of peace, get married, and catch the Portland Packet in time. But, Toby, being a golfer, believed in miracles. It was part of his psyche.

"Harriet, I've been doing some checking, and I think you'd better step on it. The map shows a turnoff up ahead about two miles. It's a gravel back road that goes over a covered bridge right into Port Henry. That should save us some time."

"I'm all for that," Harriet barked. "Just keep your pants on!" Toby intended to do exactly that for the remainder of their foray to Bloodstone Island.

Shortly thereafter, Toby, gripping the armrest, began to regret urging Harriet to "get a move on." She had Mother Tucker's truck barreling down the county dirt road, throwing gravel in the ditches, and snaking around corners as if they were sliding on marbles.

"In an earlier life, Harriet, are you sure you weren't a race car driver?"

"No." She grinned. "But you know what I think? And I'll answer that. Deep down I think you're scared of women, especially someone independent like me, quite the opposite of your mother, I suspect.

Actually, I believe you really do like women, and you drool in your sleep for their approval."

"Really, Harriet, your language has taken a bad turn, and I don't appreciate you dragging my mother into the conversation. And furthermore, I don't drool." Toby crumpled the map and jammed it into the glove box. "And you're not as independent as you think," he sputtered, "or you wouldn't have dragged me into this simple little adventure of yours."

"Touched a nerve, have I? Well, I'm sorry. But excuse me while I imagine for a moment all your bravado when you're with the boys in the locker room—you and Sydney all puffed up in your element—snickering over your female conquests and how good you are at holding your liquor."

Harriet's words stung Toby into a state of speechlessness, which was unfamiliar territory for him. He speculated that she must be the female embodiment of Dr. Jekyll and Mr. Hyde. *What had come over Harriet?* He could only surmise that the age-old clash of the sexes had surfaced, and in this battle, he visualized being the big loser. "Harriet, I don't know what's touched you off like a Roman candle, but you might slow down a little. We're coming up on the covered bridge. It appears to be a one way." Choking on his words, he said in an attempt at levity, "We're beginning to sound like we're already married. Are we practicing?"

"I'm sorry to upset you, Toby, but in a way, I guess I meant to, because I happen to care about you." Punching the throttle, she gritted her teeth and zeroed in on the bridge. "Do you realize that you've devoted your entire life to your pal Sydney or should I say Mr. Emily Post and his Brookside Country Club?"

"Indeed, Harriet, your tone is way out of bounds, and you know on the course that carries a two-stroke penalty. Besides, it's rude. Speaking of which, you're about to have a rude introduction to the bridge if you don't s-l-o-w down."

"Oh . . . oh," Harriet yelped. "I didn't realize we're doing seventy. Hold tight, sweetiekins!"

Too late to apply the brakes on loose gravel, they rocketed into the darkness of the covered bridge and shot out the other side like a clown from a circus cannon. The Port Henry speed trap set up on the far side disappeared behind them, leaving a patrol car in a cloud of exhaust fume.

In less than a mile, the fishing village of Port Henry came into view, which brought a broad smile of accomplishment to Harriet and to Toby a broader smile of relief. Flashing over a rise in the road, the wheels barely touching, Harriet glanced down at the harbor and was relieved to make out the Portland Packet among a cluster of fishing boats. Still berthed at the town's long public pier, its boiler room belched black smoke in anticipation of sailing. Toby, on the other hand, took notice of the harbor's relatively calm water inside the breakwater. But the sea beyond it roiled. This did not bode well for his delicate digestive tract.

"Toby, Toby, Toby." In her excitement, Harriet's voice reached a higher octave. "It looks like we might pull this off after all, thanks to your short cut. I hope we can find someone to ask where the justice of peace is without too much trouble."

"Oh yes." Toby's chin dropped on his chest. "I don't think we'll have much trouble finding someone. Look in your mirror. There's a traveling information booth behind us with flashing lights and a policeman in it. You can ask him."

Harriet pulled off to the side of the road and folded her arms over the steering wheel. "Please, Toby, don't say anything, not now. I'm trying to think."

The Port Henry police officer cautiously pulled his squad car in behind their Mother Tucker Chocolate truck. A large man in a too tight police uniform emerged from the '46 Chevrolet, a car much too small for someone of his girth. He grappled with his suspenders and gun belt to restore order to his britches, which he wore at low tide. As he approached, he removing his sun shades and pushed back the bill of his cap to capture a sufficient amount of light to write down their out-of-state license plate. Harriet rolled down her window and watched the officer approach deliberately like a gunslinger in a B-movie. He had a look that said, "Gotcha."

"So, little lady," the officer opened with a thick down-east accent, "what seems to be the big rush?"

"Please don't tell me I was speeding, officer. I'm on my way into town to get married."

"You don't say," pointing to Toby, "to him?"

Toby replied, "Yes, me, officer. But you needn't be concerned, because we've agreed to divorce three days from today. I have it right here in our marriage agreement." Harriet turned around to look straight into Toby's eyes with a contemptible stare that defies description.

"Really?" said the officer. His eyes rolled up in disbelief. "I guess we do live in different times after all." Returning to the matter at hand, he said, "Maybe I better have a look at your license, ma'am. You too, mister." Taking them, he began scribbling on his pad. "New Yorkers, I might have known. And I see you're no Mother Tucker either. Do you mind telling me what you're doing in this vehicle? You didn't nick it, did you?"

Harriet replied, "There's not a scratch on it. We rented it from a nice gentleman in New Hampshire for our honeymoon, and as you can see, it's in perfect condition."

The officer shook his head and adopted a cast-in-place smirk. "A lady smart-aleck, huh? Now you might as well show me the registration, please." His eyes narrowed. "And keep your hands where I can see them."

"Really, officer, there's no reason to treat us like criminals," said Harriet, trying to take the offensive. She feigned a smile. "Have we done something terribly wrong?"

The officer smiled and nodded. "Don't play little miss innocent with me. You were doing fifty-five miles an hour over the speed limit when you crossed the covered bridge." His voice became shrill, his bark self-righteous. "That's considered reckless endangerment in our town. I suppose you didn't see the speed limit over the bridge, fifteen miles per hour. Besides that, you didn't come to a stop before you entered the bridge. Going too fast to see the stop sign?"

"Officer, I'm sure you know your duty, but we're really in a hurry." Anxiety furrowed her brow. "Couldn't you just give us a ticket and be done with it? We need to catch the Portland Packet."

The Port Henry police officer had his fish hooked, and he was not about to turn them loose until he had them stuffed and mounted. "Can't wait to get on with the honeymoon, eh? After you get married, where're you two lovebirds headed in such a big hurry?"

"Bloodstone Island," said Harriet, "and look, here are the tickets if you don't believe us."

"Now why wouldn't I believe you? See here, I don't know who sold you these tickets, but you'd better get your money back. The Packet hasn't stopped there in years, least not since the owner closed the place up."

"Oh good Lord, Toby, whatever are we to do?" Harriet's eyes welled up with tears, and she retrieved her handkerchief just in time to dab them before the dam broke.

Toby's words offered little comfort. "Well, I suppose it would be too much to ask of you, Harriet, but we could go into town and get your money back on the tickets." Toby thought a bit of sarcasm could make her angry again, and she'd stop sniveling.

"I hate to break up the chit chat," said the officer. "I need you both to step out of the truck. After that, ma'am, I'm going to administer a simple test to determine if you've been driving under the influence."

"Influence of what?"

"Old demon alcohol, that's what. You think I didn't see a flask on the floorboard?"

"That's mine," shot Toby.

"Easy, Mr. Worthington. Folks about to be honeymooners are apt to share. Unless it's full, it constitutes an open container of alcohol in the vehicle. That by the way constitutes a serious violation of the law around here and a heavy fine to boot. In any case, I'll need to examine it for evidence." Toby's mouth fell open, but no words came out.

Out of the truck, the officer waved them over to the side of the road and said, "Now listen to me, ma'am, I want you to close both eyes and point your left finger at your nose until you touch it."

"I'll do no such thing. You're a bully, and I'd sooner stick my finger up your nose."

"All right, I'll just testify before the justice of Peace that you refused to be tested." The officer, now on the third page of notes, inquired, "Does either of you have any firearms with you?"

"Well, y-y-yes, officer," stammered Toby. "Just for our own protection, don't you know? Can't be too careful out here in the sticks."

"Right. Tell me where they are, and I'll fetch them." Toby told him his WWI army pistol was in his golf bag in the back with his luggage. Harriet didn't want anyone rummaging in her purse, period, gripping it with the tenacity of a bull terrier. The officer prevailed in the tugging match however and dumped the contents of her purse on the front seat to retrieve her derringer. He chuckled when he discovered her gun. "Puny little thing." Examining both weapons, he muttered, "Good, neither one is loaded." Satisfied with that, he smiled and moved on. "I suppose you've got licenses you can show me?"

"Officer," said Toby taking a deep breath, "you really are working overtime to be difficult. The pistol is a war souvenir, and the United States Army happens to allow me to keep it. The derringer was nothing more than a clever gift of costume jewelry from her late husband."

"I take your answer to be no. I think we can wrap up the rest down at the station. I'll have to hold you over until the chief gets back and decides what to do about you two.

"For now, I want you to follow me into town, so get in your truck and wait for me. I've got to go back a ways and pick up a road kill, somebody's cat. Part of my job, so wait here."

Back in the truck, Harriet glanced at Toby, her voice quavering. "What do you think he m-m-means by hold over?" Harriet quavered.

"I think we'll find out soon enough. He's coming back with the cat in a gunnysack, and I think he's going to leave it in his trunk. Yes, now he's on his way over here.

"Officer," she called out, "will we be long at the station, and we really need to be on our way?"

"Oh, you'll be a guest of the Port Henry jailhouse until my chief gets back tonight and decides what to do with you two. He's out of town and might not get back until tomorrow." An earlier self-satisfied smirk returned. "Don't you worry now. It's not the honeymoon suite you two imagine, but it's not the worst sleepover in town."

Stunned, Toby and Harriet listened in silence until Toby croaked. "You can't just keep us without charging us. I'm not totally ignorant of the law."

"Are you in some sort of a rush, Mr. Worthington? When we get to the station, I'll be drafting up the charges soon enough."

* * *

Resigned to facing an overwhelming ordeal, Toby and Harriet slouched back in their seats. All day they had fought their way through biting storms and oppressive clouds, but nothing could match the cloud of doom that settled into Mother Tucker's cab. Reluctantly, Toby withdrew his never-to-be-used handkerchief. Humidity and anxiety drove perspiration from his brow down onto his nose where it dripped like a leaky faucet. Harriet did not fare better, dabbing at the tears that streaked her makeup.

Following the officer down a winding road to Port Henry, they realized they had no chance of getting married and catching the four o'clock Portland Packet, even if it did stop at Bloodstone Island. The road led into the center of a small yet bustling village of white clapboard houses and stores stringing itself out along the jagged coastline. Fishermen were unloading and sorting their catch on the docks. The packet had taken on board most of its passengers and light cargo. Pleasure boats and small craft bobbed at their moorage, secure from the heavy sea beyond the breakwater. A pictorial cluster of inns and shops hugged Port Henry's protected harbor, providing a perfect backdrop for events more pleasant than the one Toby and Harriet faced. Looming ahead, the county courthouse came into view, bristling with its row of tall white columns. They followed the officer down a side driveway to the chief's office, parked their Reo truck in the visitor's lot, and followed lockstep behind the officer. Inside, a pudgy redheaded officer named Hester Whipple, according to her badge, greeted them curtly. Peering over her reading glasses and a stack of detective magazines, she said, "Well, well, well, Jared, what have we here?"

"You'll know soon's I tally up the charges. If we get more folks like these two comin' through town, we'll be needing extra help around here. Get yourself a coffee and bring me one while you're at it."

Judging by appearances and the way her key chain jangled when she walked, she must also be the jailer. Biting his lip Toby turned to Jared, "Do you mind if we sit down, we've had a rather long day of it, don't you know."

"Can't say that I do know, but help yourself." Jared pointed his hat toward four metal chairs in the reception area.

Before returning to her desk, Hester lit a cigarette at the coffee bar and poured two cups. The phone rang several times before she returned to her desk and picked up the receiver, "Port Henry police station, got a problem?"

Her eyes winced as if she were getting an earful of pain. She stubbed off the end of her cigarette, cupped her hand over the receiver, and murmured to Jared, "It's the judge, old *Iron Pants.* She wants to know if anyone found her cat, Moxie. He snuck out of the house this morning and wasn't around when she got home."

"Tell her we'll keep an eye out and hang up." Suspecting the worst, Jared rushed out to the ash barrels and collected the cat he picked up after citing Harriet. He removed the studded cat collar and brought it into the office. Holding it up to an overhead light, he proceeded to read it aloud, "M-O-X-I-E."

Turning to Hester, he said, "I want you to call the vet'nary and ask him to drop over here on the double and pick up Moxie. Maybe he can reassemble her pussycat back together. There's bound to be a funeral of sorts, and he might have a proper box to put Moxie in. Oh, and when you call, tell her nicely we have her dead cat here. He died instantly and didn't suffer. It might comfort her to know that we have the couple in custody that ran over her precious Moxie." Not pleased, Hester crushed out her relit cigarette and took a deep breath before taking on her assignment.

"You know," said Hester, "the vet'nary ain't going to come. He doesn't do 'dead.' You want me to call the county coroner or our funeral home?"

"Your call, Hester." Jared turned his attention to Harriet and Toby who overheard the whole story unfold. With a sense of self-satisfaction at having the perpetrators in tow, his eyes locked in on Harriet's, "You know, lady, you ran over the wrong cat."

Harriet shivered. "I don't recall running over any cat."

"At the speed you were going through the bridge, I shouldn't wonder. Little Moxie didn't stand a chance." Pleased to see Harriet shaken, he then added, "No use denying it. Pussycat twan't lying there in the road before you come cannonballing through."

Flabbergasted, Toby remained seated while a defiant Harriet stood up and folded her arms defensively. "Don't tell me running over a cat is a crime in Port Henry?"

"'Tis if it belongs to the justice of peace," he replied, smiling through a fresh toothpick. "I'll just have to tack that on to my list for old *Iron Pants* to chew on."

Harriet returned to the metal chair next to Toby and leaned toward him to whisper, "Honest to God, Toby, I thought Chief Beebe was the worst lawman on the face of the earth, but this, this Jared is the biggest lump of horse pucky in New England." Suddenly, Harriet straightened up and said," Good heavens, Toby, did you hear them refer to the justice of peace as *Iron Pants*?"

"Yes, and I'm not sure what that portends for us, but it sounds like trouble to me."

Harriet, still puzzled, said, "I'm not sure that's a term of endearment or disrespect."

Overhearing Harriet's remark, Jared butted in, "Everyone in town calls her that behind her back. But she's known it for years. Some of us think she's pretty damn proud of it."

Harriet remained curious; she wanted to know everything about the justice of peace that might be helpful in the adjudication of her traffic violations. "Would it be improper of me to ask how she came by such a name?" Toby's hand shot over to hers in an attempt to quell anything that would be interpreted as aggressive.

Jared thought for a moment, scratched his chin, and engaged in a serious debate about whether to reply. In the end, he couldn't resist the impulse to gossip. "I should tell you anyway that she's a tough judge, and people here respect that. Keeps her reelected. But the real reason has to do with Jacob Anderson, the only man in town I or anybody else ever knew who tried to, how shall I put it, 'cozy' up to her." He smiled at the image he conjured up.

"Why don't you put a lid on it, Jared?" barked Hester across the room.

Surprised to be interrupted, he replied, "When I'm good and ready." Slouching in his swivel chair, he folded his arms over his chest and took delight in answering Harriet's pointed question. "It seems that Judge Abigail Underwood represented an impregnable fortress to Jacob's advances, over a considerable length of time, I might add. He's the one that coined the name *Iron Pants*. Of course, this is just my humble opinion." Returning to filling out the traffic charges against Harriet and Toby, he stopped to look up. "You can arrive at your own conclusions about the name *Iron Pants*. I just thought you ought to know that ever since she rejected Jacob's romantic advances, her only show of affection has been for cats. And, as I said, you ran over hers."

* * *

At four o'clock, the Portland Packet pulled away from the dock right on its summer schedule. The ship's long melancholy whistle indicated another precious passing of time for Toby and Harriet. "I'm glad I'm not on that tub," Hester said. "This storm isn't finished yet. Just look outside. Rain's blowing sideways again. I'm surprised they'd leave in this weather. You know, I wouldn't trust the packet to cross my bathtub let alone the stretch of water between here and Portland." Her plain speaking words echoed Toby's thoughts that also had serious reservations about challenging the sea this afternoon.

"Don't you worry over the packet, Hester," Jared said. "That coast guard cutter that's been parading up and down our coast? It can take care of that old scow. For some ungodly reason, they've been nosing around here like there's a war on. I don't know what they're looking for between here and Portland, but it must be awfully damn important."

Hester slid out of her chair and sauntered over to Jared. "I've been wondering the same thing. Up the inside passage of the barrier islands and down the outside. Round and round like they're on a race track." She scratched behind her ear with a pencil. "Maybe it's a training exercise." She paused again. "You think its Poachers? Contraband?"

Jared, always an observer and not one given to contemplation, looked up at her and shrugged.

Toby and Harriet had other things on their mind, although they judiciously kept an ear out for what transpired in the office, especially if their name popped up in conversation. During a lull in the office chatter, Toby whispered to Harriet, "Your feelings about Jared, you're right, of course, but we're at a serious disadvantage here." Toby retrieved his pipe and, while packing it, asked, "We've tried and missed this sailing of the packet. So how much time do we have left, contractually that is, to show up and spend the night there?"

The question surprised Harriet, even though it shouldn't have, and the blank expression on her face indicated that she didn't have a ready answer. Silent, she glanced down at her lap where her fingers fidgeted as if they were operating an invisible calculator. Bracing herself for Toby's reaction, she looked up and said matter-of-factly,

"Actually, Toby, it turns out to be the day after tomorrow, plus one or two, but I desperately wanted it to be today. I thought it best to have a little extra time to cover any eventualities, you understand, and give us a little time to spend together."

Eventualities, he recalled, *plagued us ever since we left Livermore Falls.* Incensed, Toby had no ready reply for Harriet and wondered for the umpteenth time how he could have stepped into such a quagmire.

Unexpectedly, the chief burst through the door and sailed his hat across the room that comfortably missed the hat rack. "Hi, Hester. I couldn't stay away from your charm and crappy coffee." Tall, muscular, and mustachioed, he obviously continued to swagger confidently through life since he captained the Port Henry high school football team. Behind his desk, just below a photograph of President Truman, Milo McDonald's police academy photograph, high school athletic letter, certificates of promotion, and awards for marksmanship lined the wall.

Reaching for his oak swivel chair, he said, "What's on the docket, Jared?"

Catching the chief's eye, he simply pointed his finger at Toby and Harriet.

"Hello there," said Milo, "You're a nice-looking couple. What can our humble office do for you?"

Toby got to his feet and approached the chief who'd settled in behind his desk. "Well, since you put it that way, we'd like to clear up our traffic problems and move on."

"I take it you're not from around here, right?"

"No, we're from Livermore Falls in New York. Harriet and I belong to Brookside Country Club. Perhaps you've heard of it?"

Bemused, Milo said, "Can't say that I have, should I? Anyway, welcome to our little town. You probably noticed that Officer Jared just slipped me a laundry list of your traffic violations. You and Mrs. Bartholomew need to know that you shouldn't be in too big a hurry to leave town."

"Well, Chief, we admit being in a rush to get here, and now we have to leave as soon as possible for Bloodstone Island. I have good reason to believe Mrs. Bartholomew's life is in jeopardy. We were being followed most of the day by someone we think would like to see her or both of us dead and preferably before we get married and arrive on Bloodstone Island."

"No disrespect, Mr. Worthington, but this sounds like some kind of parlor game for rich socialites. You know, treasure hunt."

"Really, Chief," replied Toby, "your reference to the Edwardian age of silly games out in the country is ancient history."

Milo adopted a more serious tone and leaned forward, resting on his forearms. "So who do you think is threatening her?"

"For one, it could be her stepson, Claude Hadley. I believe he's a product of her second husband's first marriage." Toby tapped his pipe in the sheriff's ashtray.

Milo appeared puzzled and began taking notes. "Anybody else? You said for 'one.' Are there others?"

"There may be others, but Harriet believes that Claude has an obvious motive to prevent her from getting her rightful inheritance. You see, Harriet and I need to establish our presence as a married couple on Bloodstone Island. If we succeed, my fiancée inherits the island according to her second husband's will. If not, Claude will inherit. Simple really."

"You don't say, Mr. Worthington?" The chief rolled his eyes and stared at the ceiling momentarily. He grappled for a pack of cigarettes in his top pocket. "What makes you think this Claude is disposed to violence?"

"Whoa, Milo." Jared slipped another traffic violation in front of the sheriff. "I pinched this Claude character this morning. Last name's Hadley. His left brake light was out, and I pulled him over. Blue '40 Chevy Coupe, his car's ready for the graveyard, Pennsylvania plates and all. In any case, I won't forget this character right away. Real nasty out-of-state type."

Harriet came to her feet as if some internal fire alarm went off. "That's him all right, the obnoxious little creep, I have no idea what he looks like, but I know he's a couple of years older than I am." Stepping over to Milo's desk, she said, "And another thing, when he was a kid, he had to be incarcerated in a mental hospital. A psychopath or sociopath, I think the doctors said."

Chief Milo threw up both hands as a gesture for everyone to stop talking. "Let me get this straight. You don't know your stepson who's following you, but arrives in town ahead of you in an old wreck. Now you both say he's capable of murder. Sounds like a stretch to me."

Jared interrupted again, "This Claude guy is definitely creepy. His eyes don't line up, if you know what I mean. He and I were definitely at cross-purposes. He mumbled that he'd have the light fixed. Then I warned him what would happen if he didn't report back to this office in seven days."

Harriet, her face suddenly flushed, blurted out, "I told you so, Chief. And I have threatening mail to prove it." She began digging frantically in her purse. "Care to see it?"

"Not right now, ma'am. I don't know what I can do to help you two out or even protect you. But you and I still have to deal with these traffic charges. Jared was very specific as to your violations." Back at his chair, Jared's smirk returned, which he put on as if it were part of his uniform.

Milo took a long drag from his Lucky Strike cigarette. "Are you prepared to dispute the charges before the justice of peace?" He slid the list of charges in front of Harriet and waited for her response. Stopped in her tracks, she took a long deep breath in an effort collect her wits before summoning an answer from deep within. Toby crossed his fingers. Hester rolled her swivel chair closer to the chief's desk to hear Harriet's response. Jared stood silently in rapt anticipation.

Harriet fell back on two of her great inner strengths, perseverance, and self-preservation. "Chief, my life suddenly became more complicated when Toby and I crossed a covered bridge into Port Henry." She began pacing like an attorney in summation before a jury, and all eyes followed her. "I'm pleading innocent to all charges, and if this complicates your lives, so be it. I'll take my chances with *Iron Pants*."

Hester immediately spun around and turned her back on Harriet's onlookers to hide a broad grin about to burst into a chuckle. She felt a certain delight erupt within her when women took a stand; and Hester admired among others *Iron Pants* for having made her mark. As one who had been on the receiving short end in a man's world since childhood, she determined early on in life to hold her own and decided to give as good as she got, even though it might mean disappointment and heartbreak along the way. Irritated with Jared's constantly condescending demeanor, Hester knew that advancement in the department depended on cunning if she were to climb around or over Jared. Harriet and Hester chose to plow her way through a sea of men but occasionally found it necessary to tack their way forward.

When she heard Harriet's defiant plea, she empathized with her desperate position. At the same time, she suddenly recognized that she just might have stumbled upon an opportunity to further her own cause and, as a byproduct, that of Harriet's.

Donning her rain gear, she announced that she was going out to the parking lot to check on their squad cars and have a look at the Mother Tucker Chocolate truck.

Harriet unknowingly had an ally now, even though Hester was only a pawn on the chief's chessboard.

Chapter 9

Jailbirds

Harriet's innocent plea backed up the chief's office agenda and sent it down a different road. Schedules had to be adjusted for the following day appearance before the justice of peace who, without her Moxie, could either be bereaved or short tempered or both. On quiet days, her cat used to keep her company, and the town clerk saw to it that a fresh saucer of milk resided in the kneehole of her desk on days she presided. Tomorrow, absent her feline companion, *Iron Pants* could be contentious; and the chief knew it. Jared's attempt to lighten the pallor that had descended on the office fell flat when he suggested the flag be lowered to half-staff for Moxie.

Milo grimaced at the remark and rang the courthouse office upstairs just before it closed for the day. Phyllis Maybury, the town clerk, answered the call. Milo knew the practice to hold hearings such as traffic disputes and family squabbles occurred in the afternoon schedule and asked that Bartholomew and Wadsworth be included.

Phyllis obliged and scribbled in Harriet and Toby names for tomorrow's 1:30 p.m. open time slot to appear before the justice of peace. Suddenly, she recognized their names, and exclaimed, "Hold your horses, Milo. Those two were supposed to be in here today to get married. A tad bit late at the altar, wouldn't you say?"

"I suppose. They did say they were in town to get married. Well, it's partly our fault down here. We put them on hold, so to speak."

"Abigail d-o-e-s-n't take kindly to being put off. Listen, we've got a short schedule of legal matters to clear up in the morning. Have them up here by nine o'clock, and I'll squeeze 'em in."

Milo sounded relieved. "Thanks, Phyllis. I'd really like to get them out of here, out of town for that matter." He glanced over at Toby and Harriet and lowered his voice. "They're sort of a pain and you know where." He chuckled briefly. "By the way, I should tell you that Moxie, you know Abigail's cat, is no longer with us. He got run over today, and Jared claimed our newlyweds-to-be are responsible."

"Oh god! Now how in damnation is all this going to play out?" She gasped. "I don't think Port Henry's ever had a double execution before, but this could be the first. Sending a couple to the gallows the same day they're married? Milo, that cat has been a courtroom fixture as long as I can remember, a genuine all-American lap cat." She swallowed hard. "And *Iron Pants* never rendered a decision without asking Moxie's opinion."

"Phyllis, calm down. You're beginning to raise your voice. Go home and get a good night's rest."

She didn't reply and slammed down the receiver.

Hester, back from the parking lot, shook the water off her rain gear and combed her hair back with her fingers. "All's good out there, as 'spected. Sure is a nice candy truck you got there, folks."

Milo, exercising his authority like a drill sergeant, said, "Hester, be a good sport and bring me tomorrow's schedule for the judge. I want to pencil in Mrs. Bartholomew and Mr. Worthington for nine in the morning and one thirty in the afternoon." Looking straight at Jared, he said, "You need to make yourself available at one thirty, and no adlibbing on the stand. Understood?" Jared nodded like a scolded schoolboy.

"Now let me see. Mr. Worthington and Mrs. Bartholomew, I am disposed, perhaps against my better judgment, to release you until you'll have to appear back here at eight o'clock tomorrow morning. All right?" Toby and Harriet sat tongue-tied. Milo began again, "Since I've come to believe your common interest resides in getting married and jumping over to Bloodstone Island for whatever, I don't think you're a flight risk. But don't skip out of town, and please understand your vehicle is impounded." He paused, reached for another cigarette, and looked around the room again for some reaction to his edict.

To everyone's surprise, Toby took the initiative. Toby rose from his chair and folded his hands behind his back. He cleared his throat as he walked over to the front office window. Peering out, he said,

"Chief, I appreciate your trust, but under the circumstances, we're not anxious to leave these confines. Claude is probably out there just beyond these walls, either looking or waiting for us." Toby turned to look over his shoulder at Harriet, seeking some sign of approval. "I think I speak for Harriet too."

Toby walked languidly back to his chair next to Harriet. Together again, they sat erect and lock kneed, waiting for Milo's decision.

The chief looked contemplative, as if he were waiting for a play to come in from the coach. "Well, I can certainly see your point. Preferring our jail to a hotel in town at least backs up my hunch you're probably tellin' the truth."

Milo saw an opening to close any debate over the issue and leave for home. He responded quickly to Toby's concern, "Hester, fetch some sheets, pillowcases, and pajamas for our overnight guests." Looking at his two quavering miscreants, he pointed to a cellblock down the hall. "You and your fiancée won't mind sharing a cell, right?" Not waiting for their approval, e called out loudly to Hester again before she got out of earshot., "Have the Lighthouse Inn send over two chicken fried steak dinners and one for yourself at six, and charge it to our office. You know the routine."

"You're the boss," said Hester. "Anything else while I'm standing here?"

Toby interrupted and raised a finger, saying, "If you don't mind, at our age and station in life, we would appreciate a meal absent fried foods however well prepared by the inn's chef. I'd be happy to reimburse your office or the inn for say a fare of poached salmon and boiled potatoes?"

Milo, impatient, raised an eyebrow and said, "Are you absolutely sure there isn't anything else?"

"Perhaps a tomato aspic and a key lime pie or the like for desert. I don't wish to cause any inconvenience."

Milo fell back in his chair and stared at the ceiling for a moment. "All right, Hester, you heard him. I give up. Get them whatever they want and get something you'd like too." Milo thought for a sarcastic split second, *It's probably the newlyweds' last meal anyway.* Hester smiled. "As I said, you're the boss. Oh, and thank you."

The prospect of spending the night in a jail cell did not bode well in Harriet's mind, as it represented a totally foreign human habitat, except of course in books she'd read about the prevalence of prison rats preying on inmates. But by giving Toby an almost imperceptible nod of approval earlier, she had tacitly agreed with his assessment of the situation. They would be spending the night together, sharing the same cell, if not the same bunk. Still, it raised a cause of concern for Toby.

From his chair, Toby glanced up at a bulletin board covered with wanted posters of society's leading criminals. He imagined his picture and that of Harriet's being new additions. His thoughts rambled over the last ten hours, realizing, *We're probably wanted in three states by now. Beebe must have discovered by now Harriet stole her own impounded car. Brilliant! Evading a state trooper in New Hampshire, another veteran move by Harriet. Cripes, not even lunch for us at the Crooked Chimney Inn, settled for crappy diner food. Thanks now to my fiancée's driving expertise, we've landed in a Maine hoosegow.*

Head in hands, his brain chugged along down the same railroad track, *Me, a three-time loser, dammit-all. That fits me to a T. I'd like to kill the idiot that said getting there's half the fun? God Almighty, I can hardly wait for the other half.*

Instead of going to the storeroom, Hester made a detour to the mailroom where the teletype machine chattered away printing out up-to-date police bulletins. She hunched over in front of the electronic marvel as it spewed out police reports from around the region. Once it stopped printing, she tore off the messages and checked to see if the teletype needed a new roll of paper. Walking back to her desk, she scanned it intently. Attaching it to a clipboard, she moseyed over to Jared and dropped it off on his desk. She looked over at Toby and Harriet and noticed their eyes staring back at her with a look of anxiety. "Relax. There's no mention of you two here, Claude either." Relieved, Toby sighed and patted Harriet on the knee.

Toby became increasingly restless. He returned to the front window and gazed out upon the unusual triangular village green, its flagpole, white iron benches, and a pair of wooden stocks common for punishment in the days of Puritan justice. He tried to imagine how he and Harriet would look locked up in such a contraption, two targets bent over with their head and hands dangling out, unable to dodge missiles of rotten vegetables. Commenting on his observation, he said, "Chief, I'm certainly relieved to know the stocks aren't in use anymore."

"Actually, Mr. Worthington," replied Milo grinning, "funny you should ask, but that form of punishment is still on the books. It's reserved for, as I recall, 'unspecified crimes' too horrendous to punish by other means."

Toby returned to his seat and said to Milo, "Well, I'm certainly glad that leaves us out."

* * *

In preparing their jail cell furnishings, the chief obliged one of Harriet's requests by producing two rickety wood chairs they could use as improvised nightstands. Not to be overlooked, Toby asked for a privacy screen to divide the cell he'd be sharing with Harriet. Grumbling, Hester brought another bed sheet and hung it up over a close line she found buried in the storeroom. Toby expressed his gratitude to Hester, without giving an explanation.

This delicate cotton curtain provided, at best, the psychological defense Toby needed against what he perceived Harriet's nature to be, an aggressive female sex predator. Besides, he did not wish to encourage her with any unintended display of his manhood before lights out, not that he envisioned himself as the epitome of a desirable young buck. He remained committed to his prenuptial agreement, which insisted that there would be no consummation of their relationship during their brief marriage. Now he wanted to insure against the possibility of such a thing happening the night before.

Finally, Hester's nerves frayed to the breaking limit when she had to fetch two water pitchers from the lunchroom and retrieve their medications, which were locked up in the property room. Addressing no one in particular, she spit out, "Are we running a jailhouse or a goddamn guest house?" No one volunteered an answer to her question.

The twilight hours began by passing quietly. The ferocity of the storm seemed to have abated, even though the downspouts continued to gush storm water. Everyone knew that it would take only one old maple to topple over on the power lines to plunge the whole town into darkness. The lights in Port Henry had been flickering on and off all day but had remained steady the last couple of hours.

Anxious to be home in time for the family's evening meal, Milo checked out at five o'clock. Jared had left a half hour earlier to return to his favorite stake out at the Walkover Bridge, mainly to escape any jailhouse duties that he might be assigned. Usually off duty at six o'clock, his routine let him drive home to the solitude of his apartment upstairs over Hopkins's Hardware store. Alone now, Hester became the boss.

* * *

On time, a buzzer at the front door signaled the arrival of the previously ordered evening meals. Hester ushered the busboy from the Lighthouse Inn into the office, signed his chit, and directed him to leave the hot meals on the lunchroom counter. Toby and Harriet needed no coaxing to follow Hester to the table. Following the chief's directions to satisfy everyone's personal taste, she had ordered liberally from the inn's menu. Appreciative, Toby dropped a twenty into a mason jar on the table that collected donations for the Policeman's Ball. Hester took notice. Famished, the three devoured their entrées in silence.

But while they were washing their desert down with hot coffee, Hester slipped Harriet a small plain sealed envelope. In the kind of whisper that hints of confidentiality, he said, "Don't open this now, but before you get up in front of *Iron Pants,* open it and then you'll know what to do."

"Really. I guess I should thank you, even though I have no notion of what it is. But in our situation, it certainly can't harm." Harriet tucked it away in her blouse pocket. "Thanks."

"No thanks necessary. It's to my benefit as much as yours." Hester returned to her apple pie mounded with whipped cream.

Toby, sitting at the end of the table, watched and listened to the conversation. Being confused, he decided not to enter into whatever transpired, dismissing it as more *woman talk.* His only real thought at the moment envisioned a nightcap and how nice it would be before bedding down, but that wasn't going to happen.

After dinner, Toby and Harriet returned to their cell. Toby sat down gingerly in the middle of his bunk, while Harriet probed her bunk like a cautious cat with only one life left to live. Finally, both began flopping up and down in a futile exercise to check the firmness of their springs and mattresses. According to their agreement with the chief, the jail door was left open so they could, at will and as often as they found necessary, trundle off to the bathroom down the hall without having to ask for an escort.

Toby had taken the Port Henry newspaper with him to check the classified ads for charter boats as an option of getting to Bloodstone Island. His way of keeping an even keel meant looking to the future no matter how grim, ahead not behind. He constantly had to remind himself that he did promise to get Harriet to Bloodstone Island, no matter the expense. And the expense, he contemplated, could cost him both his dignity as a bachelor and his long friendship with Sydney. With Claude on the prowl, it could even cost him his life.

The storm may have been in its death throes, but the voice of God Thor still had more to say before it left town. A flash of lightening and the simultaneous clap of thunder brought both Harriet and Toby upright in their bunks. The windows replied by rattling in their frames as if they shook from fear. Lights flickered but stayed on. Like aftershocks in an earthquake, the thunder roared off to the south and west.

Hester, accustomed to nature's wrath, went into the lunchroom and poured another cup of coffee. Returning to her front desk station, she told Toby and Harriet that the storm was officially over and proceeded to settle down with the latest copy of *True Detective* to wait for her eight o'clock relief.

When the phone rang at seven thirty, she winced at being interrupted and slammed the magazine down. "Port Henry Police Station, what is it?" A long silence prevailed, which alarmed Toby and Harriet. "Oh, good God," said Hester, "I've got a great aunt on the packet. I knew I should have told her not to go." A long ominous pause followed while she hurriedly took notes. The teletype began chattering again. "OK, you people in Portland are in charge. We'll stand by if needed." She hung up and sprinted for the mailroom.

Unable to contain his curiosity, Toby called out, "What's happening, Hester?"

"Not now. I've things to do, later. The packet's run aground on Turquoise Island."

Harriet sat straight up on the edge of her bunk with the shock of the news. Her voice rattled, "Toby, we could have been on the packet."

"Yes, and it seems we're a lot luckier off in jail? I can't believe it. This is awful. I don't know how I should feel, both perhaps, sorry and angry how this accident could happen."

Toby and Harriet listened to Hester as she made a series of calls on her list in case of an emergency. Once through, she leaned back in her chair and took several deep breaths. There was nothing she could do about her aunt, except hope that she survived. As a diversion to her personal distress, she read to Toby and Harriet the stilted information she just retrieved from the Teletype.

BULLETIN: EMERGENCY 19:30 HOURS
PORTLAND PACKET STEAMER: LOST STEERAGE:
SENT SOS 18:06: ROUGH SEAS
SWAMP SHIP: VESSEL AGROUND ON WEST SHORE
TURQUOISE ISLAND 18:36: COAST
GUARD ON SCENE 20:10: RESCUE IN PROGRESS:
END

Her voice breaking, "Well, that's it. We'll just have to wait it out and see what happens."

Anxious to be with relatives, Hester already had her coat on when her relief arrived at ten minutes to eight. She quickly introduced the young man to Toby and Harriet, explaining that Spencer was fresh out of the police academy but is well acquainted with procedures. About to bolt out the door, Hester turned and said, "Perhaps there are a couple of things I should tell you before I leave about our two guests. They come across as a little uppity, old-school manners, you know the silver spoon type, but they're not a bad sort, getting married upstairs tomorrow. So be nice. OK?" Spencer nodded. Hester left in haste.

The next few hours passed in quietude except for traces of popular music drifting from officer Spencer's radio, that and the patter of rain against the windows. Even the teletype fell silent. At ten o'clock, Spencer rose from his desk to check doors, glance through the Venetian blinds at the department's parking lot, and douse the lights, except his own desk lamp and a small nightlight in the jail cell hallway.

Toby didn't realize that the nightlight cast his shadow on the sheet that separated his bunk from Harriet's. Toby complained bitterly about the tight fit of his jailhouse pajama top, knowing of course his outrage would fall on deaf ears. Accustomed to wearing a simple one-piece nightshirt, he did not bother to put on the pajama bottom.

Harriet, suspicious that Spencer might have roving eyes, crawled beneath the sheets to undress and slip into her pajamas. While climbing out of bed to fold her clothes over a chair, she looked over at the sheet. There stood Toby's full frame shadow. Yawning, Toby stretched his arms and proceeded to organize his private parts like a mechanic rearranging his toolbox, and he spent an inordinate time at his task.

Fascinated, Harriet's pulse quickened as she crouched nock-kneed, her hands frozen to the chair. Her throat tightened so much that her breath finally erupted into a crescendo of loud gasps.

Toby, befuddled, asked, "What's the matter now, Harriet, one of your nightmares?"

"Perhaps it's foretelling one. Go back to bed, Toby! Please."

Spencer came running to investigate, "What's all the trouble back here? I'll have none of it."

Harriet replied, "It's nothing, Officer. I broke my nail on the bed rail. You know how troubling that can be." Shaking his head, but satisfied, Spencer returned to his post.

Unable to sleep, Toby tossed in his bunk, hunting for a swale in the mattress befitting his ample frame. Attempting to fluff his pillow was like trying to fluff a bag of cement or arrange his toolbox.

Harriet had a measure of the same discomfort. She just had a fright and was too exhausted to drift off to sleep. Worried and frustrated over their dire circumstances, she began to snivel. Dabbing her eyes on the sheets pulled over her head, she gathered herself together once again.

"Tob-e-e-e," she said softly. "I can't sleep. Can you come over and tuck me in?"

Chapter 10

A Courtroom Appearance

Right after daybreak, Toby and Harriet awoke from a restless night's sleep. Wearing a towel around his waist, Toby was doubly worn out, having gone back and forth several times to tuck Harriet in. Anxious to tackle the day's business, they took a number of turns using the restroom to be sure they looked spiffy. Toby called out to Spencer, saying that they would like to change into clothes more suitable to go before the justice of peace. "Want to look our best, don't you know?"

"So?"

Sensing his ambivalence, Harriet appealed, "We'll need our suitcases. They're locked up in your storage room."

Reluctantly, Spencer dropped his feet off Hester's desk and proceeded to the backrooms to collect their luggage. Being quite a number of pieces and not knowing which ones to bring, he brought the lot. "And listen," he said, "I need to use the bathroom too before I get off duty."

The pair agreed to be decked out in full uniform, wearing their slightly crinkled Brookside Club blazers rather that dressing in casual summer garb. "Harriet, if we are defeated today, it'll be with our boots on and swords drawn." Toby chuckled as she adjusted his classic bow tie.

Harriet smiled. "At least we won't look like some riff-raff that gets the swift boot." Toby nodded.

Harriet retrieved the envelope that Hester gave her the night before and slipped it into the inside pocket of her blazer.

Toby yawned. "I wonder what happened to the packet last night?" Calling out again to Spencer, he asked him if he'd heard anything.

Spencer walked part way from Hester's desk toward their cell and stopped. "Guess you didn't overhear all the traffic coming through late last night. Good news. Coast guard got everybody off—thirty-two passengers and six crew. Took 'em to Portland." He retreated back to his desk to complete his activity report and said, "The packet didn't make it though. Tide dragged it back off the rocks, and it sunk. Just as well probably, everybody thought it was ready for the scrapyard."

At six thirty, the front door buzzer rang. Spencer opened the door to let Hester in, carrying a flat of freshly made donuts. "Hi, Hester. Fresh coffee's on. If you brought any crullers, let me have one. I need to be on my way."

"I can see that," said Hester. "What's the big rush? Got a heavy date for breakfast?"

Spencer tried talking through a mouthful of a cruller. "No, but it sure is good news about the packet."

"Right, and my aunt Sue's OK, except for a few bumps and scrapes. I heard she wouldn't get off until the captain came with her. Tough old bird. No call for the old man to go down with a rust bucket. Anyway, if your paperwork's done, get your tail out of here."

Hester settled in back at her desk and summoned the cellmates. "Hey, are you two lovebirds up and about yet? I've got coffee, cold cereal, and donuts ready in the lunchroom. You can't get married on an empty stomach."

"In a minute," replied Harriet, "just need to freshen my makeup. Toby's taking his tablets."

Hester knew Jared had arrived when she heard the back door from the parking lot slam shut. Hester, Toby, and Harriet had already settled in at the lunchroom table. He shot directly past them with a grunt similar to a wild boar.

"Pay no attention to him. He gets disgruntled every time he has to testify in front of the Iron Pants." Hester opened a paper bag she had brought with her and produced two boutonnieres.

"Since you'll be getting married shortly, I thought you ought to look the part."

"Why thank you," exclaimed Harriet. "What a kind thought and certainly unexpected."

"There's no need to thank me at all," Hester replied. "Just you remember to open the envelope I gave you when the time comes. Say, why don't you two freshen up, and when you come back, I'll take you up to the courtroom."

* * *

Toby and Harriet followed Hester up the back stairs of the station to the second floor courtroom, which prisoners who were headed to trial used. From the door at the top of the stair landing, they proceeded across a lobby, heading for the courtroom entrance. The grandeur of the space diminished with the pervasive smell of stale wax and polish, which blended with the odors of disinfectant emanating from the restroom doors left ajar, all too typical, Toby thought, of poorly ventilated public buildings.

The sound of their footsteps echoed as they traipsed across the granite floor. Toby surmised that Port Henry's commitment to a stately courthouse delivered a strong message that the town took the law seriously. Toby paused a moment to take a measure of the space, cranking his neck to glance at its high ceiling. Portraits and murals of the town's history adorned the walls. He turned to admire the broad steep stone stairs and ornate brass railings leading down to the street below. Hester, annoyed with Toby's progress, prodded him toward a pair of tall oak-paneled doors where Harriet waited.

There, Toby marveled at the solid brass handles fashioned after ship davits. He spoke unabashedly about his admiration for them and ran his hands affectionately over the oil-rubbed carved panels on the doors. Off in his own world, Toby was unaware of the disturbing mood his dalliance visited upon Harriet and Hester.

Inside, the bailiff, sensing visitors, swung the door open; and Toby virtually fell inside. After reestablishing his footing, his eyes popped open with a look of incredulity on his face. The courtroom overflowed with memorabilia of the town's history with the sea: artifacts and sailing ship models; ropes, pulleys, and signal flags; wood everywhere, every kind; hard maple-pegged floors, soft pine wainscots, birch and teak railings, oak captain's chairs in the jury box and visitors section, all wafting the pleasant smell of linseed oil, varnish, and hand-rubbed shellac. His gaze traveled upward where two rows of light fixtures hung from heavy anchor chains. Six proud old sailing ship's wheels had been retired to shore duty as chandeliers, shedding some light from days past, albeit electric from what used to be oil-burning brass lanterns.

Harriet, also startled, suddenly became amused and whispered to Toby, "This would make a wonderful theme restaurant, don't you think?"

At the far end of the room, on axis with the main aisle, Phyllis, the town clerk, sat erect behind a broad table, collating papers in preparation of the morning's business. Directly behind her rose the judge's bench, resembling that of a preacher's pulpit. Framing either side of the judge's high back velveteen chair, the Star-Spangled Banner and the Main State flag stood at attention.

Once again, Toby stopped in his tracks. He leaned toward Harriet and said, "Will you just look at that?"

"What?"

"That huge oil portrait between the flags, behind the podium. It belongs in the Vatican."

"Oh, that," said Hester. "That's Judge Underwood, founder of Port Henry. Better known as old Judge Keelhaul."

Harriet clutched the nearest chair rail. "You mean *Iron Pants* is a direct descendant of HIM?"

"A-yuh. Don't fret. Come on, I'll take you down to the defendant's table on the left.

Shuffling down the center aisle with Harriet, Toby took notice of the large oak-framed wall clock ticking away. The sight of its pendulum swinging with each passing minute conjured the image of a medieval axe ratcheting nearer and nearer to his neck. Sitting at the table, he reached over and took Harriet's hand. "You'll pardon me if I seem a little nervous. It's my first marriage, don't you know?"

"Well, you make my fourth, and if it's any comfort, this is by far the most nerve wracking."

Toby withdrew his hand, making a mental note that it would also be her shortest. He glanced again at the tick-tocking wall clock, which seemed to grow louder with each passing minute. *Hmmm. Only a moment or two before doomsday*, he thought, clearing his throat. *I wonder what Sydney's doing right now. No doubt he's on his way to the club, probably looking for an afternoon golf match or a game of bridge. He's no good at bridge, not without me as a partner anyway. Whenever he gets stuck in a rough patch, I've always had to come along and pull him out. Well, he'll just have to do it alone.*

* * *

More precisely, back in Livermore Falls, it was exactly 8:48 a.m. when the desk clerk at the 1876 House waved the morning paper at Sydney as he walked through the lobby. "Mr. Wadsworth, did you see the news? The Portland Packet ran aground last night in a big storm off the coast of Maine."

"Let me see that!" Sydney spun around in his tracks. *Good Lord,* he thought, *Toby and Harriet were supposed to be on that ship. I might have known. It's my fault. I never should let him out of my sight when he's with Harriet.*

Sydney resolved to kill Toby in case he survived the sinking, but his only thought at the moment was to get to the accident site as soon as possible. He would decide a suitable fate for Harriet later.

Newspaper details were sketchy and gave Sydney little comfort. The *Livermore Falls Journal* had reported:

The coast guard was on the scene and was involved in a rescue effort to save the passengers and crew. The captain of the steam-powered Portland Packet radioed that it lost power when a water pump failed to keep up with storm water entering the hold. The main boiler was extinguished. Losing power and steerage, the violent storm tossed the doomed Portland Packet on the rocks of the uninhabited Turquoise Island.

The packet was on a routine run to its homeport in Portland, Maine, when the accident happened. One of the first steel-hulled vessels, it provided service for passengers and light cargo to several coastal towns and islands.

Sydney engaged the clerk at the front desk. "I seem to recall there is some kind of air service located near town. I need to get over to the Maine coast in a hurry. There's a chance my good friend Toby Worthington was on board, and he may be alive."

"I'm sorry to hear that, Mr. Wadsworth. You two are like brothers. Perhaps he's been rescued." The clerk's fingers nimbly flipped through the phone book. He glanced up and noticed Sydney's troubled face. "Hey, maybe he didn't even get on that tub."

"Possibly, and I appreciate your concern, but—"

"Here it is, Mr. W., Monarch Airlines, *Short-haul freight, Charters, Lessons, Rescue.* Hector Monarch runs it. He's new in town. Honestly, I don't know how he makes a living. He's got a nice grass field and hangar down by the Beaverkill, but he's always plowing up someone else's pasture. He's got two airplanes and shoot, one of 'ems usually laid up."

"Yes, yes, very comforting observation. Be a good man and call him up for me."

After several rings, Sydney overheard a chipper voice on the other end, "Monarch Airlines, how may we help you?"

Grabbing the phone, Sydney said, "This is Wadsworth calling, Sydney Wadsworth. I'm interested in chartering a round-trip flight to the Maine coast, and before you answer, I also want you to know that I'm a resident of the 1876 House and a member of Brookside Country Club. Of course, I will be the only passenger, and I would like to depart as soon as you can have one of your aircraft available."

There was a short pause then, "This is Meg Monarch, hold on, please. I'll have to check with my bro, the owner." Several minutes passed while Sydney toe-tapped his frustration until Hector Monarch came on the line and introduced himself, "Mr. Wadsworth, I'll be your pilot. I'm more than happy to be of service. As a matter of fact, the *Monarch One* is fueled and ready for takeoff at a moment's notice. You can fill out the usual contract papers when you get here."

"Good, I'm much obliged. I'll fill you in with the details when I arrive. I'll be there in a few minutes after I grab a duffle bag from my room and catch a ride."

"Yes, but I should tell you that there is some nasty weather off to the east. It's beginning to spit rain here now, and my barometer tells me there's a blow coming. The storm could be bad enough that we may have to turn back."

"Yes, I understand. But let's give it a go. I'll pay up either way." Sydney hung up hurriedly and asked the clerk to dial Brookside.

Simone answered the phone with her usual charming French accent. Of late, Sydney had become vulnerable to her deep seductive tone of voice and coquettish mannerisms. He found himself increasingly in her sway whenever they engaged in conversation, and his feelings for her made him uncomfortable.

"Simone, I wouldn't think of troubling you, if it were not an emergency. Could you give me a lift from my place to the Monarch airfield? You know where it is?"

"Yes, and you will be pleased to know my driving is much improved. I assume you'd like me to come right now. You are off going to find your friend, Tobee, yes?"

"Yes, and how the devil did you find that out?"

"As you yanks say, news journeys fast. I'm on my way, au revoir."

Woody, the Brookside station wagon, was still behaving strangely under Simone's direction when it pulled up in front of the 1876 House. However, Sydney was not about to give her any grief.

They drove in silence along the Beaverkill when Simone opened the conversation. "I want to say that I think you are very brave to risk your life flying in one of those, those butterfly planes. You must love your friend Tobee very much."

"Why, yes, I guess I do. I wouldn't say love, but we've been close for many years."

"I admire that. Friendships can be so short and shallow."

"I'm sorry, Simone. It sounds as if you've had a recent disappointment."

Simone did not answer but smiled and plucked a black bow tie from her club blazer.

"Ohhh, Mr. Wadsworth, remember this tie? I want you to wear it today for good luck. I forgot to put it in the club's lost and found. Anyway, you should have it now since it seems to be a trademark of yours around the club."

Although Sydney had denied ownership earlier, he was grateful to get it back. At a complete loss for words, he managed to say, "Thanks, Simone. I hope I won't need luck today."

Simone slowed the *Woody* down as the east end of the Monarch airstrip came into view. Halfway down the airstrip, the Stebbin's old red barn now served as the hangar and terminal, a perfect retrofit. Built long before the birth of aviation, it still stood tall and proud with its handsome slate roof.

As if waiting for orders, an army surplus Jeep stood at attention next to the gaping hangar door. Fifty yards from the Millhouse River Road was the gravel entrance drive to Monarch Airlines. The American flag at the entry confirmed the strength and direction of the wind pointing west. Only the old rusted-in-place weathervane atop the barn's cupola disagreed by pointing north.

Light rain began to splatter *Woody* when it came to a stop in front of the hangar. A wire-glass door displayed a cardboard "OPEN" sign fashioned most likely with a crayon. Sydney glanced over at Simone, smiling weakly. "Perhaps I could use a bit of luck."

"You don't have to go, Mr. Wadsworth," Simone pleaded. "I'm sure Tobee would understand." She reached over to pat his forearm.

"Yes, he would. Unfortunately, Toby isn't part of this equation. It's what I have to do, what I expect of myself." Stoking up his courage, Sydney exited *Woody* with his duffle bag and umbrella in hand. He thanked Simone for the lift and shook her extended hand. After he disappeared behind the office door, she waited several minutes to see if he might have a change of heart. Not to be, she drove away, wondering if he would ever find Toby. She shuddered at the image of Toby and Harriet being shipwrecked and probably endangered by man-eating sharks.

* * *

Toby and Harriet took their seats in the courtroom and awaited the judge's arrival. They had no way of knowing that at that moment in time Sydney had arranged a charter flight to wing his way to Port Henry.

On schedule, Judge Abigail Underwood swirled into the courtroom from her chambers at precisely nine o'clock. She scaled the few steps up to her bench with surprising athleticism for a woman judge passing her middle age. Glancing around, she noticed that everyone was upstanding and asked the town clerk to lead everyone in the Pledge of Allegiance prior to her dropping the gavel and pronouncing court in session.

Seated, she said, "I see that the first order of business is a civil marriage between a Mr. Tobias Worthington and the widow Harriet Bartholomew. According to my information, this civil union was to take place yesterday." Her brow furrowed and without looking up said, "However, I understand that on your way here, you were detained by the Port Henry Police Department. Also, you spent the night in our jail. I trust you found our accommodations satisfactory?"

The room temperature seemed to drop suddenly when Abigail's icy stare sent a chill down the backs of the betrothed. "I also see we will be together again this afternoon. You've managed to accumulate an impressive number of traffic violations," her voice lowered, "along with a serious *unspecified* one."

Looking over the marriage application, Abigail could not find fault and asked Toby and Harriet to approach the bench and stand before the town clerk. Having signed off the application and license, she handed the papers to the clerk and requested the bailiff to come forward to witness Toby and Harriet's signatures. "Before this civil marriage is carried out, I have a few comments to make." Standing at the bench, she towered over the trembling twosome that looked like a pair of miscreant bloodhounds. "First, I want to tell you that I disagree with a marriage that is consummated with a scrap of courtroom paper. I can understand passionate young people with little means choosing this pathway for a life together. But, you two?"

Neither Toby nor Harriet were used to being dressed down in private or public, quite the opposite. They remained silent and suppressed their anger and impulse to explode, because they realized the stakes involved should their marriage application be denied.

"Mr. Worthington, you do have a ring for the bride, I presume?"

"Forgive me, Judge, I must have left it on my keychain in the jail's property room. I'll see that Harriet gets it later." Following the clerk's instructions, Toby and Harriet busily scrawled their signatures on the marriage license.

Abigail continued her lecture on marriage with a series of admonishments. Exhausting her series of admonishments, she concluded with, "You may kiss the bride now, Mr. Worthington. Now?"

"Certainly, Your Honor, whatever you say." In the farthest reaches of Toby's mind, he could not imagine such intimacy with Harriet. He turned to her and shut his eyes tight enough to draw tears. He moved toward her slowly like a freighter feeling its way through a fog. Harriet grasped the situation along with the collar of his blazer. Their puckered lips connected ever so gently, like two butterflies landing on a rose bud.

Fate usually has its way. A couple habitually charged with disturbing the peace failed to appear in court. Judge Underwood held a brief tête-à-tête with the town clerk and called out to Toby and Harriet, "Mr. and Mrs. Wadsworth, please return to the bench."

Perplexed, they turned about and reluctantly approached Abigail. Their attention suddenly back on high alert, Toby whispered, "Confound it, Harriet. What's that vulture want now?"

Abigail said, "You have an appointment with me at 1:30 p.m. In the interest of saving everyone's time as well as the court's, are you prepared to have your case heard now? If so, I will summon arresting police officer to attend."

"We're certainly ready when you are," said Harriet. The town clerk invited them to be seated at a table for defendants to wait for the arrival of the arresting officer. Toby nudged Harriet and agreed with her, saying, "Might as well get this over, old girl. We're in this together now."

Jared's keychain jangled to the beat of his heavy footsteps marching down the aisle. Turning to face the accused, he fixated on Harriet and delivered his best sneer meant to intimidate her; but having never lost a stare-down to date, she would have none of it.

Abigail asked Officer Jared Peabody to take the oath and reminded the newlyweds that they were still under oath. Cocksure of his charges, Jared relished the idea of bringing these two outsiders to his system of justice, which excluded the slightest shred of charity or mercy. Jared removed his hat and with great deliberation entered the witness box. Finally seated, he flamboyantly reached in his shirt pocket for his notes.

Abigail, anxious to proceed, became annoyed with Jared's theatrics. "Officer Peabody, please get on with the charges against the Worthingtons."

"I'm just coming to that, Your Honor. In my twelve years on the force, I have never witnessed such a flagrant abuse of Port Henry's traffic laws. And I'm here to state as emphatically as I can that I trust this court will make an example of this driver and her companion to the extent the law allows." He reached in his shirt pocket once again, this time for his reading glasses.

"On the afternoon in question, yesterday, I was parked on the east side of the Walkover Bridge. That's when a 1939 hopped-up Chevy panel truck bearing the name *Mother Tucker's Fine Chocolates and Confections* shot past me. After I pulled their vehicle over, I ascertained the driver to be a Mrs. Harriet Bartholomew, sitting over there with her companion, one Mr. Tobias Worthington."

"For your information, officer," said Abigail, "as of a few minutes ago, they are Mr. and Mrs. Worthington."

"Doesn't surprise me one bit," observed Jared. "With out-of-state people, everything has to be in one hellava big rush, same's they drive." Pleased with himself, his sneer returned in full bloom. "As you know, Your Honor, there is a stop sign on the west side of the Walkover Bridge. Their speed coming out of the bridge was so fast they obviously didn't stop before entering the bridge."

"I'm sorry to interrupt, officer, but that sign is outside the Port Henry jurisdiction, and we cannot levy a fine for violations outside our city limits."

Tripped up, he flinched but recovered quickly. "You're quite right, Judge. I only bring it up as a measure to show how fast they were traveling. It's my professional opinion, as an officer, that they were traveling seventy miles per hour at the time, throwing gravel in every direction. That puts them fifty-five miles per hour over the speed limit. In my book, that's reckless driving and public endangerment."

"Quite right, officer," said Abigail who listened intently. "How fast were they going when you managed to overtake them?"

"Well, they were doing the speed limit, but they probably slowed down when they spotted me sitting by the bridge." Jared squirmed in his chair, uncomfortable with Abigail's pestering questions. Sweat laced with salt poured from his brow, stinging his eyes and clouding his vision. Clearing his eyes with a handkerchief and wiping the fog from his glasses, Jared continued, "Even more serious than excessive speeding, Your Honor, is the fact that her reckless driving involved alcohol. On the floorboards, I observed an open flask of what apparently contained hard liquor. And you, Judge, if anyone, knows how strict our laws are related to open containers in a vehicle." Abigail found his familiarity repulsive. He turned to look at her, hoping to see some sign of approval for his keen observation.

His appeal went unrequited. Jared persisted with his charge of driving a vehicle under the influence of alcohol. "I asked Mrs. Bartholomew to step out of the car so I could administer the city's standard sobriety test. She insulted me and flat out refused. She did.

From the reckless way she drove and her refusal to take the test, I think it's highly likely that she's downright guilty."

Harriet noticeably gasped at this point in his testimony. She whispered to Toby how she wished that one of the charges against her included the strangulation of a police officer. As Jared's catalog of charges continued to pile up against her, she remembered the envelope that Hester had given her. Desperate to turn the tide, she sought help, and this might be as good a time as any to open her envelope. When she read Hester's hand-scrawled note, she couldn't restrain herself from leaping out of her chair and bellowing out, "Well, wouldn't you just know it!"

Startled, Abigail raised her voice in return, "One more outburst like that, and I'll suspend this hearing. Agreed?" Harriet nodded and sat back down. In the dark, Toby gave her no comfort.

Abigail settled back in her chair, "Officer, you may continue with your charges."

"Thank you, Judge. This couple from New York acted nervous and suspicious. Gave me a story about having to go to Blood Island on the packet, when everybody knows the packet hasn't stopped there in years. So naturally, I inquired if they had firearms. They each had a handgun, and you'll find them on the clerk's table offered in evidence. They had ammunition with them, but no license for them, least not in their possession. The law in Port Henry is very clear about possession of handguns." Jared continued to alienate Abigail who did not appreciate being brought up to date on the law.

"Just to be clear on the record," said Abigail, "it's Bloodstone Island in spite of its more popular name in the community." Glancing over at the clerk's table, she remarked, "The large revolver resembles an antique collector's item. And the jeweled one appears to be in the same category, looks to me like a fashion statement or a cigarette lighter." Pausing for a moment, she said, "Officer, you might do well to look deeper into the matter."

Jared flushed at Abigail's observation and acknowledged her request with a disgruntled, "Ayah," knowing full well that the weapons the judge described existed outside the requirements for a license. But Jared had saved his best card to be played last, the coup de grace.

"Your Honor, it grieves me deeply to bring to your attention to an 'unspecified charge,' because I understand your personal pain associated with it." He paused and bowed his head. "The fact that you must invoke the penalty makes it all the more difficult." He folded his glasses and tucked them away in his shirt pocket. Slowly, he raised his hat from his knees and placed it over his heart.

"Your Honor, everyone in Port Henry knows how dear your cat Moxie was to you. Moxie died an innocent victim of a reckless driver, one Harriet Bartholomew. There are no laws, no punishment to fit this crime. Yet a crime it is and must be punished, or there is no justice for the loss of Moxie. That's why I'm bringing an 'unspecified charge' before this court for you to adjudicate and set a precedent for similar cases." Jared dropped his hat back down on his knees and concluded, "Not to do so would be a travesty."

Abigail did not need Jared to remind her of her grief. Once again, she turned away to gaze to the overhead chandeliers. She had become consumed with vengeance when she learned from the police department that Harriet had run over her cat. Her tears had dried quickly, however, and she needed to fight back against her feelings toward Harriet, which included bodily harm. A faint smile drifted across her face and back again. After all, she had just married Harriet and Toby, and her mind raced to the thought, *I married her to that old curmudgeon, and that might be sufficient to punish her for the rest of her life.* "Officer Peabody, if you have no further charges, please step down and make yourself available in case you're needed." Abigail stood up and announced, "I believe this is as good a time as any to take a ten-minute break before we begin the testimony of Mrs. Worthington."

Harriet took the opportunity to shove Hester's letter over into Toby's lap. "Just look at this, Toby. I bet Jared's ears are burning up."

Putting on his "readers," it only took a moment for Toby to read it and reply, "His pants will be on fire too when the judge gets a look at this. Well, I never in all my days, humph."

Abigail appeared annoyed when she returned from her chambers. She revealed the state of her temperament when she slammed the gavel down hard three times as if she were driving a bent nail. Calling the court back in session, she invited Harriet to take the stand in her defense.

Before speaking, Harriet sat in the witness box, refreshing her makeup. After returning her compact and lipstick to her purse, she retrieved Hester's letter and began, "Your Honor, I wish to begin my defense with the last charge of killing your Moxie. I did not, and if I may read the contents of this letter, I think it will have a bearing on the rest of the violations I'm being charged with."

"Please begin, Mrs. Worthington. You have my full attention. It will be entered in evidence."

Harriet held the letter out at arm's length to focus on the handwriting. "This letter is written on Port Henry Police Department stationery as follows:

> *To: Mrs. Jeffrey Bartholomew,*
>
> *On the evening of the arrest of Mrs. Jeffrey Bartholomew and a Mr. Tobias Worthington, the charge of reckless driving resulting in the death of Moxie, the cat, was discussed.*
>
> *I felt duty bound to see if there was evidence on their vehicle. There was none.*

Harriet paused to search a reaction from the judge. However, she did see her clench her fists together in a knot tight enough, as the local expression goes, to choke the life out of a horse; but Abigail held her tongue. Harriet drew in a long breath and held it momentarily during which time she puckered her lips pretentiously before speaking. Her eyes narrowed and dropped down to glare at Jared like a she-wolf eyeing Mary's little lamb. Only then did she raise her chin aloft to read again from the letter,

> *I checked the police vehicles parked in our lot. In spite of heavy rains, I discovered a small amount of cat hair and remains on the left side of the bumper on the squad car driven by Officer Peabody, the arresting officer. Obviously, that of Moxie. I retrieved a portion of the cat's remains and logged it into the evidence room. While I realize that an animal killed in a driving accident is not a criminal offense, I felt it was my duty to identify the driver, should it for any reason became an issue of law raised before the Port Henry District Court.*
>
> *Officer Hester Whipple*

The town clerk took the letter from Harriet and handed it to Abigail. Phyllis waited anxiously for her to finish reading the letter so that she could enter it in evidence and have done with it. Phyllis, a native of Port Henry, had no appetite for any disturbances on her way to retirement. She sensed that another kind of storm was about to hit the town, this one at the hands of *Iron Pants*.

Between shock and anger, Abigail struggled to compose herself in order to react to this new evidence with a measure of civility demanded by her station and status in the community. Jared sat perfectly still, much like a child who believed that if he didn't move, he would disappear. Toby, on the other hand, sat on the edge of his seat, quite animated, nervously tapping his pipe on the chair rail.

Abigail turned to Harriet; her voice shook with irritation. "You may step down with the court's apology. All the charges against you and Mr. Worthington are excused. I speak for the town of Port Henry in expressing how sorry we are that you have been unnecessarily detained, and I trust that you find this apology acceptable. This court finds that the testimony of Officer Jared Peabody not to be credible but prejudicial and as such inadmissible." Abigail stood to look down from the bench at the evidence table. "Please take your firearms with you when you leave here and don't forget any of your other possessions in the property room. You're both free to go."

Chapter 11

Sydney Takes to the Air

Hector waited for Sydney inside a makeshift office. Through the office windows, Sydney could see him at work. A phone in one hand, he was seated at a table that spilled over with maps and charts. Coffee mugs served as paperweights. One did double duty as an ashtray. Unkempt as the office appeared, Hector, in uniform, was a pleasant contrast; and his deliberate hand and body gestures oozed confidence.

Beyond the office, Sydney spotted the Monarch's silhouette in the open hangar door. A female figure was placing chocks under the front wheels. Sydney stopped to contemplate the plane's delicate frame showing through its thin skin and wondered if it would fare any better than a kite in a gale.

When Hector noticed Sydney taking a visual inventory of his facility, he went to the door and waved him to come in. "No worries, Mr. Wadsworth. That's our recently acquired Piper J-3 out there, 65 horsepower gassed up and ready to go." Completing a short stack of paperwork for the flight, he said, "So where is it down Maine you want to go? Southern Maine is within our nonstop range now that I've added a small reserve tank."

"Good," said Sydney. "It's Port Henry, south of Portland, on the coast. I estimate it's about 320 miles as the crow flies."

Hector glanced at his watch, now approaching 9:15 a.m., and then back at Sydney who was busy fiddling with the zipper on his Brookside rain jacket. "I charge twenty dollars an hour for time in the air plus expenses. I hope that sits all right with you. Since you're a resident, your check's good. By the way, call me Heck."

"Very well, Heck it is. I assume you're the new owner of this establishment, yes? How long have you had your license?"

"Flying? Shoot, a ten-year-old can fly our plane solo in a week." Hector donned a well-worn WWII jacket and bill cap. Sewn on patches spoke of combat and action in the European Theater. "Funny you should ask. My first real experience flying was in '41 in North Africa. I was a crew member at the time on a B-24. Great bomber, but slower than molasses in December. Returning from a bombing run, we lost an engine and got separated from our group. Two Jerrys shot up our plane, got our pilot and copilot pretty bad too." Hector picked up his briefcase and a thermos of coffee and walked toward his plane. "The short of it is that I managed to get behind the wheel, feathered the engines, and ditched it on a beach in the Med. Got a medal and a disability too. I loved flying long before that experience. Ever since that day, aviation's been my life, and I've never looked back."

Sydney noticed that the only evidence supporting Heck's license was a good old war story. Nonetheless, he followed Heck to the plane, where a young lady waited with a footstep. Against his better judgment, Sydney dismissed the obvious risk to his person and focused on the outside chance that he might be reunited with Toby.

Heck called over to Sydney, "That young lady holding the steps, she's my oldest sister. Meg's a good pilot on her own." He chuckled. "We had quite an argument about who was going to fly you this morning, but she's too good a mechanic to spend her time upstairs.

Arriving at the plane, Hector chided Sydney. "Please don't lean on the plane, Mr. Wadsworth. Its skin is very sensitive to stress." Sydney nodded and stowed his belongings behind the seat. He crawled in, assisted by Meg's firm shove on his buttocks. Heck popped in behind the wheel and helped buckle Sydney in.

Sydney asked, "What's the weather report say, Heck?"

"Pretty sketchy. Low cumulus three thousand feet. Altocumulus, twelve thousand feet. Scattered thundershowers, wind from the northeast, 25–30 knots, gusts to 40. Could be a nasty system heading our way."

Having already checked the falling barometer in the office, Heck scanned the instrument panel and adjusted the altimeter accordingly.

Completing his checklist, he waved Meg off and engaged the whining starter motor he had the shop incorporate. Slowly, the prop revolved until suddenly the engine turned over and the prop turned into a whirling blur. Heck adjusted the mixture and throttle until the engine idled comfortably. In Sydney's mind, the sound of the engine had finality to it, as if it were telling him there's no turning back now. Meg pulled the chocks free, and *Monarch One* began inching its way out onto the runway. The engine sputtered and coughed again, as if to clear its throat before having to sing one perfectly pitched high note.

As they taxied down to the west end of the field, Heck handed Sydney a paper bag and kept one for his own use. Sydney was mystified and inquired what he was expected to do with it.

Heck smiled. "It's in case you get air sick. I get sick every time I go up. Can't help it."

"Well, I don't get sick," said Sydney. "Navy man, don't you know?"

"OK, but don't expect to share mine. And if you need to take a leak, you can't go over the side," he jabbed. "There's a plastic jar behind you."

"Very thoughtful, Heck. Anything else I should know?"

"Nope, here we go." Heck lowered the flaps and opened the throttle. *Monarch One* bounced down the grass runway into a strong headwind, and it became airborne before it reached the hanger at halfway point. A crosswind gust yawed the piper out over the Beaverkill River before Heck could right his ship again. He circled back over the hangar and gave a wing dip wave to Meg.

After easing back on the throttle, Heck set a course east-northeast. "I'm going to take us upstairs over this cloud layer. There are some high mountains in southern Vermont and New Hampshire, and we need to be at four thousand feet to clear them." Sydney nodded. Heck continued, "This headwind doesn't help our ground speed either."

Bouncing about in the clouds like a beach ball, Sydney realized why Simone referred to the Monarch planes as butterflies because they reacted violently to the slightest variations in the weather. Sydney constantly checked his safety belt. Sometimes the ride reminded him of an old truck on a lumpy hayfield. It was as if the clouds resented their presence and tried to shake them out of the sky. He thought back to his limited days in the navy and preferred a high sea in a thick fog to this experience. It seemed that for every one hundred feet they gained in altitude, they lost fifty, and Sydney's patience wore thin.

"An hour of this," Sydney shouted, "and my bladder's going to explode."

Without looking over, Heck said, "Another hour of this, and we're turning back." He called Meg at the home field for a weather report. He listened intently to her reply then turned to Sydney, "Well, Mr. Wadsworth, we're committed now. Our home field is socked in. Heavy rain and visibility's three hundred feet."

Sydney reached for the flask of scotch inside his rain jacket, which he kept for emergencies. He took a long drag and winced before he took another nip to chase it down. "It helps settle my bile condition," Sydney explained. "Doctor's orders." Before he replaced the flask, he said, "Under the circumstances, skipper, perhaps a swig might sharpen your senses?"

Heck, not looking too well, said, "Maybe, when we're safely on the ground."

"Of course, I was only trying to make light of our situation, don't you know?"

Rainwater streaked across the belly of the wing and fled like sweat from a boxer. The cloudbank was so dark and dense that Sydney could barely see blinking running light on the wing tip.

Sydney noticed a strange faraway look coming over Heck's face as if he were possessed by a demon. Grimacing, Heck's skin turned to a shade of putrid yellow. Staring blindly ahead, he fumbled for the airsick bag under his seat. Fortunately, he found it just in time. Retching, he filled it to capacity.

"It's all in your mind, don't you know?" said Sydney.

* * *

Finally, after what seemed to be an endless battle of wills, the *Monarch*, in a brief moment of victory, broke through the layer of clouds at three thousand feet. Although they could see some distance ahead, neither found comfort with the realization that they were sandwiched between the scud below and a dense layer of roiling alto cumulous overhead. This weather system seemed to have no quit in it and proved larger than anyone had forecast. As if it had a mind of its own, it would remain stationary in an area; and instead of moving on, it would back up and retrace its steps as if it hadn't done a proper job the first time.

Heck told Sydney that he decided to fly between the layers but needed to take the *Monarch* up another thousand feet to clear the mountains. "I don't want to alarm you, but this headwind is eating up our fuel." Sydney did not respond, and the next couple of hours passed in silence. Weather conditions continued to improve, and the lower layer of clouds opened up occasionally to views of the countryside passing below. Sometimes a window would reveal enough so that Heck could confirm his course by recognizing a river or highway. Away from the mountainous area, Heck dropped down to three thousand feet just above the broken layer of clouds where he could get a better look. The rain had tailed off and visibility improved, but more and more, fuel became an issue.

Since they left Livermore Falls, the plane had behaved like a cocktail shaker in the hands of a zealous bartender. Now in a stretch of relative calm air, Sydney could read his pocket watch: 12:45 p.m. He calculated that Port Henry must not be much farther ahead.

His thoughts turned to Toby and Harriet, and he ran the gambit of what could be the best and worst scenarios of their fate. Closing his eyes, he first off imagined that the Portland Packet had sunk, leaving Toby and Harriet adrift at sea, clinging to one life jacket. In his dreamlike state, he blurted out, "Oh God, he's going to give the jacket to Harriet."

"Give what to Harriet?" said Heck.

"Nothing, nothing. This is my nightmare. Private, don't you know?"

Returning to his thoughts, he wondered if they were still alive, and if they were, what was really happening to them? Deciding that he had worked himself up into a state, he consoled himself with the thought that *they must have missed the ferry and being married were now engaged in having a gay old time of it without a worry in the world. While I'm risking my life, they're probably on some mystical island rolling around in a meadow of nuptial bliss. What a disgusting picture. And then, of course, if I survive, I shall have to give my blessings to the happy couple.*

* * *

Their ETA placed them close to the Maine coast and their destination, Port Henry. Heck got on the radio to call the airfield, check the weather, and receive landing instructions. After several attempts, it was obvious that Heck was either not getting through or receiving information he didn't want to hear. His voice became agitated. It was obvious that something was definitely wrong.

After an animated conversation, Heck turned to Sydney and shouted, "You stupid idiot, Wadsworth! There's no airfield in Port Henry."

"Don't look at me. You're the goddamn pilot, Hector. It was your job to find out!"

"It isn't even an emergency field now. The stupid town closed it down after the war!"

"Well, there's got to be a farmer's field, road, or something to land on. Be a little creative, Heck!"

"I know my business, so just mind your own. If you can't, go take a hike." Heck dropped the *Monarch* through an opening in the clouds to scout out a possible landing site. At one thousand feet, Heck estimated their visibility was about a half a mile. He asked Sydney to look too and began his search by flying in wider circles. The countryside was sparsely populated and consisted of small farms, patches of forest, and dirt roads that avoided hills and hugged stream banks. Nothing of real promise showed up.

Suddenly, the engine sputtered and coughed a few times to let the pilot know that it would need more fuel if they wished to keep flying. He dropped the nose of the *Monarch* to keep it from stalling and dropping like a rock. The propeller came to an abrupt stop in the upright position, and the comforting sound of the engine was replaced by the wind whistling beneath its wings. The *Monarch* was no longer an airplane but a glider. Heck frantically radioed a May Day call, giving their approximate position.

Sydney shouted, "On the starboard side, five o'clock. There's a decent stretch of straight road running up to a covered bridge. The road's got to be at least a couple of hundred feet long."

"Good work. It looks like our best chance."

"Well, do your best, Heck. I'm not ready to cross the bar yet."

In spite of a brisk cross wind, Heck managed to align the aircraft over the narrow gravel road just before touching down. Bouncing its way toward the covered bridge, Sydney said, "I think you could apply the brakes now."

"Brakes? The brake pads are shot, Wadsworth. If you want brakes, open the door and drag your foot!"

"Listen, Heck, I was only making a suggestion. Let's not quarrel. Look, it might be wise to keep us on line with the bridge opening. I don't want to end up in the drink."

"Jeeeezus, Mother of Mercy, we're going in. Brace yourself!"

Both wing tips sheared off as they plunged into the darkness of the bridge. The propeller caught in the deck timbers, and the plane nosed over. Continuing its forward progress, the tail section rose up and sheared off in the heavy timber rafters. The collapsed landing gears folded up and were ripped off when they snagged against the side rail timbers. Bouncing back and forth, the old bridge peeled the plane like an orange. The cockpit jettisoned from the fuselage and continued its journey toward the open end of the bridge.

Finally, only the topless-doorless cockpit of the plane remained skidding to a rest outside the bridge in the middle of the road. The two men, still seated, remained motionless and fixated on the crumpled cowling hovering over an engine gasping in its final death throes.

Sydney broke the silence, "I should sue you, don't you know? That or at least get my money back."

"No, I don't know why you should sue me, but I'm sure you'll tell me." Heck was still dazed and looked as if he just returned from the gates of Hades. Bloodied, he slowly checked himself for broken bones or serious cuts and then looked back to see where his beloved plane was scattered.

"Breach of contract, Heck. As a retired attorney, need I remind you that you're under contract to get me to Port Henry?"

"Well, why don't you take the trouble to look behind you and read the sign over the bridge?"

Hiram Walkover Bridge 1842

PORT HENRY TOWN LIMIT

Stop before Entering: Then Proceed: Speed Limit 15 mph

"I stand corrected, Heck. Lucky for you." Sydney began to chuckle, even though he felt a wince of pain in his chest. "You don't seem to be a bad sort of fellow. You look a little pale under that scrape on your head. Now how about that scotch?" Sydney took a serious swallow and pointed the flask at Heck.

Heck took a sip first then a healthier swig. Clearing his throat, he managed to say, "That's damn decent of you, Wadsworth. I should be happy I'm alive, but my business is scattered around in that bridge. My reputation too. No insurance is going to cover this."

"Don't be so sure you're ruined. Join me in a cigar?"

"Might as well since we aren't going anywhere. I'll probably end up in the clink for this." Heck slumped back. "Thanks for the smoke, and I wouldn't mind another shot of that good scotch of yours to go with it."

"Sure, but I want you to remember that it was your heroics that saved the life of your passenger. I could have been killed. So look here, now, I'm willing to testify to your steady hand and how most pilots wouldn't have survived this storm.

"Really?"

"Yes, and after everything gets put right again, and it may take time, I might even help you get an airplane with brakes that work."

Heck perked up at the prospect, changing the subject. "If you don't mind my asking, why was it so important you had to fly over here today?"

"Well, I decided to take an outside chance that I could find my friend, Toby Worthington. He was on the Portland Packet that went down in the storm last night. I still have some hope. At least I've come this far, and I've you to thank. So let's toast the fact that we escaped the Grim Reaper."

The men emptied the flask and smoked Sydney's last two cigars. It seemed like an eternity before a patrol car from the city police department pulled up, lights flashing, in front of the remains of *Monarch One.* The officer eased out of the car, clutching a radiophone in his right hand, and draped himself across his open door. The engine ran while the lights and wipers continued about their business in a light drizzle. He gazed at length before reporting the scene of the most unusual traffic accident he'd ever seen. "Come in, Hester. This is Jared."

"This is Hester. What's your problem now?"

"Just listen up. You and I have a lot to talk about later. I'll tell you what I've got here. I'm on Cottage Grove Road on the east side of the Walkover Covered Bridge. In the middle of the road, there are two men, soaking wet, one's holding up an umbrella, kinda crooked. Well, they're seated behind an airplane engine with half a propeller."

"Are you imagining things again, Jared? Where's the goddam plane?"

"I don't know where the friggin' plane is. They must have left it in the bridge. They're laughing, smoking cigars, and it appears to me they've been drinking!"

"If I know you," said Hester, "I'd say you're the one on the sauce. Over."

Jared signed off with Hester and approached the two men in what remained of the *Monarch Butterfly* cockpit. Reality had finally sunk in for Sydney and Heck as they sat there, quite wooden in the drizzle. They had fallen into a stupor and couldn't respond in a rational manner to Jared's questions, who was completely befuddled by what he saw and unable to comprehend what could have happened, let alone the circumstances leading up to such a horrific accident. Jared did what he knew best and arrested them.

Exhausted and completely drained of adrenalin, all their physical and cerebral resources had departed like the smoke from one of Sydney's Havanas. Jared, of course, advised them as best he could that they were being arrested for, among other things, *unspecified* charges. Annoyed with having to deal with the accident, he proceeded to unload them like two limp sacks of grain from the cockpit and toss them into the backseat of his squad car, ignoring Heck's plea that they might have need of medical attention. Jared slammed the door shut, picked up what he could find of their scattered belongings, and threw them in the trunk. Before leaving the scene, Jared remembered to trot back to the scene, drop a number of traffic cones, and close the bridge on both ends with reflective tape.

Speechless since their arrest, they spread out in the backseat like a pair of jellyfish.

The short drive in the patrol car to the Port Henry police station proved both unpleasant and uneventful.

Jared sped his squad car toward town with lights flashing and siren blaring. His eyes fixed straight ahead, he spoke with his usual thick clipped-down Maine accent. "I don't know what we're supposed to do with the likes of you two. We've got our hands full 'nough with the locals, let alone you newcomers." He radioed in to the station. "Hester, come in. This is Jared, again. I'm bringing in the two men I just 'rrested for flying their plane into the Walkover bridge. I'll work up a list of charges when I get in the office. Over."

"Gotcha," replied Hester. "I'll let the sheriff know, anything else? Over."

"Ay-uh, get Henry and his wrecker out to the bridge. Ask him to clear the road and haul everything to his scrapyard. And tell him to collect every piece. It's evidence. Out."

The washed-out road into Port Henry did little to restore Sydney and Heck back to consciousness. When the squad car came to a stop five miles later, Heck was the first to regain some sense of his whereabouts. He nudged Sydney, but there was no response. The backdoor opened, and Jared ordered them out of the car.

Heck replied, "Officer, you better think about getting us to a damn doctor before you throw us in jail. Wadsworth's old and probably in a state of shock from the looks of things!"

Sydney opened his left eye far enough to get a blurry look at the officer. "Thank you for coming by when you did, officer." He took a feeble breath that sounded like a straw dragging the bottom of an ice cream soda. "I'll be sure to put in a good word for you." His eye closed involuntarily before he dropped back into unconsciousness.

"Did you hear that, officer? Those could be his dying words," Heck wailed. "I want you to think on them real hard when you bring us in."

"How was I ta know he might be a goner? When I found you two sky jocks, you were having a fine time of it."

Heck raised his head and turned to Jared. "Well, maybe that's the way it is right after you cheat death. Chew on that for a while. Now can we just get him to a doctor?" Jared slammed the car door and, without a word, drove up Main Street to Doc Harwood's home where he kept his office on the first floor.

Doc Harwood stood in the doorway to the waiting room, his rotund form silhouetted by the brightly lit exam room behind him.

The medicinal smell of antiseptics swept past him to a number of his patients that ran the gambit from children with drippy noses to hypochondriacs in search of conversation. Before he could say, "Next," the front door to his office flung open. "Well, Jared, what have you brought me now?"

Doc's patients knew him as a no-nonsense man who had experienced every medical malady and calamity known in the area. Every accident or illness passed through his doors before a patient ever reached the hospitals in Portland or Boston. Although one is never a prophet in his own country, Harwood achieved that distinction more than twenty years ago.

"I got two new patients for you, Doc. They've been in a bad plane accident, so I drove 'em around to your back entrance and parked there."

Together, Jared and Doc's nurse, Jenny, carried Sydney and Heck on stretchers into the operatory where they could have their injuries examined. They stretched Sydney out on the exam table first where Doc loosened his clothing and removed his valuables. Stripped of his shoes and wet outer garments, a cursory examination revealed that Sydney hadn't received any life-threatening wounds or broken bones. Other than a few cuts and contusions, Doc thought he survived the crash remarkably well.

However, Sydney continued to be in a semiconscious state. Heck conveyed that right after the accident, "Sydney, I should say Mr. Wadsworth, seemed quite alert until he went into a state of shock after a cigar and a dram or two of scotch."

"I shouldn't wonder," Harwood said. "He's had a pretty traumatic experience. Pretty shaky, but we should be able to stabilize him." He instructed his nurse to attend to Sydney's injuries and turned his attention to Heck. "Jared tells me that you're the pilot. You're both very lucky."

"Yeah, I guess. But I don't feel so good myself right now. Hurts to breathe. I can't raise my left arm either."

"I've a feeling you're just beginning to hurt. First, I'm going to give you some relief for the pain. Next thing is to get you on an ambulance to Portland. You could have some internal injuries."

"Hold your horses right there, Doc. These two are responsible for damages to the Walkover Bridge, and they'll have to pony up for it. Can't let this pair go Scot-free without them posting bail."

"You can't be serious, Jared. I'll tend to my business. And if you tend to yours, I imagine you'll be getting their names and particulars to give Chief McDonald."

Chagrinned, Jared said, "Sorry 'bout that, Doc. I'll set to it right now. Just tending to my duty as I sees it."

"Good. I'll be sure that Wadsworth gets the proper care he needs. When I think the old bird's up to it, I'll make sure he has a bed tonight up at the clinic."

Examining Heck, still seated, Doc asked, "What were you thinking of trying to land in Port Henry? We haven't had a field here since the war."

"I just found that out, didn't I? When we ran out of fuel, I didn't have too many options."

Doc Harwood smiled. "I suppose that covered bridge looked like a hangar to you. If I might ask, what brought you to Port Henry, especially today in the weather we've been having?"

Heck groaned as the doctor continued prodding for injuries. His voice raspy, he said, "Wadsworth here chartered my plane. He found out about the Portland Packet going down and thought his friend might have been on board. His name was Toby something."

"Jeeeezzzus, Mary and Joseph. We had a Toby down at the station! Would his last name be Worthington?

"Yup, that's it."

Jared grabbed his gear and didn't stop to put on his hat and coat before he scrambled out the emergency room door. No one gave his flight much notice. Doc assumed his departure meant a trip to the station to report the details of Sydney's arrival.

Doc Harwood and Nurse Jenny were much too busy to be concerned about Jared's duties or hasty exit. The doctor's concern at the moment focused on stabilizing Sydney enough to have him delivered to the local clinic where he could be observed and cared for overnight. Jenny bagged his clothing and underwear, all in a state of disrepair too embarrassing to make a charitable donation. In a separate bag, she placed his personal belongings: watch, cigar case, tie swag, money clip, golf ball markers, tees, bills and coins, and to her surprise a small matchbox filled with small-caliber bullets that looked like ones her brother used in his .22 rifle. When his wallet slipped from her hands, a couple of his credentials fell out, which included professional and country club memberships. Jenny giggled at a membership card certifying his honorary status in a fraternity club known as the Mystic Order of Stags and Wags.

Doc Harwood had left Sydney with Jenny to care for his other waiting patients waiting anxiously in the waning hours of the afternoon. Checking back in an hour, the doc examined Sydney, still twitching and murmuring occasionally in a state of semiconsciousness.

Doc called to Jenny, "He's safe enough for shipping. Ring the ABC Ambulance Company and have him picked up for delivery to the Seamen's Clinic."

"On it." She had already organized most of his personal effects, but she didn't know what to do with his umbrella, one that seemed inordinately hefty. In a quandary, she folded it up and tucked it up under the sheet between his legs where it became securely entrenched and someone else's problem.

The grandfather clock in Doc Harwood's waiting room chimed five o'clock when the ambulance drove up for Sydney. Only eight hours earlier, 9:00 a.m. to be exact, Sydney had taken off from Livermore Falls on his mission to rescue Toby and Harriet in Port Henry. While Sydney and Heck struggled easterly in the skies over Vermont and New Hampshire, by eleven o'clock that morning, *Iron Pants* had already married the betrothed pair and exonerated Harriet from her array of traffic infractions, including an apology from the court.

Chapter 12

The Honeymoon Suite

Elated to be free, Harriet and Toby swept up their firearms, tucked them into their blazers, and scampered down the aisle like two arthritic gazelles headed for a watering hole. Toby glanced at the courtroom clock, noting that it was still forenoon. Plenty of time, he thought, to find some mode of transportation to Bloodstone Island tomorrow.

Jared, hat in hand, raced ahead of them down the back stairs with the intention of arriving in the police station before they did. Toby gathered that the purpose of his haste focused on confronting Hester at her duty station.

As shouting matches go, Hester had a reputation of holding her own. When Jared arrived, the debate of course centered on Hester's letter to the judge, which served to torpedo his case against Toby and Harriet. Milo walked into the office and shot past Toby and Harriet to break up the argument.

Milo stepped between them. "You two got something better to do? Break it up or I'll lock you both up for disturbing my peace. Whatever it is, we'll settle this up later. You, Jared, get back on the road. Hester, not a word." He paused to compose himself. If it had not been for the chief's arrival, this discussion might have continued out on the parking lot similar to the finale of a 'B' Western movie. "By now you know these folks are free to go." Milo turned to the Worthingtons. "Sorry, folks, we don't always behave like this, must be you bring out the worst in us." He hitched his belt and launched into Hester. "So fetch their belongings, will you, and be lively about it."

Chucking their luggage into the Mother Tucker Chocolate truck, Harriet and Toby once again set about the task of chartering a boat. Harriet drove, while Toby looked up and down the piers fronting Main Street in search of a likely candidate capable of ferrying them to what the inhabitants refer to as Blood Island.

Toby's earlier telephone inquiries, made from jail, had produced no results at all. A veil of discouragement settled over them when they realized that virtually all of the boats in the harbor consisted of types manned by lobstermen or commercial fishermen. None of the vessel owners had an interest in providing them with, in their opinion, a "joy ride" to an outer island.

The afternoon dragged on, and both of them realized they had crossed the threshold of both physical exhaustion and emotional stress into a state of near total collapse. Toby admitted defeat first and suggested they retreat to the Lighthouse Inn for the night. At least they knew they enjoyed the jail food from their kitchen, and Harriet agreed that it seemed useless to press on into the evening hours.

Weary, they entered the small yet quaint lobby whereupon Harriet slumped into an overstuffed chair. Toby approached the front desk, and the clerk greeted him with a polite, "How do." He asked the young man if the inn had two rooms available, just for the night. Harriet overheard and flinched.

The clerk leaned over the registration desk to speak confidentially to Toby. "Aren't you the two birds that got married this morning? Does this mean the wedding's off?"

"No, no, guess it just slipped my mind."

"I thought it might have, for a man of your years and experience. I'm authorized to give you our honeymoon suite at our standard rates. Third floor, room 301. It's our signature room." The clerk winked along with a wry smile and said, "Just sign the register and give me a few minutes to make sure housekeeping has your room ready. Oh, if you have any luggage, sir, I'll bring it on up for you."

Too tired to protest, Toby agreed and pointed to the drive-up. "Bring us our overnight bags in the back of our truck, if you would be so kind, and park it for us, will you, like a good lad. You'll be tempted to joy ride, but I'm counting on you to resist such a temptation."

"Certainly, Mr. Worthington, and you'll be staying with us for dinner? The baked cod is our special tonight, and the dining room is open till seven thirty. Of course, we do provide room service until then."

"We'll certainly keep that in mind." He turned to Harriet whose legs had parted company in opposite directions over the footstool where she had kicked off her shoes. "All right, Harriet, on your feet, get shod, and grab your purse. We're in for the night." She responded without a word.

Arm in arm, they struggled up the staircase. By the time they had reached the second floor, the clerk had squeezed past them with their luggage and placed them inside the door of 301. When they arrived at the top floor landing, the clerk stood waiting for them in the hallway with the expectation of a good tip. He informed Toby that he had taken the liberty of having the parlor maid leave a bucket of ice on their bureau. The young man struck a chord with Toby who reminded him of his caddy at Brookside Country Club, and he rewarded the hop-to-it clerk with a generous gratuity. The clerk winked at Toby and dropped the room key into Toby's outstretched hand.

Harriet, focused on finding something soft to dive into, bolted into the room. Toby had the same thing in mind but was late off the mark. In midstride, she stopped in her tracks and gasped, "Good God, Toby, will you just look at this room? I've never seen anything so repulsive."

"I certainly can't disagree." Rolling his eyes and rubbing his chin, he posited, "I'd say the decor is Early Parisian Whorehouse."

Harriet, not amused, said, "As if you would know. I suppose you'd also like to explain the reason we're in a round room?"

"There's a reason for everything, Harriet," Toby said. "It's not always apparent, but I suspect it is either meant to resemble a lighthouse, which seems to be a recurring theme hereabouts, or it's to prevent the bride from being cornered."

Confounded by his behavior, she said, "Honestly, Toby, you're suddenly in bad form. I don't know what's gotten into you.

Toby contained an urge to laugh, realizing that he had turned the tables on Harriet. On the subject of *amour,* Harriet played defense for the first time on their expedition. The suite's unabashed tawdry furnishings also startled Toby, but he continued to press his advantage. "Don't you find the red chenille bedspread rather suggestive with all those lacy heart-shaped toss pillows? And look at this, a Victorola, right under our very noses. They've certainly thought of everything. Ah, a nice selection records too. Hmmm. Bolero by Ravel, commendable choice, yes?" Perhaps the more nauseating he made the room seem in her eyes, the better his chances were to remain chaste during the night.

Calling Harriet's attention to the bedroom's high conical-shaped ceiling above the bed, he pointed at a gaudy crystal chandelier. Below it dangled a life-size sexually explicit replica of Cupid. Feigning disappointment at Harriet's total lack of interest, Toby lowered his voice, "I hoped you'd be pleased."

Harriet planted herself face down on the bed in a gesture of total despair. Toby, sensing she would suffocate unless she came up for gulp of fresh air, stepped over to the French doors and pulled back the red velveteen drapes. The doors led out onto a small circular balcony overlooking the harbor and a magnificent seascape. He returned to Harriet and whispered, "Come on, old dear. Give me your hand and come out here on the deck with me. Great view, and I promise to stop being a tease. I do believe the staff sized us up and decided to have us on, don't you know?"

Toby caught a glimpse of himself in the bureau mirror as he towed Harriet across the room. His reflection told him that he's much too old for this kind of activity. "We must look like juicy gossip or good sport for the locals."

Stepping out on the balcony, she broke her silence, "Well, after what we've been through, I'm not about to give the natives any satisfaction."

"Neither am I. They expect us to scream bloody murder about the room, but I intend to shower them with compliments on their tasteful accommodations."

They stood close to each other for a moment, quietly scanning the horizon. Beyond the breakwater, the remnants of the rainstorm could be seen in retreat. Rays from a late-day sun poked through the overcast to open the sky, reminding Port Henry that it had not departed with the tempest. An offshore breeze from the west drew the heavy air out of town and out to sea, and both took long deep breaths of the invigorating air. The cries of seagulls overhead proclaimed the end of the storm and a better day ahead.

Toby glanced over his shoulder at two bentwood chairs obviously designed for their artistic merit instead of comfort. "Let's sit here for a moment and take in the air. I'll bring out a couple of pillows for the chairs. The deck's puddled, but the chairs feel dry." Harriet sighed in resignation and did not require any further encouragement to stay put.

When Toby returned, he suggested, "Harriet, there's ice on the bureau, and I've an ample supply of scotch in my bag for emergencies. A splash will do you good. Shouldn't let good ice go to waste."

"What a good idea, Toby." Harriet smiled, tossed her head back, and jostled her hair with both hands. "After all, it is our wedding night."

Toby produced a faint smile and feigned he didn't remember. "So it is. Really, Harriet, in all the excitement, I must have forgotten that we were married this morning. Before you say anything, this does call for a celebration, right?" Toby stepped back into the suite and, after a brief detour to the bathroom, began his duty as a bartender.

When he returned to the deck, he found Harriet in a contemplative mood. She leaned forward and pointed out over the railing. "Toby, squint your eyes and look at the horizon. That dark lump you see out there is Bloodstone Island."

"You don't say. Yes, I do see it. We're sitting here when we should be sitting over there looking back at Port Henry. As it turned out, we couldn't have made it across anyway. So we didn't find a boat today. There's still time left to make it under the wire. Today's just the seventeenth."

"I suppose. Let's toast the Greek goddess of good fortune and hope my demented stepson doesn't show up on the island ahead of us." Fortified with a sip of scotch, Harriet rose from her chair with glass in hand. "I'm going to freshen up and get out of these clothes."

"All right, but don't panic when you see the bathroom and put something on. You don't want to get a chill out here."

On the way back, she stopped to freshen her glass. "Toby dear, let me fix you another."

"Good idea, but just a pinch. We need to be off at sun up. I've been thinking just now about you and me. Perhaps we are different, but not as much as I previously thought. The scrapes we've been in together since we left Livermore Falls? Well, I think they've brought us closer together than I could ever imagine. Battling the elements, evading the law, having to bed down in jail, beating a bum rap . . . things I didn't bargain for."

"You've been a good sport, Toby. You know that steamer trunk of Jeffrey's you were eyeballing, the one in that stack of luggage stacked in my hallway? Well, you can have it. I don't want any of his things, and just looking at his stuff makes me miserable. I don't know why you want it, but I've got an idea you know what's in it."

"Yes, I do know, and I'll be eternally grateful to you. Believe me, the contents already have a good home." Harriet did not express an interest as to what home he meant. Nonetheless, her gesture overwhelmed Toby. "Someday, when you're ready, I'll share with you the story that goes with that trunk."

Time slipped over the railing and over the horizon with each refresher of scotch. The view and salt air had a mesmerizing affect, not to mention the presence of Johnny Walker's Black Label. When Toby finally checked his pocket watch, he noticed the hotel dining room had closed for the evening. He nudged her gently. "It's too late for dinner now. The dining room is closed. I vote that we stay in for the night."

"That's good with me. I can't even think of food. It's getting dark too. Why don't we have a nightcap and turn in?"

Toby agreed. "I'll get it for you if you turn down the covers."

"Fine, but I'm not going to bed with Cupid and his thing hanging down over me from the chandelier."

Toby fully understood her reasoning, but the logistics of removing it in his present condition seemed well beyond his capability. What scotch had done for his bravery; it did not do so for his dexterity. Aware of his limited mobility, he still had to deal with her problem. "Harriet, it's so high up I couldn't possibly reach where it's attached without a ladder."

When Harriet returned carrying both glasses of scotch, she suggested putting a chair on the bed and offered to help. "Toby, why don't you get yourself ready for bed first? I'll bring one of the wicker side chairs over and set it on the bed. I'll steady the chair for you while you climb up and get Cupid and his appendage down."

"Good idea, Harriet," Toby mumbled, "but I still don't think I'll be able to reach where it tied on."

Challenging his manhood, she said, "Well, you could at least give it a go."

"All right, all right," grumbled Toby. It only took a couple of minutes to change in the bathroom and return in his flannel knee-length nightshirt and patent leather slippers. Harriet already had the wicker side chair positioned in the center of the bed, its slender legs poking into the bedspread. Toby scanned the situation. "Where did you find that chair? Some circus lion tamer probably left it behind. I bet he couldn't tame the cat he brought with him."

Harriet pleaded, "Let's get on with it, Toby. Upsy-daisy. I've got a good grip on the legs. It's armless so hang on to the back. You can do it."

Toby climbed aboard the bed opposite Harriet. The real difficulty arose when Toby brought his second knee up onto the chair. It tipped toward Harriet. She pushed back too hard. Toby leaned forward too far. Toby and the chair lurched back and forth like a metronome until he decided to abandon ship and roll off the chair onto the bed. "Enough, Harriet, I'm spent," he gasped. "The chair legs sink into the bed when I get on it, and I can't reach all the way up there anyway."

"Can't you try just one more time for me? I have an idea. Listen to this. Instead of trying to unfasten Cupid from the chandelier, let's just drape a pair of your briefs over his 'naughty parts.'"

"If that will make you happy, Harriet, fine. Let me tell you our circus act will never make center ring." Toby returned to the room waving a pair of his neatly pressed briefs like a white flag of surrender. To screw up his courage, he stopped by the Victorola to find a suitable musical accompaniment for his feat of daring. He chose the recording of Ravel's Bolero that he took notice of earlier that evening. As the music began, Toby rubbed his hands together and cracked his knuckles as he called upon all his scotch-impaired manual dexterity to accomplish a feat of such daring. To keep his hands free, he placed the briefs between his teeth where they would stay until he reached for them to hang on Cupid.

The second assent progressed much better than the first. Once again, the chair legs settled into the bedding. Toby with one hand on the back of the chair slowly rose to his feet, which he placed on the chair's narrow circular rim.

Harriet, head down, dared not look up for fear of witnessing Toby's privates for a second time in as many days. "Hurry up," Harriet groaned. "I can't hold this chair all night."

Toby calculated in his muddled state of mind that he could not reach up and secure his briefs on Cupid unless he jumped up and committed both hands to the task. Bending his knees ever so deftly, he sprung up; the chair followed him part way in spite of Harriet hanging on to it. At the apex of his leap, Bolero reached climactic crescendo.

On his descent, Toby's feet burst through the chair's wicker seat. When he hit the mattress like a spent cannon ball, the bed slats gave way, which sounded like the crack, crack, crack of a small-caliber pistol. The chair's round seat frame lodged itself just above his buttocks and fit Toby like an undersized girdle. Gift wrapped in a chair, it took but a fraction of a second before he teetered over onto the mattress and rolled face first onto the floor with a resounding thump and the groan of a wounded wildebeest. With a free hand, he felt for his nose to make sure it was in its proper place between his eyes.

Harriet yelled, "Look, Toby. Jumping Je-e-sus, you've DONE IT."

Toby grunted and glanced up. With a smidgeon of pride, he said, "So I h-a-v-e. You know I don't think I broke anything except the chair, and I'm stuck in the damn thing." He rolled back and forth on the floor in a feeble attempt to shake it loose. "I need your help, Harriet. I can't get out of this infernal trap. Bring me some soap or whatever that greasy stuff is you plaster on your face. Maybe between us, we can slip it off, don't you know, like a ring off a finger?"

Harriet obeyed but did not find his insensitive remark flattering. On her return trip from the bathroom, she navigated around the listing bed to witness Toby continuing to squirm on the floor. Amused, she began to giggle. Soon the giggle soon turned into a muffled laugh. As she made her way down to the floor behind him, she couldn't contain the urge to tease. "Toby, you do have a rather nice bottom. I just love those rosy cheeks of yours. I do believe they're blushing." Toby bit his teeth down into the deep pile carpet to keep from bellowing an appropriate profanity. She smeared her fingers into a jar of cold cream and cooed, "I can see this is going to be a lot more fun for me than you."

Before Toby could respond, they were startled by a loud rapid knock on their door followed by a key rattling in the lock. A young man burst through the door wearing the vest and attire of a night clerk. He also wore the expression of one having just discovered a crime scene. He fumbled for words. "Holy Mackerel, what have you done to this room?"

"I was about to ass . . . ask you the same thing, young man," Harriet replied. "It's perfectly dreadful, isn't it? The room, that is."

The eyes of the young clerk popped open. "What do you think you're doing, half dressed, flopping around on the floor at your age? Some kind of new parlor game for the elderly?"

Toby sputtered, "Don't you dare be judgmental with us. In the morning, I will be registering a complaint to the manager in the st-strongest of terms. It's outrageous to let a room with such flimsy furniture. As to the present condition of the room, the fault, dear Brutus, is yours, not ours."

"Perhaps so, sir, but the racket going on is ALL yours, and it's disturbing our other guests." The clerk adjusted his bow tie, cleared his throat, and said, "One of our guests thought they heard shots and were going to call the police but decided to call me first. I said that I would call the police if I couldn't get your promise to stop whatever it is you're doing."

Harriet rose to her knees. "We'd love to stop." Pointing to Toby, she said, "As soon as I get Mr. Worthington out of the chair he's stuck in, you won't hear another p-e-e-p from us."

On his way out, the clerk observed Toby's briefs hanging high over the bed. Thinking, *Well, they are New Yorkers*, he rolled his eyes and left, saying, "Remember, you promised."

They both fell silent and remained motionless until they heard the clerk's footsteps reach the staircase. Finally, Harriet whispered, "Well that s-u-r-e took the fun out of everything."

"Forget that. I've had quite enough frivolity for one night. Now help get me out of this chair."

Toby thought it would take a bit of twisting and turning to disentangle himself, even with Harriet's help. Agreeing on a strategy, she sat behind him and assumed a rowing position by placing her feet under his armpits. In this position, she pulled back on the chair legs as if she were rowing. Like getting the first olive out of the jar, it took a number of attempts. Finally, with one mighty heave, Harriet sprung Toby from his snare and fell backward with the chair coming to rest on top of her.

Completely done-in for one night, they stretched out on the floor, trying to catch their breaths for the struggle that lay ahead of them, being able to rise from the floor and crawl into their respective sides of the bed.

Earlier, Harriet had chosen the side of the bed closest to the bathroom, which now listed decidedly over to Toby's side. When he observed the broken bed had left the mattress cockeyed and sloping toward him, it did not take a long mathematical calculation to know, with the help of gravity, sometime during the night Harriet would likely be invading his space.

By the time Toby rose to his feet and could stand without hanging on, Harriet had already slipped between the sheets. A sore back and painful nose became his companions, both of which changed his mind to turn in for the night. He decided to have a pipe out on the balcony. Foraging his way through the personal effects in his luggage, he sought out his tin of "Three Nuns" tobacco and Dunhill pipe. He muttered, "Nothing like a good smoke to clear the air I always say."

He continued his wobbly trek to the balcony and grabbed his paisley smoking jacket from the closet. *No sense risking a chill,* he thought. He stopped by the bureau mirror to see if his eyes had turned black yet from the injury to his nose. To check on the soreness he felt around his midriff, he opened his jacket and raised his nightshirt. Alarmed, he whispered, "My eyes still look all right, but holy cripes, am I ever going to have a nasty bruise around my equator?"

Glancing around for Harriet, Toby verified she had decided upon an early retirement for the night. He felt an instant sense of relief. She had already crawled into her side of bed and had fallen asleep without so much as a simple "good night." In haste, she hadn't bothered to remove her peignoir with its boa of pink feathers that when she breathed fluttered back and forth. At least for a few hours, the burden of being married had been lifted from his shoulders. He experienced a twinge of empathy for Harriet, feeling that perhaps he had misjudged her and her checkered past, one that led him to believe some time ago that she had terminated two of her previous husbands, both of whom died from a strange stomach ailment.

He tiptoed toward the bed with the full intention of tucking her in and covering her feet sticking out from under the covers. But he thought better of it, knowing the risks involved of waking her; after all, she'd need a good rest to get her bearings come morning.

On the balcony, he leaned his deck chair back against the outside wall and lit his freshly packed pipe. The rain-washed, heady sea air rejuvenated his spirit and turned his mind back to a different uplifting fragrance, new mown grass at Brookside.

Toby clenched his pipe firmly between his teeth and muttered, "No looking back now, you old sot. You'd better find a way to get Harriet to Bloodstone Island and back. And try not to get both of us killed in the process."

He relit his pipe and watched the white smoke curl and disappear into the darkness. In a moment of whimsy, Toby wondered if the smoke would find landfall on Bloodstone Island, a place quite close in terms of miles but an eternity away if recent events portended the future. Overhead, the moon gradually peeked beyond the eave of the balcony. It reminded Toby of a great ship sailing inexorably through a sea of stars. He watched at length. With a deep sigh, his mind gave way to contemplate the state of his own ship, which seemed to be rudderless, going absolutely nowhere. Not wishing to dwell on the subject too long or risk falling asleep outside, he rose to knock the spent ashes from his pipe on the palm of his hand.

As he returned into the well-lit bedroom, he stopped by Harriet and noticed that she hadn't moved an inch since he left. Her feet still hung out over the bed and beyond the covers. He reckoned the old bird had had enough excitement for one day. So had he, but as he went to turn off the lights, he turned around and tucked her feet under the covers.

Chapter 13
The Morning After

"Toby, T-O-B-E-E, where are you?"

"I'm over here on the floor, Harriet."

"Well, for heaven's sake, what are you doing down there?"

"I fell out of bed last night. And it was too hard to get back in." Toby rolled onto his knees and peered over the edge of the bed at Harriet.

Rolling over toward Toby, she whispered, "Toby, we didn't, did we?"

"I don't think so, if I take your meaning. Does it make any difference?"

"I suppose not. I just felt like I should know." Harriet's eyelids, stuck together with makeup, refused to open properly. In desperation, she pried them apart with her fingers. Sitting up, she stared at him, her vision still impaired. "Toby, are you wearing sunglasses?"

He realized instantly the nature of her remark. As he feared, the collision between his nose and the floor had provided him with two black eyes. "I'm not wearing sunglasses, Harriet, but I will be soon, whether I need them or not. I'll explain later. It's time for us to hit the deck if we're going to find passage to Bloodstone Island."

"It seems like you've already hit the deck, Toby. I don't think I care to get up right now unless I have a Bromo first." She ducked back under the covers and plunged her face into a pillow. "Would you be a dear and bring me one?"

"Yes, right after I see what's in the envelope shoved under our door." Rather than get off the floor, he calculated it would be easier to retrieve it by crawling the short distance to the door. "Probably a notice that our business is no longer welcome in this establishment." Addressed to the Worthingtons, he casually tore it open. Even without his glasses, he could easily decipher the message written in large hand-scrawled letters.

YOU HAVE BEEN WARNED. GO HOME AND YOU LIVE. DEFY AND YOU DIE.
IF YOU TRY TO CLAIM BLOODSTONE ISLAND, THE ISLAND WILL CLAIM YOUR BLOOD.

Toby sat silently for a moment, while a shiver ran its course up and down his back. *I walked into this mess right up to my neck,* he thought. *Now, damn it all, I'm even married into it. I've been to jail, to the altar, and probably be in a funeral home by tomorrow night.*

Blaming himself for his naiveté, his shoulders drooped as he slowly returned the life-threatening note back into the envelope. Toby's usually even temperament turned indignant when he recalled that he had packed for a three-day retreat on a secluded island, all with the noble intention of helping out a member of Brookside. Angry, he still felt a responsibility to resolve this predicament before it turned macabre. *What to do? First things first,* he reasoned. *Get Harriet a Bromo.*

* * *

Valuable morning hours slipped away as they stumbled around between the bathroom and the bedroom like two zombies trying to locate their day clothes. Fortuitously, Harriet ordered coffee and sweet rolls from the kitchen and wisely asked that the tray be left outside the door. Meanwhile, Toby removed a long-handled broom from the maid's closet and proceeded to jostle "Cupid" until he managed to snag his "never to be left behind" pair of summer weight briefs. It floated down and landed just beyond his reach on the bed. When every muscle in his body ached and resisted any command to move, he spread out on the bed where he could take inventory of his injuries and reclaim his briefs.

A knock on the door signaled that the coffee had arrived. "Be a sweetie," said Harriet, "fetch the coffee, won't you?"

"Harriet, I will, if you promise to talk to me." She managed a weak nod of approval and looked away disinterested, as if to avoid conversation. Toby returned with the coffee tray and poured two cups. "Let's take a chair out on the balcony where we can collect our thoughts." Harriet tagged along behind, shielding her eyes from the sun.

"I don't wish to alarm you, Harriet, but we received another life-threatening message this morning." He reopened the letter and handed it to her.

She said, "This is what was under our door?" Still clutching it, her hands dropped into her lap. She looked at Toby, and her voice cracked when she exclaimed with a dash of sarcasm, "Not exactly a wedding present, is it?"

"No, and that brings me to my first question?" Toby stood, cup in hand, and asked, "Why should our lives be threatened if we go to Bloodstone Island? What we are trying to do is a simple enough task, but we seem to keep getting in our own way. Obviously, anyone could stop us by bumping us off right here in Port Henry."

"Oh, Toby, I think whoever wrote the notes just wants to scare the poo-poo out of us so we won't dare to go."

"Well, it apparently scared Jeffrey enough, since he just stuffed the first note in his desk drawer." Toby glanced out to sea. "Maybe that note written to you frightened him. On the other hand, he might have felt that you two didn't need an island that belonged to Duckie." Toby sighed and sat down again. "Conceivably, he didn't want the aggravation of owning a small remote island, plus the attention it might draw to his past. Sink me if you wish, Harriet, but Jeffrey and the law were not on the best of terms."

"I know now about his past, but I want you to believe I really loved him. In ways I couldn't with Duckie, you do understand?" She dabbed her eyes with one of the inn's linen napkins and proceeded to complain about the wretched sun ruining her complexion. Toby recognized it as a diversion to the matters at hand and let her diatribe run its course until she said, "As I told you before, I need this property to secure my future." A faint cynical smile appeared. "Toby, you must think there's uranium deposits over there, but I assure you there aren't."

The more coffee Harriet consumed, the more she engaged in the seriousness of the conversation. “Toby, if owning this island is so damn important to my son-in-law, I don’t know why he doesn’t confront me face to face. Maybe we could have worked something out. Unless he’s the greedy—excuse me, Toby—little bastard I think he is. I haven’t the faintest notion where he’s been or where he is right now, but he seems to be closing in and knows our every move, doesn’t he?”

It was a rhetorical question that startled Toby because her face ran a gambit of expressions from quizzical to anger. Her mood swings did not escape Toby’s attention. “All I know is that if we don’t show up on the island, Claude will gets his hands on the property by default.” She took another long gulp of coffee before putting a point on her thoughts. “Right now he probably is thinking how to kill the both of us. I wonder if he has the nerve for murder.”

Toby rose again to look out over the ocean at Bloodstone Island. “Well, I for one am not anxious to test your theory.” Clutching the railing, he posed another problem to her. “The chief here explained they aren’t about to protect us. So that leaves us with our limited skills in martial arts and our two guns of questionable merit.”

Not to fall prey to Toby’s argument, Harriet closed her eyes in reflection and said, “So if our antagonist is Claude, at least we’d have him outnumbered and outgunned.”

“Another assumption.” Toby chuckled. “Like Officer Hester, I think you’ve read too many detective stories.”

“Don’t poke fun at me, Toby. You come right over here and pour me another coffee. I’m being perfectly serious.”

“Yes, I gathered as much, and did you ever shoot anybody with that pea-shooter pistol of yours?”

“No, but I was going to once. You were in the army during the war. You must have at least shot at somebody with your pistol.”

“I was in the artillery, Harriet. We sent shells over the enemy lines, and I don’t know if we hit anybody on the receiving end. A sad time in my life, I tell you, and I really don’t care to dwell on it. Besides, it’s irrelevant, and there’s no more coffee. From what you’ve told me about Claude’s youth is that he’s cunning but maybe short on brains. Seems he doesn’t know right from wrong either.” Toby sat down close to Harriet and showed her the note again. “Look, it’s all too clever by half. Obviously, the staggered block letters were used to disguise the writer, typical of a criminal element. But the rhyming element suggests, at least to me, that more than one individual is involved. Yes?"

Harriet fidgeted. "You could be right. I haven't given it a lot of thought."

"Personally, I think there's something going on over at Bloodstone Island that doesn't bode well. What's lurking behind us—and I mean Claude—may represent much less of a danger than what lies ahead of us." With a degree of difficulty, Toby stood up and headed into the bedroom.

"Harriet, better get a leg on if we're going to find a boat today." Harriet grumbled a couple of unintelligible course epithets beyond Toby's earshot.

Inside, he looked around the honeymoon suite and made a mental note that even though the room looked disheveled and suffered a measure of superficial damage, he concluded the inn had not suffered any structural harm. "Harriet, just in case we might not be welcome here any longer, I think we would be wise to pack up our luggage and have it at the 'ready' by the door, don't you know?"

"All right, Toby, but why don't we slip out the back stairs?"

"Thoughtful of you, Harriet, but the second exit's an outside fire escape. So much for that idea."

* * *

Dressed in their informal summer togs, Toby and Harriet left the honeymoon suite prepared to meet head on a challenge at the front desk. At the top of the stairs, Toby stopped and remembered to put on his sunglasses. Recalling her last look in a mirror, Harriet decided to put her sunglasses on as well.

Toby paused again and said, "Before we go downstairs and through the lobby, we should appear as if nothing out of the ordinary happened last night."

"Humph. Nothing important anyway," Harriet said with a trace of sarcasm.

"Right. Ignore everyone until we're through the lobby. Chin up, Harriet. Think of us as being on parade. Arm in arm now."

Harriet, perpetually struggle with the battle of the bulge, discovered the sound of stairs squeaking under her weight just as annoying as the sound of stepping on the scales. She complained to Toby.

"You should expect the stairs to creak in any inn, especially one that's over a hundred years old. But I sometimes think stairs in old hotels were meant to squeak from the day they were built. It served as a way to keep tract of guests and their whereabouts."

"You don't say."

"Yes, I do say. Having worked as a part-time night clerk in college, I speak from experience, even though I only held the position for six months. I could tell a guest's weight and age by the pace of their stepping and rather the stairs creaked or groaned. Information I thought might come in handy one of these days, like today." As Toby and Harriet descended into the lobby, they felt as if they had just stepped into a lake full of piranha that hadn't had a good meal for a month.

"Don't let these people trouble you, Harriet. Take my hand and follow me to the front door. We're newlyweds, and they just want to see what we look like in the flesh." Toby smiled, brushing back those standing in their way. He tipped his cap, but the assemblage did not return his cordial gesture. On the contrary, the whispers he heard floating about lobby turned into an angry buzz. Toby interpreted it to mean that he and his bride had provided the inn's guests with a sleepless night. Some voiced that he should pay their hotel bill too. A more vocal group of wives suggested that Toby's prurient behavior could do with a dose of old-fashioned bodily harm.

Before Toby and Harriet could weave their way to the front door, they heard a shrill shout that beckoned Toby. "Mr. Worthington, Mr. Tobias Worthington, would you please come to the front desk?"

"Yes, give me a minute. Please everyone let me come through."

He turned to Harriet and gave her hand a squeeze. "When there's an opportunity, head for the front door, get outside, and wait for me. Trust me, I shouldn't be too long."

Hat off, Toby worked his way to the front desk and removed his sunglasses. "Well, here I am. What's so urgent you have to discuss?"

"I'm the manager here, and to start with, our guests are outraged by the ruckus going on in your room last night. I haven't assessed the damages to the honeymoon suite, but as soon as I do, I expect you to be responsible for every penny before you and Mrs. Worthington check out." The agitated manager rapped his knuckles on the registration counter hard enough to shake the ink out of its well. His cheeks flushed, and he puffed enough to fill an airship. "And I assume that you'll be checking out shortly."

Toby removed his sunglasses and said, "First of all, you have grossly misjudged us, sir. And it is you and your staff that will be apologetic." A collective gasp ran through the group eavesdropping in the lobby. Those who followed Toby and Harriet to the front door suddenly turned around to witness the confrontation. With two black eyes, it looked to everyone present that Toby had already lost the first round.

The contentious manager managed to provoke Toby. Even though Toby was known for his even temperament, he could easily have exhibited his rage, but when he visualized how an incident in the hotel could bring Officer Jared through the door, he bit his lip at the thought of being escorted to jail for another stay.

Composed, Toby said, "Do you really think this is the time to discuss last night's events in the honeymoon suite? Frankly, I'd like to put this matter to rest."

"So would we all," replied the manager as he straightened up behind the front desk, placing his thumbs into his vest pockets. "Why don't we hear your explanation first? The floor is all yours."

"Thank you. It seems your staff was playing a little joke on us last night. Before going into our room, they had time to decorate your so-called honeymoon suite with sexually explicit ornaments befitting a French house of prostitution. Hardly appropriate for young marrieds, let alone us, wouldn't you say? And as to the rickety furnishings and a shabby relic of a bed that crashed down on us, your establishment has a great deal to answer for. It would be within our rights to demand damages."

Toby paused before driving home the last nail into a suddenly wooden manager. "I think you should know that I sit on the National Board of Directors for Independent Innkeepers. I see you display our plaque with a measure of pride as a four-star member. Take a good look now—go ahead—it may be the last time you see any stars on that plaque."

The manager's face flushed, and he took a step back from the front desk. "Of course, Mr. Worthington, I wouldn't wish to compromise our reputation and membership standing. I will look into the matter directly. You can be assured that I will take immediate steps to rectify this indignity." He rang anxiously for a bellhop. "Perhaps I can mitigate this whole embarrassing situation if you and Mrs. Worthington would consider yourselves as my guest for last night?" He began to stammer when he observed the looks on his clientele. "May I inquire if perchance you might need, need, need a room for another night's stay? I know the owner would be pleased to have you as our g-g-guest. We'd like you to leave here with a good impression of the Lighthouse Inn."

The battle won, Toby accepted the invitation, but to pour salt into the manager's wound, he feigned reluctance. Dejected guests turned away and left, disappointed by the complete capitulation of the manager. "As a matter of fact, we would like a room. Perhaps you will be so kind as to find us another, this time with twin beds." A sheepish-looking bellhop arrived at the front desk where his irate boss waited. "Oh, and please transfer our luggage. We've already packed and left it by the door to our room a few minutes ago."

Outside, Harriet stood by waiting for Toby until the melee surrounding him had calmed down. With little to do other than pace back and forth, she retrieved their truck keys from the doorman and fetched their vehicle. She pulled into the front door drive-up, left open the passenger door, and kept the motor running, just in case they needed a Hollywood kind of escape.

Once outside the hotel door, Toby, dragging his 7-iron, half-skipped, half-walked to the truck and did a clumsy landing on the passenger seat.

"Drive on," he puffed.

Chapter 14

Sydney and Toby Reunited

"Harriet, I thought I saw a clinic driving around yesterday. Do you know where there's one?"

"Well, forgive me, but it's been about ten years since I've been here. And then I didn't come over here every time Duckie did, just once in a while to get my hair done." Looking over at him, she asked, "What's the matter, Toby? I saw you holding onto your chest this morning."

"I didn't notice it until this morning, but I'm sore all over, especially my ribs. You know I might have broken my nose. It seems a little loose and swollen." Harriet had only driven a hundred yards when she came to a screeching halt. "Look, how's that for luck? Across the street. A clinic." The irate truck driver behind them did not share their enthusiasm but expressed his opinion of her driving with a long blast on his horn. Harriet responded with a less than polite hand signal.

"Good eyes, Harriet. Pull over there, and maybe they'll have a nurse or somebody that can check me over."

She drove into the clinic's off-street parking lot just as a Port Henry police car sped from there on the way out. Harriet recognized the driver as Officer Jared, but fortunately, he did not notice them. Inside the small waiting room, the medicinal smell of disinfectants permeating it told them they were in the right place. At the far end, a reception counter in front of a sliding glass window separated the nurse's station from the waiting room. A sturdy middle-aged woman in uniform came to the window and asked them to sign-in on the clipboard.

"I'll be back in a couple of minutes. I have a difficult patient to attend to in the ward. Doc Harwood sent him over here last night after a bad accident. You know the story. Superman wants out of here."

"Oh yes," said Harriet, "I know the type."

Minutes later, they heard a loud harangue going on coming from the ward. As it became more heated, Harriet became concerned for the nurse's safety. Toby on the other hand assured Harriet that she seemed to be holding her own and that she looked perfectly capable of managing a situation that became physical.

The nurse opened the window again and poked her head part way through. "This is going to take a little longer than I thought. He's really, shall we say, unhappy. A police officer was just here and served him a summons to appear in court."

Back in the ward, the voices became louder, and now the altercation could be heard in the waiting room. The argument centered on what clothes leave in, because he declared that the clothes he wore when admitted were in an unacceptable ghastly state of repair.

Toby turned to Harriet and said, "If I didn't know better, I'd say that was Sydney's voice."

"Of course, it isn't, not unless his voice came here without him." Painfully, she looked into Toby's blackened eyes. "It is him, isn't it?" Toby stared past her at a duck print on the wall, as if she didn't exist. "Maybe."

The nurse returned and exclaimed, "I don't know what to do with him. He wants out, and I want him out. But I can't put him out on the street in his gown and socks. I'll get fired." She doubled back to glance at the clipboard then over at Toby and Harriet. "Oh, so you're Toby Worthington. You two must be the couple that got married yesterday. Congratulations. I must say you've cut quite a swath since you arrived in town. Officer Peabody said you two might be acquainted with this patient. His name is Sydney Wadsworth."

"Did you hear that, Harriet? Sydney is here. I wonder what he's doing in Port Henry." Toby's brain checked out temporarily into space. Fortunately, Harriet had been seated, or she would have been lying in a dead heap, staring up from the floor. Her initial shock however turned to anger, and Toby knew he lay directly in the path of a hurricane.

"I think I know the answer why he's here," said Harriet. "Someone broke their word and let Sydney in on our plans. How could you, Toby?" Furious, her voice shook. "Darn it all, I trusted you."

"Now, Harriet, let's not jump to conclusions. I'm sure Sydney has a logical explanation."

"Toby, I can hardly wait. Let's pop in for a visit. Coming with me?" She turned to the nurse and asked, "Please, show us to Sydney Wadsworth. I think we can sort everything out rather quickly."

"Right this way," said the nurse, leading the way, with Toby dragging up the rear. "I'd appreciate any help you can give me. I'd like to get off when the night shift relieves me. Oh, and I'm sure his medications haven't worn off yet. When you leave, I'll give you the doctor's prescription for pain."

* * *

They discovered Sydney sitting straight up on the edge of his bed, his street clothes tossed over the end of his bed frame. "Harriet! Toby!" exclaimed Sydney. "Thank heavens you're safe and all that. I'm glad to see you're both OK, except you, Toby. You look terrible. I thought you were on the packet when it went down.

"No, Sydney, we never made here in time to catch the packet before it left. Anyway, it doesn't stop at the island we needed to go to. And by the way, how the devil did you know about the packet sinking?" Toby turned to look at the nurse and said. "You may leave us now. We'll be on our way soon."

Harriet, still indignant, began to rail on Sydney, "So, Sydney, you came all this way to see if we were all right? Or just Toby?"

"I'm sorry, Harriet. Of course, I'm concerned about you as well, as I would for all the ladies at Brookside. You and I have had our differences, but Toby is not just a close friend. I'm his solicitor and the executor of his estate. He acted properly to keep me aware of his whereabouts." Harriet, silent, disbelieving, retreated to the water cooler a few steps away and dapped her brow with cold water.

From behind Sydney's curtain, the only other patient in the ward pleaded. "Will all of you please shut up and get out of here? I need my rest."

The nurse shared the patient's feelings. "He does have a point, and I'd appreciate it if you would pay the bill and take your problems someplace else."

"She's right," said Sydney, turning to Toby. "Let's move on, old fellow. I'll need a lift from here to pick up some of the 'ready' at the nearest local bank."

"Sydney, you're in hospital dressing gown. Do you think you should go into a bank looking like this?"

"You'll be with me. And it should be obvious to anyone, especially a banker, that I need, among other things, a completely new wardrobe." He picked up his patented leather dress shoes and tossed them into a wastebasket. "So, Toby, if you'll take care of the bill here, we'll be off. I'll repay you, of course. While you're doing that, Harriet and I will go to your car."

Harriet couldn't get a handle on the evolving course of events, and she was too befuddled to get out in front with her own agenda. Frustrated, she decided to play along with Sydney and Toby. The thought of escorting Sydney out of the clinic in a hospital gown repulsed her. Leaving the ward, she said, "Wait here, Sydney. I'll bring the truck up to the ambulance entrance, and Toby can bring you and your things out. And don't forget to bring your summons. It's on the end of your bed."

From behind Sydney's curtain, the nurse said, "Finally. Good riddance to the lot of ya."

* * *

The morning slipped away as Toby and Harriet shuttled Sydney around Port Henry. Sydney had to take up residence in the back of Mother Tucker's Chocolate Truck, cramped between his meager luggage and Toby's overabundance.

Toby shouted over his shoulder to Sydney. "As long as you're here in town, you might as well stay on a while and have a look about." Harriet's wince went unnoticed. "I'm glad you brought your umbrella along. We might need it later, if you take my meaning. I'll explain as we go."

First stop, the bank. Harriet pulled up in front of the Portland Trust Bank and said, "Toby, you'd better go in there for him. If he goes in with that hospital gown on, Jared'll be here to arrest him."

Sydney, who Toby thought could do no wrong, said, "The bank would never give me Sydney's money. Just wait here, old dear. We shouldn't be long."

Harriet dropped her forehead on the steering wheel and closed her eyes. Since the arrival of Sydney, she realized she no longer held the same sway she had had over Toby; and her hope of his help depended on his honor, not as a husband, but as an upstanding, however gullible gentleman. Without him, the short crossing to Bloodstone Island looked to her as daunting as swimming the English Channel solo.

* * *

Seemingly aloof from his surroundings, Sydney strutted barefoot from the truck into the bank entrance as if he were wearing the "king's new clothes." He strode past two aghast women tellers straight into the manager's office as if he were the bank's chairman of the board. Toby followed close behind, holding his blazer open like a scarecrow in an effort to provide a modicum of modesty.

"God man, what do you mean by coming in here looking like . . . like—"

Sydney cut off the manager who struggled for a metaphor. "Good heavens, sir. I see you're Mr. Blankenship. I didn't come into your bank looking like this by choice, especially since I am here to garner a reasonably large sum of money from my bank account in New York. If I were an embezzler or some such sort, I would have arrived here in suitable business attire. Now then, will you'll hear me out?"

"Yes, state your business, but be quick about it." Unnoticed, Blankenship buzzed the tellers to alert the chief of police two blocks away. "Who are you and who's your friend standing there holding his arms out?"

"I'm Sydney Wadsworth, and this is my close friend, Toby Worthington. I'm in need of some 'ready' from my bank account to cover my travel expenses while I'm in Port Henry." He turned to Toby and said, "I'm sitting down now, Toby. Please seat yourself down. We'll only be a moment."

Sydney turned to the manager and said, "I need to put in a call to the Highlands City Club in New York. To speed things up, here's the number." Toby volunteered that he would reimburse the bank for the call after he recognized a reluctance of the part of the manager. Buckingham's eyes rolled but decided to play along, quite certain that there was a criminal scam to unfold.

Sydney said, "Ask for Rodney. He's the retired CEO of the Republic National Bank. I still bank there, of course. Describe me to him, and he'll vouch for me. He'll have the bank send a draft to you for, let's say, $3,000. He should be playing dominos with Pinky about this time of day."

Unfortunately, Pinky took the call from the desk and said that Rodney was losing and in too foul a mood to come to the phone. When Pinky finally understood the nature of the call, Sydney was relieved to know that he would soon be receiving a bank draft wired in care of Blankenship.

When Chief Milo burst into the bank lobby, the matter had already been settled. He looked through the glass wainscot to the manager's office and saw exactly who had been the cause of the entire ruckus at the bank. Milo thought for a moment and took his hand off the firearm on his belt, turned around, and returned to the station.

Armed with cash, Sydney paraded next door to the bank into the town's best and only clothing store, MacLearnon's. Toby and Harriet waited for him to emerge back on the street. To the delight of its elderly Scottish owner, Sydney paid cash for a complete off-the-rack outfit of a summer suit, shirts, shoes, boater straw hat, and other matching garments and accessories. The news of Sydney's recent exploits spread throughout the town.

Chapter 15

Sydney and the Judge

Jared entered the courtroom and approached the prosecutor's table as if he were walking through a jungle rife with cobras. He had suffered a bitter defeat at the hands of Judge Underwood the day earlier, and as a result, he realized that he had jeopardized his standing in the chief's department and perhaps his job too. With a measure of trepidation, he sat on the edge of a chair, waiting to be called to the witness box for his testimony. The hat he usually wore at a cocky tilt conformed now to uniform regulations right out of the police academy. The seldom-buttoned collar of his shirt strained against his throat, causing his cheeks to balloon and turn redder than the buttocks on a baboon.

When Judge Underwood entered the courtroom from her chambers, on her way to the bench, the town clerk invited everyone to be upstanding as was the usual courtroom custom. *Iron pants,* through perseverance and with the family name Underwood, had achieved the high station of judge, hitherto unheard of up to the present day, at least in this part of Maine.

Through years of Yankee self-discipline, she tried not to register emotion of any kind, believing it may be construed as a sign of weakness, especially in a woman. However, Abigail's self-restraint collapsed when Jared came into full view. She stopped in midstride, suddenly aware that Jared looked like a bloated bullfrog. "Officer Jared Peabody, remove your hat and unbutton your collar before you explode and find yourself scattered all over the ceiling." When pressed, her sharp tongue often cut like a knife, and just then, her remark revealed that her mood did not bode well for the defendant in this afternoon's final case.

Before resuming her march to the bench, she paused again to glance around the courtroom, sizing up those in attendance. She was not startled to recognize the cub reporter for the town newspaper standing by the back entrance with the bailiff, but became rather bemused at the sight of Harriet and Toby comfortably perched in the front row of visitor's seating. Again, she could not contain an impulse to blurt out, "Are you two planning on spending your honeymoon in my courtroom?" Not waiting or wanting a response, she swept past the speechless Worthingtons.

When the judge whisked past Sydney, he stood motionless beside a table usually reserved for defendants and their legal representatives. He surmised that Abigail imagines that she is some sort of sprightly yet premature granddame. On second thought, an entrenched spinster? His first impression of her floundered, however, because she didn't seem destined to conform to any of his preconceived notions of the female species, which he had taken pride in developing over several decades of acute observation. In a strange way, this pleased him.

While Judge Underwood ascended a short flight of stairs to her desk and posh high back swivel chair, the town clerk, Phyllis Maybury, bade everyone to be seated. After Abigail saw that Phyllis had finished sharpening her reservoir of pencils to take shorthand of the proceedings, she settled in and gaveled that court was now in session. She paused a moment to glance into the knee hole of her desk, staring at the saucer of milk reserved for her beloved, now deceased cat, Moxie. The saucer would have to remain filled for the time being, she thought, until an old myth had proven itself wrong, that Moxie had one more of his nine lives to live.

She sighed and returned to the business at hand by looking up from her desk and squinting at the defendant who had decided to challenge the charges brought against him by the chief's Police Department. Sliding her bifocals up the bridge of her nose remedied the blurry image of Sydney. She conceded that he looked like someone better suited to a boardroom chair than a courtroom seat. To her eyes, he represented a well-dressed piquant gentleman of means and no doubt one versed in polite society manners. Ah, she thought, if only such a man existed that possessed both qualities. Jacob Anderson hardly measured up.

However, after a few years on the bench, she had ample reason to doubt her own judgment and to be suspicious of strangers that attempted to deceive her by their suave appearance and put-on-airs to curry a favorable decision. Abigail usually bristled at any such attempt and threw the book, so to speak, at those who did.

She swiveled her chair around to face Jared, a man whom she found just as contemptible for different reasons. "Officer Jared Peabody, approach the clerk, take the oath please, and enter the witness box."

Jared, noticeably uncomfortable, squirmed and fumbled with his citation notes. *Iron pants* captured his attention with a shrill announcement that could be heard in the next county, "Officer Peabody, this is a hearing to determine what legal recourse is to be taken with respect to your arrest of Sydney Wadsworth and one Hector Monarch, both of Livermore Falls, New York. The clerk will take note that Mr. Monarch is in absentia."

For Jared, getting on the stand was no less nerve wracking than arriving at the end of a diving board over a frigid pond. He knew he'd be all right once he got in the water. So once again, he managed to compose himself, cleared his throat, and said, "It's this way, Your Honor." He began with some temerity yet confident that the facts, as he saw them, would support his contention that the defendants in this case should be convicted of "unspecified charges" and punished accordingly.

"When I arrived at the scene of the airplane accident at the Walkover Bridge, I found two gentlemen sitting in the middle of Cottage Grove Road, drinking alcohol and smoking cigars, rather pleased with themselves, I might add. One of them was Sydney Wadsworth, the man sitting over there behind the table. The other man, Hector Monarch, had to be taken to the hospital in Portland for observation. The date and time is in my report on your office desk."

Abigail interrupted his testimony to ask, "On what charges did you arrest these men?"

Jared referred to his notes and citation sheet. "I was just getting to that. First off, they were guilty of flying and drinking on a public road."

"During or after the accident?" Abigail inquired.

"Shoot, I can tell when someone's under the influence of demon alcohol, but I couldn't provide any hard evidence, 'cause I couldn't get either of them to walk, let alone respond to my inquiries. Judge, I ask, who would fly into a covered bridge unless they were dead drunk?"

Abigail said, "So you don't know. Go on, Officer."

"Almost all of the airplane stayed inside the bridge. Obviously, they were traveling well over the speed limit and failed to stop before entering the bridge as required by law. My only choice was to charge them with speeding, reckless driving, and public endangerment. Of course, under these circumstances, it would be to the letter and extent of the law. You do see my logic? I'm acting in the best interest of Port Henry."

"It's becoming all too clear," she said with a noticeable overtone of cynicism. "Please continue and tell the court what's the estimated damage and disposition of the airplane and the bridge. Roughly."

"This, Your Honor, is where the events surrounding the accident gets a little tricky." Jared asked for a glass of water and took a healthy gulp prior to flipping through his notes. The storm had left town, but the humidity stayed behind to augment a torrent of sweat running down Jared's forehead. "You see, I had two jobs, well, maybe three. Besides getting the two men into our police station, I had to clear the road—and the bridge—to make sure it was safe for traffic. I discovered that most of the plane was turned into scrap metal inside the bridge. I had Hester order Henry's Wrecking Yard to clear everything up and keep every scrap at his place as evidence. The mess will cost Port Henry a bundle, no telling how much right now just to repair the bridge. Thousands probably."

"Question," said Abigail. "Stop there for a moment, Officer Peabody. You did have authority from the sheriff to order removal of the evidence? Yes?"

"Nope. In the heat of the moment, it didn't occur to me. Besides, Judge, he wasn't around anyway. Jest trying to do what Sheriff Milo would have done under the circumstances."

Once again, Jared proved a great disappointment to Judge Underwood. She tapped her pencil on the desk, hoping to drum her temper back into submission. It would be useless, she thought, to ask Jared if he took photographs of the accident, since there weren't any in the file. Pictures, she thought, would have gone a long way to substantiate his account of what happened at the bridge. "All right, Officer Peabody. If you've nothing further to present in the way of evidence, you may step down. Oh yes, and please remain available until court is adjourned for the day."

Spinning around in her chair, she turned her attention to Sydney. "Mr. Wadsworth, I see. I'll be most interested to hear your defense in light of the officer's charges. Please step forward. The clerk will administer the oath, and you are invited to take your place in the witness box. Again, this is a hearing before the court, and it is understood that Mr. Monarch is not able at this time to testify in his own behalf. When you are ready to give your testimony, please feel free to begin."

As Sydney passed by the bench, Toby and Harriet leaned forward in their seats, clasping the rail in front of them with both hands in rapt anticipation of what Sydney was about to say.

"Harriet," whispered Toby, "you are about to witness genius at work. He's in his element now."

"Well, Toby dear," raising her voice, "Port Henry isn't New York City, and he's up against *Iron Pants*, not some drop-out sissy boy from the Harvard law school."

Abigail lowered the gavel with a sharp rap and scolded the two to be quiet in the courtroom. Her admonishment quickly ended the couple's first fight since their marriage. Embarrassed, they sheepishly sank back into their chairs. Meanwhile, Sydney had entered the witness box. With studied deliberation, he raised a finger to his pursed lips and closed his eyes as if deep in thought, waiting for quiet, searching for a place to begin his oration.

"Your Honor, the story of my journey to Port Henry began routinely yesterday morning in Livermore Falls, New York, when I received news that the Portland Packet had sunk the previous evening. I had every reason to believe that my dear friend Toby Worthington and his traveling companion, Harriet Bartholomew, were aboard that ship. They anticipated being married prior to boarding the packet on their way to Bloodstone Island. I learned after my arrival here that instead of embarking, they were quite fortunately detained by the Port Henry Police Department."

Abigail waved her hand to interject. "Yes, yes, I'm quite well acquainted with their circumstances, which I believe you know have recently been adjudicated. I find it ironic that you and they have a, uh, long history together. Go on."

"Quite so. In fact, we three belong to the same private country club in Livermore Falls, New York. Upstate, don't you know? Brookside by name. I have both the distinction and pleasure of being its founder. Of course, I have long since retired from my law practice in New York. But forgive me, I digress."

Abigail always tried hard not to let her suspicions about outsiders show through in either her body language or facial expressions. But when she turned her attention away from Sydney to raise her head back and gaze hawk-eyed at the chandeliers, Toby could see that any mission to impress and patronize a small-town female judge would run amuck, especially if he persisted in marching down the same holier-than-thou road.

Sydney also realized that he had just lost his audience and needed a quick change of course. "When I learned of the predicament my friends could be in, I sought out my only recourse to come to their assistance, trusting of course to the Almighty that they might still be alive. I chartered a plane owned and flown by Hector Monarch. Almost as soon as we took off, we encountered the same violent storm system that engulfed the whole New England region. If I may say so, our little aircraft was tossed around like a cowboy on a mad steer. Yet we bore on, and I can attest to the pilot's extraordinary proficiency at the controls."

By cleverly asking the judge for a glass of water, Sydney drew her attention away from the chandeliers and back to him. Harriet, watching intently, elbowed Toby and whispered, "Pssst. Just now when Sydney asked the judge for a glass water, did you notice him give her a pretentious shudder for dramatic effect?"

"Yes, he does it all the time on the golf course to glean sympathy, a trick that's more than worn out on me and the regulars. Now shush and don't jab me again."

Experience taught Sydney that even the briefest of respite provided an opportunity to decide strategy and what to posit going forward. He cleared his throat to beseech her attention before he began again. "I and everyone in Port Henry can take comfort in Heck Monarch's skill as a pilot. We were forced to make an emergency landing. Our only alternative was the short straight road leading up to a one-lane covered bridge. With buffeting winds and no power, this pilot was able to keep the aircraft on dead center with the mouth of the bridge when we entered it. Through a tunnel of certain death, we burst out the other side." Sydney paused and looked heavenward momentarily. "Had he, Hector, been unable to exercise all his abilities as an aviator, well, it's extremely doubtful that either he or I would have survived a head-on collision with the bridge." His voice trailed off deliberately as he wagged his head slowly from side to side, "And yes, the bridge too would have been severely wounded and put out of service."

Abigail seized an opportunity to interrupt Sydney and ask a salient point that she thought went to the heart of the court case. It triggered in her mind that if the accident was indeed a forced landing, perhaps it wasn't the result of recklessness as Jared had earlier claimed. "In your defense, Mr. Wadsworth, perhaps you would care to expand on your definition of 'forced landing.'"

"Certainly, Your Honor. When Hector and I were flying a few thousand feet over Port Henry, we ran out of fuel, and our only option was to attempt a, shall I say, nonlethal landing on either a field or a straight stretch of road."

Abigail, fully engaged in Sydney's saga, could not hold back from asking, "But running out of fuel seems quite reckless in itself, wouldn't you agree?"

"Yes, but under different circumstances. When we left for Port Henry, the aircraft had sufficient fuel, even taking into account the possibility of strong headwinds. I was on a mission of mercy for my friends that I might be able to help, in whatever small way, hoping of course they were still alive."

The cub reporter's ears must have perked up, because he left his seat by the back entrance and moved down to a chair in the front row next to Toby. Meanwhile, Jared had stepped outside to reward himself with a smoke. He found satisfaction in believing that Wadsworth faced certain doom because he'd given such a litany of damning testimony. Surely, he reckoned, the results of this hearing would convict Sydney. He mused that his proficiency as an officer would be vindicated, and for what it was worth, his stature in the police department would be restored.

Inside the courtroom, Sydney crossed his legs and folded his hands against his chest to strike an even more effective pose. He began speaking in a slower more deliberate manner, hoping that his points would neither be overlooked nor misinterpreted, especially by the recording town clerk. "Before taking off from Livermore Falls, all the most recent charts indicated Port Henry had an active airfield. As a publicly owned facility, it no doubt found some use by small private planes and serve as an emergency field for the region." Sydney paused again to take on water and resumed his previous posture. "After I checked myself out of your clinic, I made some inquiries while I was in town. At your local bank, I stopped in to replenish my dwindling supply of resources. While I waited, the vice president and I chatted at length, and he informed me that the airfield had been rezoned and converted into a commercial shopping area. According to him, this change took place right after the war, sometime in early '46. About two years ago, I calculate."

Abigail tapped her desk to attract Sydney's attention. Her voice suggested a decent amount of impatience when she said, "Excuse me, Mr. Wadsworth, I assume this line of testimony is somehow linked to the events of your forced landing? If not, please move on. The hour's getting late."

"Linked? Oh, indeed it is." Seizing an opening to thrust home a fatal blow, he said, "The problem, Your Honor, is that the town of Port Henry never advised any federal or state aviation authority that the city no longer had an airfield, even though its license had been renewed. Consequently, we had every reason to believe Port Henry still had one. I'm sure this comes to you as a shock. In my modest legal opinion, this means that the town of Port Henry, through its negligence, is responsible for all the damages related to our forced landing."

Abigail bit down hard on her tongue to keep from uttering a stream of epithets that would make an old salt blush. She flung herself back in her chair and, as one rarely lost for words, quickly returned to sit upright and inquired, "Assuming for a minute, your outrageous claim is valid, what do you mean by 'all the damages'?"

On the sidelines, Toby's back stiffened, and he elbowed Harriet. "See, I told you he's a genius. A premier escape artist, he makes Houdini look like an amateur." Harriet returned the blow.

"In this case, Your Honor, 'all the damages' would include the replacement of the Monarch's recently acquired aircraft, damages to the historic Walkover Bridge, medical expenses, long-term injuries to one's person and psyche, loss of business, court costs, legal fees, and of course collateral damages. I don't believe I've left anything out, but then I haven't practice law for some time, don't you know?"

"I know enough," Abigail said, "enough to declare this court adjourned." The gavel crashed down hard. Everyone in the courtroom jumped to their feet and watched her leave the bench, not retreating to her chambers, however, but marching to the witness box where Sydney, nonplused, remained standing. "Mr. Wadsworth, if you're not too busy," she said, wetting her lips, "I'd like you to join me in my office where we can chat confidentially about your testimony. Tea?"

"Not busy at all, and tea would be most welcome for one as parched as I seem to be."

"Good. Then please follow me." As she passed by the town clerk, she ordered, without so much as a sideways glance, "Tea, Phyllis."

Phyllis glanced up and mumbled, "Here we go again. This poor sap is going to wish it were whiskey instead of tea when she gets through with him."

Chapter 16

A Tea Party

Sydney followed Judge Underwood to her chambers. He quickly observed her quarters as spacious and very well appointed, akin to the tastes of a man of substantial means and well acquainted with the sea. Abigail pointed to a chair, invited him to be seated, and asked him to wait while she hastened off to her cloakroom for a change of attire.

* * *

Meanwhile, Harriet, in the lead, with Toby close behind, ambled down the center aisle toward the exit. The bewildered look on their faces indicated that they didn't have a strategy for either their individual or mutual problems.

Harriet had to admit that Sydney turned the tables in his favor with regard to *Iron Pants.* This did not change her unfavorable opinion of him. Sydney had seldom appeared in her grand designs, except when it concerned Toby and the timing of his arrival in Port Henry couldn't have been more disruptive. Angry that only Toby could have disclosed their whereabouts to Sydney, her wrath simmered to a boiling point. *How could he betray me like this?* she wondered. *Men. I can't even trust Toby, and it kills me to think I still have to.* But she was not about to confront either of them. Already, her cup runneth over with disasters, and adding one more unpleasant scene served no purpose. Without question, she suspected that Sydney had come to wreck her marriage plans, not to rescue her and Toby from a shipwreck as he so eloquently described on the witness stand. But she did not wish to throw this issue into the mix of her problems. *Cripes,* she thought, *the law probably wants me in three states, and I've got a crazy son-in-law who wants me dead.*

Toby, trailing behind Harriet, had his thoughts focused on finding a boat of any size or shape to take them to Bloodstone Island. So far, he had come up empty. The few boats available for charter and sport fishing refused to venture out into a heavy sea. Earlier, Toby scoured the docks on the waterfront to entice a skipper that would take them over and back from the island. But when Toby mentioned the name of the island, he received the same answer.

"Bloodstone Island you say? Nope."

Clearly, this island must have, at best, a sullied reputation, based on everyone's reluctance to even discuss it. Not about to give up but nagged with a sense of hopelessness, he didn't know where to turn. Once outside, Toby's spirits brightened when he muttered, "Toby, you idiot, Sydney's here. He'll know what to do, if the judge doesn't skewer him first."

* * *

Meanwhile in the judge's chambers, Sydney put aside the offer of a chair and instead elected to tiptoe around Abigail's office, inspecting a treasure trove of relics from sailing ships, ship models, bronze sculptures, and paintings that gave homage to life at sea. Consumed by his natural curiosity, he set about exploring the artifacts that embellished every wall, shelf, and niche. He thought, *So this is what it's like to discover King Tut's tomb.* Behind her desk on a credenza, a collection of trophies had been assembled, presumably in order of significance. Crystal vases, silver plates, etched decanters, Wedgwood china, and vessels of every type and description. With rare exception, all the awards bore a nautical theme depicting sailboats. He surmised, *No doubt a reflection of the accomplishments of the men in her family.*

He wondered about her appearance sans judicial robes. Could she be, as Toby described, lanky and cranky. *Unlikely on both counts.*

Stealthily, Abigail crept up behind Sydney and announced, "In case you're wondering, those awards are mine."

Startled, Sydney, off in his own world, turned around and replied, "Really, yours? That's quite remarkable."

"You mean, of course, remarkable for a woman?"

Caught off guard and mentally rocked back on his heels, he replied, "Good heavens, no. I meant that even the least significant of these trophies would be a lifetime's *fait acompli* for any man or woman."

"Yes, well. Let's get on with the business at hand." Abigail smiled courteously and retired to a period wing chair opposite Sydney, who awkwardly squirmed his way into an antique Shaker chair.

Sydney, to his surprised, soaked in her new image, which obviously was meant to reveal her femininity, but in a way totally unfamiliar to him. He unexpectedly found favor in her chiseled uncomely features of high cheekbones divided by a prominent nose he could best describe in nautical terms as a well-proportioned bowsprit. Not gangly, as Toby suggested, but tall, athletic, and slim in stature. Her long silvery hair that earlier that day had been woven into a bun similar to a sailor's knot now flowed like gentle waves over her shoulders and down a white billowy knee-length tunic snugly tied off at the waist with a braided leather belt. He detested cosmetics; and when Abigail revealed herself, absent makeup, he saw her as a worldly woman comfortable in her skin of weathered face and hands. Perhaps she approached sixtyish, he thought, but certainly one who carried herself as one considerably younger. Everything about her spoke of the sea, and he found this aspect of her delightful and charming for one of his taste sensibilities.

She began their conversation with, "Assuming you're right about the charts and the airfield, what course of action do you plan on taking? Your testimony leads me to believe you've already thought things through." A long pause ensued. "Mr. Wadsworth, you're staring."

Caught out, he replied, "Yes, yes. My mind was elsewhere. Forgive me, but I'm quite enchanted by the necklace you're wearing. It's very much like, but quite different from, the one belonging to a friend of mine, if you take my meaning."

"I understand, but please, your course of action?"

"Well naturally, I expected some simplistic routine charges on the part of Port Henry, and that I, and Hector Monarch too, would be a defendant. Our option would be either to admit wrongdoing, cut our losses, and capitulate or sue the town. But this whole 'event,' shall we call it, needn't be as bothersome as it might appear for either party."

"You don't say?"

A loud knock on the door interrupted their conversation. Outside, Phyllis Peabody announced, "Tea, Your Honor." Holding the door open with one foot, she rolled in a complete tea service cart embellished with homemade jellies and scones. Phyllis did an obvious double take when she saw the judge's attire but waited to roll her eyes until after she skedaddled out the door.

Abigail's choice of clothes was no accident. She had also calculated that making use of her finishing school manners could work to her advantage, which would portray her as a genteel vulnerable woman. She was confident that her best tactic was to manage her adversary instead of confronting him. "Allow me to pour," she purred. "Do you take sugar, cream?"

"Yes, thank you, one lump and just a splash of cream. You're much too kind," replied Sydney.

"Oh, piffle."

Sydney seized an opportunity to engage in idle conversation. "I must say that I am at a loss when it comes to covered bridges. Apparently, the debate goes on as to why they are covered in the first place. I'm a lawyer not an engineer, but I'm sure you could make a decent argument about, the why, that is, when we might find a more appropriate time.

"If I may, might I make light of my unfortunate introduction with the Walkover Bridge? I know they were designed for horses to cross streams, not airplanes." He paused to sip his tea. "I also know if the Walkover Bridge didn't have a roof over it, we would have landed without incident, gladly extending our wings out over the side rails. All of which means we wouldn't be having tea this afternoon."

"Of course, but what you've just said is all palaver, so please go on."

"Certainly. It's just my opinion, of course, but I think if an engineer inspects the bridge for damages incurred by Hector's aircraft, he would be hard pressed to find any. By virtue of my first-hand experience, I believe the bridge suffered no more than a few scratches and gouges here and there. Certainly, no structural damage. *Butterfly Number One* was no match for the bridge, and Henry's salvage yard will testify to that. The salvage proceeds could easily cover bridge repairs, don't you know?"

He paused to catch her reaction, yet she remained as unaffected as an audience still waiting for the punch line. "Actually, I think the town should consider the plane flying through the bridge as a historical event. It would make a fine tourist stop. It's not every day an airplane flies into a covered bridge. Yes?

"I'm suggesting the town should be reluctant to file charges on that damages to the bridge. Fortunately, I, like the bridge, didn't suffer any structural damage, only a few nicks and scratches. As for liability to my person, I'd be willing to call the damages a draw."

Abigail winced and asked, "So you say, but aren't you forgetting Hector?"

"Of course, there is Hector, who has hospital expenses and loss of income, not to mention his airplane. He will offer his own defense, through his own attorney or his insurance company's lawyer. But I must caution the town that his position has considerable merit, and I am just one of his witnesses.

"To wit, if Hector Monarch had the slightest concern about the availability of an airfield in Port Henry. Well, he'd have flown us to the closest alternative airport. But, of course after we arrived here, it was too late. And as a consequence, we ran out of fuel. His company's prospectus and modus operandi does not include flying around the country, crashing into buildings. As I testified earlier, usurping all our fuel was neither his nor his company's negligence, but the town's negligence."

After Sydney's long soliloquy, Abigail felt her nerves stretched to the breaking point and decided to refrain from commenting. *Horsefeathers,* she thought. *If Sydney's right about the charts, the town council's in trouble and likely liable for a big lawsuit.* She needed to frame at least a plausible retort. "Naturally, your argument depends on the town's negligence, other governmental agencies, and individuals. Are you sure your evidence is clear enough to litigate? Perhaps you would care for more tea, Mr. Wadsworth?"

"Yes, thank you. And to your first question, I believe your airport should be officially closed before some other poor chap tries to land in the middle of your new business center."

Abigail tried not to show alarm or sign of agreement but scribbled a note to have the matter looked into first thing in the morning.

When she looked up, the expression on Sydney's face compelled her to ask, "Now what are you staring at?"

"Something I can't believe that I completely overlooked. Behind you in the far corner. A set of vintage golf clubs in a leather bag."

"Oh that," she said, cranking her neck to look. "The clubs belonged to my father." The complete change of subject provided a welcome relief for her. "Turned out I was his only child. He never said, but I'm sure he wanted a son to provide him an heir. I didn't take up golf, never had the patience. But I did try to please him by being a good sailor. I'm glad we spent a lot of time together on the water."

"Well, I must say you succeeded admirably." Abigail could take his genuine remark as patronizing and that, he thought, would be disastrous if he continued down that path. He bit his lip. Still, his interest in the clubs persisted. "I know we have much to discuss, but do you mind if I have a closer look at them? Shan't be a moment."

Abigail nodded approval and found herself amused with Sydney, that he could, even at his advanced age, still be consumed by a sport like a kid at his first ball game.

"Hah, these clubs are a real a prize. The heads need a little buffing to get the rust off, don't you know? Popping a bit of shellac on the hickory shafts and they'll be good as new. Leather grips are cracked but easily repaired in a golf shop. What gems you have. Hmmm, blade putter, niblick, mashie-niblick, mid-iron. Good-looking spoon and brassie too. They need sprucing up with a fresh coat of varnish. Pre 1920, I'd say." He rifled through the side pocket of the golf bag and retrieved two vintage balls and dropped them on the floor with the intention of putting them across the room.

"Mr. Wadsworth, perhaps later, I think we should move on."

"Yes, of course, silly of me. As I mentioned earlier, there is no need to make a big ruckus over this accident." Sydney returned to his chair and sipped his tea. "Between you and me, I believe if you replace Hector's modest aircraft with a new one and a like amount of cash, he would be pleased to forget the whole thing and jump on the next bus out of town."

"You really think so?" Abigail leaned forward to place her empty cup on the tea service.

"Of course, I haven't spoken to him, but he's a reasonable man. I would think the town's insurance company would be delighted to get off so cheaply and without a long drawn out court case that could be embarrassing as well as costly for everyone."

Abigail's shoulders fell, and she tossed her hair back. She felt relaxed for the first time today. Sydney represented a solution instead of a problem. "I will certainly take your suggestions under advisement. I'll have to prepare a report with my recommendations for the next meeting of the town council."

"Good," said Sydney. "Cooperation is so much preferable to confrontation, don't you know? But were I you, I shouldn't linger too long. Perhaps a special meeting of the selectmen would be more in order, and I would be available in the wings, so to speak."

"Thank you, Mr. Wadsworth, but there's another matter I'd like to discuss, a question really. I'm afraid I gave your two friends—the Worthingtons—a rather difficult time of it this morning. I need to deliver an apology. I couldn't have been in a worse frame of mind. It's no excuse really. But you see, my cat, Moxie, had been run over the day before I married them. And I was led to believe they were the culprits."

"I'm really sorry to hear that. It can be devastating, I know. I love cats myself." Sydney hated cats, hair and all. He couldn't believe what he just uttered and thought, *How could this woman bring me to say such a fib? It's just not my nature. I must have hit my head in the accident.*

"As for an apology, I wouldn't worry. Perhaps you'll have a chance while they're in town. They're staying at the Lighthouse Inn. If not, I'll pass your thoughtfulness on to them in the meantime. To digress, Toby and I have been close friends for as long as I can remember. Confirmed bachelors, we are. Harriet's been a member of Brookside going back, let me see, during two previous marriages. No doubt you wonder what's the urgency for a life-long bachelor to marry Harriet who tragically lost her first three husbands."

"Well, y-e-s," said Abigail. "From what I can tell, they don't appear to be all that well suited, except that they both wear club blazers, like scotch and carry firearms." The image she described for Sydney caused them both to smile. "But then without any personal experience, I'm hardly a judge of what makes a marriage. And what's all this about, Brookside?"

"Strange as it may seem, Your Honor, it's all about Brookside."

"Perhaps we could drop the formalities? Why don't you address me in private as Abigail? Please go on. I find this all quite interesting."

"Of course, Abigail. Likewise, I prefer just Sydney," he said, moving to a more comfortable chair closer to Abigail. "If I may digress again, marriage can take on many forms, and people of every station in life hold on to those things they cherish and discover a willingness to protect them at any cost. Chaps like Toby and I aren't much different. We're just friends, but each of us has a bond with Brookside Country Club going back to its inception. As its founder, I understand these things."

"And Harriet also has a Brookside bond?" said Abigail.

"For Harriet, it's not quite the same thing. Hers is a family membership by marriage, not by her choice. Nonetheless, she's still a de facto member as long as she is married or remarries within a year."

"So that's it." Abigail waived a finger at Sydney to express her surprise and disbelief. "A marriage to Toby would keep her membership at the club?"

"Good heavens, no, not at all," Sydney protested, tendering a sardonic smile. "Toby has always held her in contempt and suspected her of having done-in her first two husbands. Always referred to her as an 'old trout.' Her last husband, Jeffrey Bartholomew, was a 'rotter.' Toby and I discovered him to be a thief and murderer. We were with him when he committed suicide, just a couple of weeks ago actually."

Puzzled and annoyed, Abigail said, "This Jeffrey thing is all too much to digest now. So what in the devil is this Worthington marriage all about? You'd best believe me when I say I won't have my court made a mockery."

"Bear me out, please. As simply put as possible, Toby agreed to marry Harriet so that she could meet the terms of her second husband's will to inherit Bloodstone Island. As irrational as such a demand seems, she's required to spend a night on the island as a married woman accompanied by her husband."

Abigail stood up to confront Sydney, "You expect me to believe that rubbish, do you? Why would your old pal Toby do such a ridiculous thing?"

"As I said, he's a member of the club. Toby felt duty bound to come to the aid of another member, along with his time-honored compassion for any woman in distress, and I might add Harriet has a genuine fear for her life."

"Honestly, Sydney, what's going on?" She walked over to the golf bag, took out a club, and began swinging it around and thrusting it like an epee. Raising her voice from across the room, she said, "Fear for her life? What kind of pish-posh is that?"

Abigail hardly bought into all of Sydney's spiel. Confused by the maze of bizarre events taking place and the confluence of characters the likes of which she'd never encountered before except in fiction, she found it difficult to follow Sydney into such uncharted waters. Yet she found the whole scenario intriguing, like a puzzle that only she could solve. And in the process, she discovered, to her surprise, being strangely attracted to Sydney. However, her basic instincts told her to be cautious of "Brookside" folks whose type fell well outside her comfort zone. Not a knight in shining armor flying into town, he nonetheless represented a breath of fresh air bearing the manners of a gentleman.

Sydney, still composed, inspected his fingernails. "Pish-posh, you ask? It's impossible for you to have known. To begin with, she has a deranged stepson, Claude Hadley, from her second marriage. He's intent on keeping her from inheriting Bloodstone Island, because he's next in line and wouldn't stop at murder to get it. Putting it mildly, he's a sociopathic misfit. That's why Harriet had the Derringer in her purse when she was arrested. Claude's around town, and I believe Officer Peabody has already had a minor encounter with him. You can check with Sheriff McDonald." Sydney rose and walked over to Abigail, holding out his hands. "Here, let me show you how to hold the club. We wouldn't want to knock anything over."

She flinched in retreat. "How can you be so calm?" She turned away from Sydney and dragged the putter over to her chair and collapsed with the club firmly clutched between her knees.

Sydney returned to his chair and sighed. "I must confess that when the two of them embarked on this journey, I felt that I had been betrayed by my best friend. I flew here with every intention of stopping this ridiculous marriage." Out of habit, he reached for his silver cigar case, but before opening it, he thrust it back in his breast pocket. "I've since learned that this whole mission of Toby's was something he felt he could handle on his own without troubling me. He knew how busy I was at the time.

"You see, Governor Dewy will be coming to Brookside in a few days for a campaign appearance, and I'm in charge of the preparations for his visit. Ostensibly, the governor's visit is to award Toby and me a specially struck medal for being citizen crime stoppers. The two of us managed to break up a syndicated crime ring operating out of the Chicago area. The governor is big on stopping crime, don't you know?"

Abigail threw both hands in the air. "Let's stop right here and please examine your nails later. I'd like your full attention." Trying to absorb Sydney's story line a mile long with no finish line in sight wore on her nerves because she had another more important issue on her agenda.

"By all means, Abigail, I apologize for rambling."

"Yes, well, excuse me for interrupting," she said. "This is all quite fascinating. But I too have more than a passing interest in Bloodstone Island. For one thing, this island and a number of the other barrier islands are in my jurisdiction, and I like to keep abreast of what's happening. All of a sudden, this uninhabited island lying dormant off our coast has become a place of interest. A couple of parties, besides you and your friends, have become quite exercised over it. Perhaps there are others interested, and maybe there's a connection. I don't know, but I think it's about time I find out."

She stood up and returned the putter to the golf bag across the room. The brief silence gave her time to gauge her words and thoughts more carefully now that she had decided to change the subject. "We've noticed a coast guard cutter, the *Leslie*, cruising up and down our coastline, looking for who knows what. Couldn't miss it, one of the guard's largest during the war. Sheriff McDonald's taken notice too. Still commissioned, he said the *Leslie* should be scrapped. Said it couldn't catch a bootlegger in a rowboat.

"About ten days ago, the *Leslie* anchored out, and a few hours later, the skipper, a young lieutenant, came ashore in his gig. Marched right into the clerk's office and asked a lot of questions about Bloodstone Island. He got whatever he wanted from Phyllis Peabody, but when she asked why he needed the latest skinny on the island, he stonewalled her questions with the standard cliché, 'just routine.'

"Oh, and before I forget, an attorney type who said he was from Portland logged in with Phyllis and began asking a raft full of questions about the island's ownership. She got suspicious, and after he left, she couldn't find him in the Portland directory. So naturally, when Toby and Harriet arrived here with their Cinderella love story, my ears really perked up."

Sydney rose to his feet. "Well, I should think so. Everyone should go to battle stations."

Abigail sighed. "Yes, Sydney, but not right now. I'm exhausted." She smiled. "And it must be past five o'clock."

"Right you are. I'm a bit fatigued myself." Sydney confirmed the time and decided to capitalize on the moment. "Perhaps you'd care to join me in a beverage? I'd be delighted to have your company and someone like you to suggest the best setting."

Abigail responded favorably, "Well, I do know a couple of watering holes just a short walk from here. Wait here while I get my purse. I won't be a moment."

Chapter 17

An Alliance Emerges

Pleased with the prospect of being engaged for the cocktail hour, Sydney began to hum old Navy ditties while he paced impatiently around her office.

Emerging from her dressing room, she announced with a pinch of glee, "We do have a selection of places to choose from. Now don't laugh, but it's all right if you do."

"I'm sure any one you select will be most satisfactory."

On their way from Abigail's chambers past the town clerk's station, she said, "Good night, Phyllis. Be a dear and see things are locked up, won't you?" Agape as a surfacing swimmer out of breath, Phyllis could not recover her composure in time to assemble the slightest response. The sight of Abigail stepping out with a perfect stranger struck her dumb.

"Now then, Sydney, we have the 'Laughing Lobster' to choose from right here on Dock Street. It's usually filled with humorless old fishermen. By ten o'clock at night on weekends, they're fighting out in the street. So let's give that a pass, shall we?"

Sydney nodded in agreement. "Yes, and I think we should avoid the Lighthouse Inn as well. The Worthingtons are staying there, and I for one would not like to cross paths at the moment."

"Now there I'm in agreement." Abigail's thoughts buzzed around to find a way to sequester Sydney, learn more about him, and nail down his relationship with the Worthingtons. She prattled on, almost giddy, about the drinking establishments in Port Henry. "There's the uppity 'Reluctant Snail' lounge a block up on Main Street. But any reference to escargot is mistaken, so that's definitely out. Half a block down is the 'Red Herring' bar in the SeaVue Inn. After the library closes, the intellectual crowd heads for it since it's right across the street. There's nothing worse than—forgive my language—overhearing snockered poets read for their inebriated audience. Yes?"

"I most certainly agree with you on that count. But I'll wager there's a place you have in mind?"

"Indeed, there is. It just came to me. It's one block over. After a sailboat race, my father and his crew made it their favorite watering hole. I haven't been there in years. It dates back to 1841 when it was a stage stop. Originally, it was called a tavern. Now it's called Ye Olde Oyster Bed and Breakfast. The place had been falling apart for quite some time, but the new owners are trying to restore it as best they can. Nice couple, I hear."

"Sounds inviting, Abigail. Let's see how they're progressing? I'm dry as a bone."

"Why not?" She led the way, ignoring a sprained foot acquired a few days earlier.

A neatly attired middle-aged woman greeted them at the front desk and asked if they were looking for lodging, dinner, or perhaps some refreshment in the lounge? Sydney took the helm and suggested the lounge. He politely refused a window table in favor of a quiet corner in the back of the room where he chucked his valise and umbrella onto a nearby settee.

A barkeep emerged from the kitchen to wait on them and introduced himself as the new owner of the bed and breakfast and welcomed them to the Snuggery. He scooted them into their pillowed captain's chairs facing each other, placed two cocktail napkins on their table, and hovered close by with his pencil and paper at the ready. Abigail deliberated about what to order that would be bold yet feminine and appropriate for the occasion. Waiting for her decision, Sydney told the owner, "I must commend your taste in restoring the old tavern. Very clever of you to fashion this table out of an old ship's hatch, wormholes and all."

"I agree with him," said Abigail, looking up at the owner. "Oh, and I think I should like a vodka tonic with a dash of lime."

Sydney said, "Good choice for a warm evening, Abigail. I favor a Johnny Walker scotch on ice, a twist of lemon, and go easy on the ice, please."

"Certainly, sir, I shouldn't be a moment, and thank you for your kind compliment." Noticing the late sun in retreat, he lit the candle in a glass chimney on their table. To the trained eye, the interior décor recalled the inn's history quite accurately and obviously leaned heavily on the owner's attendance at local auctions and their "good eye" for antiques. Sydney restored his tired eyes on the immediate surroundings, but Abigail found the "comings and goings" of the new owners more interesting. She lowered her voice and said, "I think they've identified us, and we'll be the talk of the town tomorrow morning."

"Too bad," he blurted. "I was just thinking of staying here overnight. Alone, of course—I didn't mean—I meant I'll have to reconsider, of course, and make do somewhere else."

"Yes, I'm sure you will." Abigail smiled weakly at his clumsy remark and wondered if he had just made a simple Freudian slip.

The owner brought a plate of salty snacks with their drinks and asked if he could bring them a hors d'oeuvre. "This afternoon, we received a bushel of fresh oysters. I can do half-shell or Rockefeller?"

Before Abigail could protest, Sydney ordered a dozen raw oysters to share and another beverage to wash them down. "Now that that's settled," he said. "You must tell me more about yourself."

"There isn't a whole lot to tell, but as you know, I'm very fond of cats, and I'm going to miss Moxie terribly. You heard, of course. And then there's sailing. I loved competitive sailing as you observed in my chambers. That and my job, which seems like I've had forever. I take it very seriously. It could be one of the reasons I never came close to marrying, not very close anyway."

She laughed and groped for words to explain her marital state and decided to made light of it. "The pool of eligible men in Port Henry has always been, shall we say, shallow, and I've put a good number of them in jail at one time or another. Not too many men want to be married to their jailer. And I wasn't interested in somebody with a record."

Smiling again, she took the straws out of her tonic and set them aside. She chased an oyster down with the remainder of her drink. "I dated a little at Colby, when I had time, but Daddy succeeded in scaring them off. Don't misunderstand me. I loved my father, but Mom died when I was thirteen, and I was all he had left."

Sydney pressed his hand on hers and said, "I'm sorry to hear about your mother. Filling the void in your father's life must have come at a great personal sacrifice." As a sympathetic gesture, he politely patted her hand before gulping two oysters in succession. Waiting for their eyes to meet again, he said, "If I may be so bold, I wouldn't have given up so easily on being one of your suitors." He thought, *I can't believe I just said that. Queer. It rolled off my tongue without the slightest hesitation.*

"You flatter me," said Abigail. "But I wonder. You're a confirmed bachelor, aren't you? You and your friend Worthington? Certainly one of you must have been considered eligible in your day. I don't wish to pry, just idle curiosity. By the way, the oysters hit the spot. Haven't had them in an age, not this good anyway."

"I'm glad, about the oysters, but I don't know if I can satisfy your curiosity about either Toby or me." Sydney tossed down another oyster, which gave him a moment to collect his thoughts. "I don't know too much about Toby's early days other than he was a bounder. Toby is an intelligent chap, but one of those fellows who could never really find a niche in life, don't you know? He married quite young, but only for a few days. She ran off, and he never saw her again, very sad state of affairs. I think he said the marriage had been annulled by her parents. And, if you'll pardon me, he mentioned to me years ago that he'd sworn off women in perpetuity."

Abigail broke out in a string of uncontrolled giggles. "So Toby came all the way to Port Henry to get married again for a few days. I don't believe it. I don't know if that's a little 'in' or 'out' of character?" Abigail's expression quickly turned sour as she slumped back in her chair. "I warned the Worthingtons not to make a mockery of my court."

Her terse remark sent a shiver down Sydney's back. "I doubt if there was any intent on their part to sully either your reputation or the court's. As Toby's attorney, I certainly would have him plead innocent. Only Don Quixote could defend the honor of a woman better, especially if she were a member of Brookside Country Club. To top it off, no man I know of is more gullible when it comes to the aid of a tearful woman. To make things worse, he becomes befuddled when he's outside his element, shall we say. Then he runs amuck of his better judgment. If he were sitting right here, he'd agree with me."

With a backward tilt of his head, Sydney deftly consumed his last oyster. "In conclusion, I have to keep an eye out for him all the time. Heavens, it seems I've finished my drink, you too. It's not too late to order another."

To deflect the conversation going any further in this direction, he looked about and asked Abigail, "Since we're here, perhaps you'd care to join me in a light supper before I head out to find lodgings? Busy day ahead."

"I'd like that, but the oysters seem to have quelled my appetite."

"Mine too. Instead of a cocktail, perhaps an aperitif would be nice for now, so we can resume our chat?" Sydney signaled to the innkeeper chatting at the front desk. "I think we could do with your menu and list of spirits."

Abigail pressed on another subject troubling her. "Four marriages and Harriet's a helpless, tearful woman?" Abigail sat upright on the edge of her chair.

"Perhaps, right now, Abigail, the less you know about her, the better. It works for me. Let's just say she has had her way with men."

Abigail pressed her advantage and impulsively tacked onto a different course. "And you, Sydney, have you had your way with women?" Immediately, she thought, *Good God Almighty, what's the matter with me? I want to know, perhaps more than I'm entitled to, about Sydney's personal life, but how much then do I really want to know? It must be the vodka talking.*

Embarrassed by the question, Sydney coughed in his napkin while he prepared a response. "I wouldn't call it 'having my way.' I describe it more like 'staying out of the way.'"

The owner with menus in hand arrived at their table in the nick of time to rescue Sydney before being pressed to deliver a drawn-out soliloquy about his love life. Sydney's past had been kept in a vault the architects of Fort Knox would envy. Typically, he would be offended by a question that invaded his privacy and would either dodge the question or terminate the conversation altogether. But this evening, he was bent on puffing up his image in Abigail's eyes. Fascinated with her, he decided to answer her query as soon as he had sufficient time to untie his tongue and deliver a credible spiel. Meanwhile, the owner stood by waiting for their order.

At long length, Sydney peeked over the top of the wine list, with the full intention of impressing Abigail with his prowess and knowledge of wines. "Isn't it remarkable that so soon after the war, we're able to import fine wines again? Not that a pleasant domestic can't be found. I see that the house keeps a fine selection." The owner smiled. Sydney slipped into his old habit of name-dropping. "My friend, Baron Louis d'Chard, is a distributor for a number of old French wineries. I see a few of his labels here. Perhaps I can make a suggestion for you, Abigail, unless you have a particular preference."

"Thank you," she replied. "But perhaps we should look at the menu first?"

They both settled on the "catch of the day," baked Haddock, and a bottle of the baron's best, Chateau d'Seine. Abigail giggled when she read aloud a critic's review on the label: "a *discreet little wine with a charming but naughty bouquet*." "Really, Sydney?"

Sydney, embarrassed, shrunk in his chair but regained his composure quickly. As he had suggested earlier, each ordered a small glass of the "house" sherry to relish while they waited for their first course to arrive. The time had finally arrived for Sydney to open his "diary" and provide Abigail with a biographical sketch of his experience with the opposite sex.

He began by telling Abigail that he discovered the great love of his life as a law school student. "I was young, impressionable. Unbeknownst to me, she had a number of liaisons with other students in the past. I'll just call her by her first name, Cynthia, because even now I don't wish to besmirch her character. We became engaged about a year after graduation, and then virtually the day before the wedding, she left me at the altar, so to speak." He took a deep breath. "Perhaps she felt unworthy of me?"

"I was humiliated. The presents had to go back. My family was mortified, and our families never spoke again. It just about broke my heart, and I vowed to avoid any relationship that would end up leading me down the aisle. Any thoughts of marriage sailed away with Cynthia."

Sydney explained in a plodding manner how WWI came along and with it a short stint in the navy. The war was over before his first assignment in the Department of Naval Justice. As such, he was never aboard a ship of war, but he didn't redress introductions intended to flatter him as if he had singlehandedly sunk the German fleet. To Sydney's credit, he never elaborated on his naval career, since in truth, he never went to sea. If ever his expertise at sea should be called upon, he would have to depend on his year in the Sea Scouts and canoe lessons at camp Winakaka in Maine.

Even to his own ear, he sensed the treatise on his love life had become tedious and simplistic. He decided to wrap everything up quickly from Cynthia to the present. "After the navy, I spent most of my time quietly building a law practice in New York, that and lowering my golf handicap. Before I knew it, Abigail, I was fortyish and quite satisfied with my role as a sought-after eligible bachelor. The simple life agreed with me." He stopped to clear his throat and sip his sherry. "I found myself content with being a fair dancer and respectable at light conversation. Ha, and a good deal happier than, if I may, many of my classmates I represented in divorce court."

Abigail broke in. "As you might expect, my scenario's not all that different." Her voice choked. "Let's change the subject, shall we? I shouldn't have brought it up."

He remarked, "Nonsense, I'm glad you did. Clears the air, at least for me, don't you know?"

"I suppose, and let's not spoil our dinner. It must be ready by now." After the innkeeper removed a collection of dishes and glasses, he replaced the spent candle in the glass chimney.

The entrees arrived on scalloped china plates resting on top of warmed pewter platters. A traditional white sauce immersed the fillet of white fish, and small boiled potatoes garnished by freshly chopped parsley and dill. On the inner rim of the plate was a row of buttered baby carrots, a picture-perfect presentation according to Sydney who praised the innkeeper profusely.

Sydney and Abigail hardly spoke to each other during dinner until they found themselves sated with fish and wine. The innkeeper returned and took notice that his wife's good cooking had found approval when he saw the dishes were almost too clean to wash. He inquired if they would like to consider a portion of the Snuggery's homemade ice cream and berry pie for dessert.

While the dishes were being removed, Abigail said, to Sydney's surprise, "I'd like to stay for a little while, but I don't care for dessert. Guess I'm having too good a time tonight, except for my left foot. It's been killing me for over a week now."

"I noticed. You've been favoring your left side walking over here. I'm pretty good at massage. Picked it up from the masseuse at my club. Why don't you let me massage that game foot of yours and take the kinks out? There's no one here to complain. Look around. Everyone's long gone."

Abigail hesitated to give her approval, especially for such an unusual request and in a public place with a "heaven knows who." She rationalized, *What harm can there be in it anyway? He can't be one of those weird foot fetish characters. Besides, my foot does ache.* "OK. Sydney, but be careful, I've only got two feet."

"Well then, kick the deck shoe off, remove your sock, and shinny up to the front edge of the table." Sydney gave her a reassuring smile. "Now I want you to raise your leg up so that I can catch your calf and cradle your foot between my legs. You might need to lean back in your chair a little so I can get the proper leverage."

Why am I letting him do this to me? Abigail thought. *But what have I got to lose?'*

Sydney gently ran both thumbs up the sole of her foot until he reached her toes where he spread them apart by kneading them like dough in the skilled hands of a baker.

"Oh, Sydney, this feels marvelous," she moaned softly. "You're quite the talent?" With both hands, she hung on to the front edge of the table. She bit hard on her lower lip and fastened her eyes shut. Sydney slowly rotated and moved her foot back and forth, using his fingers to run up and down her foot with such dexterity. She implored, "Don't stop. Your hands are so sen-su-ous." Her long hair waved back and forth over her cheeks. Each time Sydney pushed his thumbs deeper into her foot, she would sigh and groan with delight.

The sounds of heavy breathing and murmuring reached the eavesdropping innkeeper. He burst through the café doors into the bar and marched straight to their table. His voice, high-pitched, said, "Is there anything I can get for you? Perhaps a room?"

"That won't be necessary. Thank you," replied Sydney, looking up. "I believe we've had a gentile sufficiency for the evening."

"I should think so. We're closing now. If there's nothing else, I'll get your bill."

"Oh my, Sydney," Abigail squealed, "the stories that will hit the streets tomorrow morning. But thank you for a most enjoyable evening." She tossed her head back and swept her hair back over her shoulders. "I have a strange urge to smoke. Perhaps now you would offer me one of the cigars you showed me in my office?"

Taken aback, he said, "My pleasure, Abigail. I was quite lucky to find my brand in a smoke shop this afternoon." Sydney groaned, "As much as I would like to spend the wee hours with you, I have to make an early start in the morning. I'm obliged to help the Worthingtons, and I need to find a boat for them by tomorrow morning, and I suppose if I have to, I'll buy one. They've hit a patch of bad luck and haven't been able to roust up as much as an inner tube to get to Bloodstone Island. They're up against a deadline, and their time's running out."

"Listen, Sydney, I've got a boat, a good one. As I said, I need to go to the island anyway. Why don't we all go over there together? It's in my line of duty. Besides, I think it would be a good idea if I disappeared for a while. On the way out of here, I'll call Phyllis at home and ask her to cancel my schedule for the next two days." She thought, *I'm definitely going mad.*

She crossed her legs and paused a moment to search Sydney's eyes for a sign of approval. He listened intently. "After all, I need time to grieve for Moxie, which I know Phyllis won't believe, even though she knows how much I loved that puss. But at least it will give her a cover story for my whereabouts. Clever, yes?"

"Quite, and thank you, Abigail. We'll go together," said Sydney. "You've an excellent idea, and we might need each other's help if there's a spot of trouble on the island. Strength in numbers."

"I suppose, and tell the Worthingtons to look for the *Star Splitter* on Dock C."

"Excellent, I'll call Toby now and fill him in on our plan. They're certain to be pleasantly surprised. What time should I ask them to be here in the morning?"

"Let's say seven thirty. One condition, it would help if you could persuade Toby and Harriet to stand clear while I do the piloting. And you, Sydney, being an old navy man, can be my boatswain mate. What do you think?"

"Aye, aye, Skipper."

Chapter 18

Down to the Sea

After slipping her deck shoe on, Abigail struggled to her feet. "Oh, oh, Sydney, I'm a little wobbly."

"So am I. Hold on a minute while I pay the bill and toss my luggage out on the veranda. Don't go away. I'll be right back for you. We can make our calls in the lobby on the way out."

Before long, they stood together on the veranda, enjoying the balmy summer evening. Lights inside the inn shut off one by one until they were completely surrounded by darkness. He snipped a cigar for her. She held it up to her nose and breathed in its aroma along its length then took it to her lips, rolling it around, back and forth, before holding it out for Sydney to light. Abigail delighted in all the attention. She did not inhale but obviously savored the taste and fragrance of an excellent cigar. Sydney reveled in her enjoyment and attempted to show her how to blow smoke rings.

"I've been thinking, Sydney. Since you're taking up my offer, you might as well sleep on board tonight. My boat's a short walk. If it weren't so dark, you could spot it from here." She changed the subject to let Sydney mull over her invitation. "By the way, how did the Worthingtons react to your call? Better than mine to Phyllis, I'll bet. I caught her in the middle of making tomorrow's lunch for her husband."

Sydney smiled. "The Worthingtons are definitely on board for tomorrow. Itching to go, so to speak. I think you'll find them most appreciative and cooperative." Sydney fell speechless. He thought, *Has my brain gone soft? Am I too numb to understand the ramifications of accepting her offer, sleep on board?* Still, he did not wish to reject her proposal and embarrass her by having to withdraw it. He struck boldly, "Why not? Sounds like a good idea. It'll give me a chance to become acquainted with your boat. Oh, but what are your plans tonight?"

"I might as well sleepover too," said Abigail. Sydney coughed and blamed his discomfort on the night air. "It's shorter going to my boat than walking to my car at the courthouse. And I wouldn't want Jared pulling me over tonight on one of his stakeouts, not after the hand I dealt him today."

Sydney managed a smile, thinking how Jared's ears must be burning. Tired but excited by the prospect of a sleepover on the *Star Splitter,* he also wondered about his newfound relationship with Abigail. Could this become the kind of liaison that would lead him down the aisle? He worried for a moment about his lack of experience or recent expertise on the subject of intimacy. But he quickly dismissed his concern, thinking, *I doubt if Abigail knows what she's getting into any more than I do. I'd give a lot to be thirty years younger. She probably would too.*

Before stepping off the veranda, Abigail locked her arm under his; and they drifted off, zigzagging their way toward the harbor, still smoking like two steamboats racing each other at sea. In haste, she chose a gravely pathway for a shortcut and slipped. With all the gallantry and strength he could muster, he tugged her arm firmly against his side and pulled her upright again. Abigail smiled gratefully, and they continued on, this time in lock step.

The onshore breeze swept over the breakwater, filling the air with heady, familiar scents of the sea. The distant rhythmic sound of waves splashing against the boulevard seawall beckoned them toward the ocean. On the greensward, dew shimmered like tiny stars as if the sky had been turned upside down. An empty park bench offered a romantic setting pointing out to sea, an invitation to stop and listen to the cadence of one wave after another pounding against the sea wall, wild, wet, and sensuous. They passed it by.

Their jovial mood prevailed as they laughed and paraded along the boulevard walkway toward the *Star Splitter.* Abigail could not resist giggling like a schoolgirl as she relived and described in vivid detail the outrageous scene they made in the Snuggery. How it would play out tomorrow morning in the coffee shops around town did not trouble her.

* * *

The town's marina harbored pleasure boats, which adjoined the commercial fishing fleet moorage and extended northward to where the boulevard dead-ended. Comfortable for both cabin cruisers and sailboats, the Port Henry facility easily accommodated a hundred watercraft, thanks to the foresight of Abigail's father who had been the captain of the Yacht Club as well as a town selectman.

Abigail proudly elaborated this part of her family history as they crossed the parking lot and walked past the marina offices. Holding hands until they arrived at the main pier, they stopped for a moment to catch their breath before traipsing their way down to Dock C. Abigail took out her keys to open the security gate and fumbled nervously to find the right one.

The night guard, who had been watching the pair, startled them witless when he trained his flashlight on their faces. "Oh, it's you," he said. "Sorry to bother you, Ms. Underwood. I couldn't recognize you and your friend in all the dark. You just go on about your business."

He winked and turned away. "I've got my rounds to tend."

"I imagine so," said Abigail. "Good night, Clarence." Keeping her voice down, she turned toward Sydney. "I'm sorry, but this little encounter with the guard will just add to the town gossip tomorrow."

"You don't mean we'd be suspected of this, that, and the other?"

"Yes, I do, especially the other."

"Of course," said Sydney, surprised and a little indignant. "Let him blabber. After all, we are adults."

The thought of Clarence gossiping sobered both of them. The gate open, Sydney followed her down the ramp with his umbrella at left-shoulder-arms and his luggage dragging behind. Ten slips down, Abigail stopped to announce, "Here we are, Sydney. What do you think of her?"

Sydney let out a long low whistle. "My, oh my. Very impressive." *Perfect,* he thought. *Now here's a ship worthy of rough seas and open water.* "Must have a ten-foot beam at least. What's her length?"

"Thirty-four feet, sleeps four, and has twin diesels. Lots of get-go. More boat than I need really. You look surprised, Sydney."

Reverting to form and long-held old prejudices, Sydney said, "I am. And you can handle this boat without help?"

"You think it's too much for a woman? After I sold Dad's sailboat, I bought this one at auction, must be eight or nine years ago. It was a wreck, but the price was right at the time. Restoring it turned out to be more of a challenge than I had anticipated. Still, on the water, it's a lot more manageable than my father's sailboat. You and I shouldn't have any difficulty tomorrow. Let's not stand about all night."

"Right, but this is going to be an overnight stay, and I don't wish to take advantage of your generosity. I hope you'll allow me and Toby, I mean the Worthingtons, to contribute to the expense."

"Have you forgotten already?" said Abigail. "It's part of my job to keep tabs on this archipelago. As you'd probably say, I have reason to believe something's afoot on Bloodstone Island. I have to admit it's been quite some time since I've been over there. So our trip with the Worthingtons tomorrow is on the house, and don't worry about groceries. I keep the *Star Splitter* well stocked with food, drinks, water, and a full tank of diesel. When I get the urge to be on the water, I'm not wasting my time making a shopping list."

She stood on the dingy platform and reached over the gunwale to unlatch the half-door to the deck. Still a little on the wobbly side, she climbed aboard and asked Sydney to hand his luggage over to her. Gripping the railing, she extended her free hand and hoisted Sydney onto the deck. They stumbled into each other's arms to keep from falling. Out of breath again, they collapsed together on the fish box hatch. In the private mêlée, Sydney's umbrella dropped from his hand and skidded across the deck.

Abigail rose to her feet first and picked up his umbrella. "By the way, you've got an awfully heavy umbrella. You're never without it, are you?"

"Yes, that is, no. It comes in handy when there's a spot of trouble."

Abigail grinned. "Do you plan on taking it to bed with you? You're not expecting any trouble tonight, are you?"

Her sexually charged innuendo flew right past him. He held his painful ribs with both hands. Rising from the fish box, Sydney grimaced and crouched with his hands on his knees, hoping to regain his balance. "My medication must be wearing off," he puffed.

Abigail, disappointed and deflated by Sydney's physical condition, said, "You'd better come to bed." She took his hand to lead him forward. The emergency lights on, she led Sydney down a short ladder to the galley, pointing with pride to her store of soda crackers, kippered herring, jars of jam, and cans of meat, fishballs, and vegetables. "If you're hungry, I could fix you something. On the other hand, you look more in need of a seltzer or a couple of aspirin."

"No thanks, Abigail. If I may comment, it certainly looks like you're ready for any eventuality, including a first-rate war. That in mind, I'm curious, do you have any weapons on board?"

"What a silly question. These aren't pirate waters. Whiskey runners and pirates? Not for a long, long time." She wondered, *Why would he ask about weapons at such a peculiar time.* And she decided to answer his query then-and-there, so she wouldn't have to later. "I keep a box of flares, a hand axe, and two extinguishers, if they count as weapons." She laughed. "Why do you ask?"

"Oh, just curious. Can't be too careful out on the water."

"Yes, well, I trust your curiosity doesn't have to do with our trip tomorrow. In any case, up on the bridge, I have a ship-to-shore radio, and we're not going to go look at it now. So follow me."

Continuing the tour, she directed his attention to the galley, dinette, and sitting area. Sydney, still in tow, hardly noticed passing the lavatory she properly referred to as the "head." On the opposite side of the passageway, an open closet displayed her clothes and alongside it a bank of drawers that overflowed with garments. A couple of steps farther toward the bow, she opened the cabin door to the master bedroom. Abigail's voice resumed a tone of authority consistent with her position as a justice of peace, "Well, Sydney, this is it. This is where we sleep tonight."

Sydney bit his lip. "Together, I see. Cozy, yet comfy." Sydney had no fight left in him. There would be little difference between him and a spent trout being dragged straight into a net. He flopped on the bed face up, staring at the spinning overhead.

"Sydney, Sydney, listen. You can't go to bed like that in your good pants." In a semiconscious state, he hadn't the strength to argue against a reasonable observation.

"I don't suppose you brought pajamas?" Her question sailed past Sydney. In tight quarters and tired, she struggled to remove his shoes, strip his belt, and drag his pants off. She draped his pants and belt on a hangar and decided to add his rumpled tie to the collection. To give them a good airing, she wound her way back to the outside deck and hung them from the overhead next to the saltwater fishing rods. She returned to find Sydney in a fetal position, halfway under the sheets, with one leg hanging out. The sight deflated any hope she had of consummating a romance that evening. The night air had revived Abigail, but it evidently had the opposite effect on Sydney.

What have I done? she thought. *I've brought a complete stranger into my bed. And it looks like a harmless one at that. I must be made of mashed potatoes, flipping like this for a couple of drinks and dinner.* Staring down at him, she contemplated what she should, or shouldn't do: stay on board or walk all the way back to her car? *I'll only have to come back here in the morning. Anything I do now won't make much difference at Mel's Diner.* Without overly weighing the options, she decided to don her summer pajamas and crawled into bed alongside Sydney. Just wanting her share of the covers, she tried not to wake him but managed to anyway.

"Abigail, is that you?" he asked, his voice dry.

"Were you expecting someone else?" Sydney detected a hint of exasperation in her voice.

"No, but I did wish to talk to you about our day together. I'll not forget it. I want you to know that I feel like we've known each other a lifetime, even though it's only been a few hours since we left your office."

"Life works that way sometimes, Sydney. At least lightning does, hits you before you can get out of the way." She turned off the nightlight. "Didn't it ever occur to you that a few hours might be more than enough for two people to connect, even romantically? After all, look at us. You didn't have to be here in my boat now unless you wanted to be."

Sydney, facing the bulkhead, said, "True, but what I mean, Abigail, is that I've taken a strong liking to you, and I don't want to risk losing whatever we have by getting off on the wrong foot." He rolled over to her side of the bed and said, "I just don't want you to think I'm trying to take advantage of you."

"Too late to worry about that, Sydney. I'm not in your boat. You're in mine. You should be worried instead about me taking advantage of you."

Shocked into silence by Abigail's overt remark, he nonetheless found it exhilarating, and it sent his imagination reeling.

"Are you listening to me?" she said.

"Sorry, yes, of course, I am."

Sitting up in bed, she giggled softly at the thought of compromising Sydney by stripping his rock-ribbed inhibitions right down to the bare bones. The thought made her blush when she recognized her deep-seated reticence in sexual matters and disappointment with men in general.

Sydney inched his way closer to Abigail and said in a whisper, "Put in this situation, I suppose we should be cautious about our feelings for each other. Passion vs. good sense and all that." He placed his head on her lap. She smoothed his thin black hair back and massaged his forehead, stroking it gently.

Locked in Abigail's arms, Sydney drifted off into a deep sleep. *Just as well,* she thought. *I'm not up for any more activity tonight than he is.* She smiled, kissed her forefinger, and pressed it on his brow. Abigail lay awake, wrestling with the realities of the morrow. Based on her long experience as a justice of peace, she knew that when Clarence gets through with the night shift, he'd show up at Mel's Diner to spin a yarn about her and Sydney that would shock everyone in town.

Abigail's thoughts returned to the events of earlier that evening. She managed a smile and reflected how smitten she was with Sydney. Worried that the optimism she had for their relationship could wane, she too drifted off to sleep.

* * *

True to form by six in the morning, Clarence, his step more jaunty than usual, had already opened the dock gates and greeted the harbormaster coming on duty. As a bachelor night watchman approaching his retirement years, there were few things that brought him as much satisfaction as being the town gossip. Although the town thought of him as a first-class scandalmonger, he featured himself as the town historian.

Meanwhile, Sydney and Abigail slept heavily. A thin layer of early morning steam fog blanketed the surface of the sea, waiting for the morning sun to rise and burn it off. No crowing of the chanticleer to herald the dawn, not at the marina anyway. The duty of waking the harbor fell to squawking seagulls. Before dawn, however, several boats in the fishing fleet had already slipped out of the harbor. Restlessly, they continued to sleep well past six and through the cawing of seagulls. Their sheets wound between their arms and legs in a knot any Eagle Scout would be proud to exhibit.

A loud tapping sound on the cabin porthole awakened them. Wrapped in each other's arms, they struggled valiantly to unscramble the sheets. Sydney tucked a corner of a sheet under his chin and with his free hand parted the cabin curtain to peek outside. "Oh God," he whispered, as he stared out into a pair of deck shoes and the club head of a 7-iron. "It's them, Toby and Harriet," he whispered to Abigail. "What in heaven's name are they doing here this early?"

"Don't ask me," she replied in a gravely voice. "My head's splitting, and I'm too annoyed right now to be nice to anyone. You'd better go do something. I'm not getting out of bed."

He couldn't avoid facing Toby and Harriet in his underwear, and his only alternative meant greeting them face to face. He felt sheepish going about it, since his encounter with Abigail would seem entirely out of character for both Harriet and Toby. Sydney, for the most part, had done his best to cling to his Victorian manners and principles in a losing battle. But then he smiled to himself wryly and thought, *Why should I be embarrassed? In fact, I should take some pride in being considered sexually attractive for a man of my age and station. But I am disappointed in Toby's lack of judgment, seduced by Harriet of all people.* After being caught out sharing the same bed with Abigail, Sydney realized that any attempt to prove he didn't would turn out to be quite ludicrous. Sydney found his clothes where Abigail hung them outside the night before, and it pleased him to see how well she had cared for them. As if nothing was amiss, he said, "We weren't expecting you yet, but now that you're here, you might as well stay. I know you'll excuse me while I dress."

"So sorry if we're a little early," said Harriet, her cheeks red, her voice fluttering.

Toby jumped in to douse the fire. "I think we all know each other here, yes? So I'll get on with loading our baggage. Want to get a good start, don't you know?"

"Well, do it then," Abigail shouted from below. "As soon as you two get aboard, we'll cast off in twenty minutes."

Chapter 19

Burning Tree

Today, the sea rested except for rolling swells. In the washboard troughs, Bloodstone Island would disappear, and on the crests, it would reappear to give its audience another glimpse. The captain of the *Star Splitter* and its passengers had more than a passing interest or idle curiosity in this little island simply named after a semiprecious gem.

To the casual observer, Hadley's castellated summerhouse appeared from a distance to have been thrust out of the sea generations ago. From a promontory located on the west side of Bloodstone Island, it resembled an impregnable medieval fortress. At its foundation, rock outcroppings along the shore fended off both high seas and any would-be curiosity seekers.

As the summerhouse came closer into view, Harriet began describing to her attentive audience the mansion's many floors, six or seven, she thought. Trying to remember exactly, she squinted her eyes and began counting the stories on her fingers. Abigail offered her field glasses to Harriet, but she bushed them away. Harriet's method of counting floors proved inadequate, since every story swept its way up awkwardly behind turrets, numerous embattlements, and parapets originally designed to shield archers in medieval times. Chimneys rose high above the rooftops like small forests, suggesting a fireplace in every room, if not more.

Harriet made several more attempts to count the floors, which proved futile. Frustrated, she summed up her extemporized dissertation with, "Anyway, there were plenty of rooms for all of Duckie's guests."

A few moments later, Harriet felt compelled to prattle on and boasted that Duckie, her second husband, had hired a New York architect for the project. "He always wanted the best, you know. I seem to recall him saying that his architect found favor with Elizabethan architecture."

Sydney cringed and interrupted, "Suffering Jehosphat, Harriet, even from this distance, any novice in architectural history can see that your fortress represents the earlier Tudor period of the 1500s. And I'd say it possesses a smattering of flashbacks to the typical Middle Age castles in Europe."

Frowning, Harriet shot back, "Of course, Sydney, you're so right about everything."

Abigail, sensing a referee should intercede, suggested that the success of this trip requires cooperation, not competition. "Enough one-upsmanship. Can't you put aside for one minute whatever's eating you? Can we try to get along until this cruise is over tomorrow?" An icy gaze accompanied her anger. She cut the engine and spun the wheel back in the direction of Port Henry. "I can visit Bloodstone Island anytime. What's your decision?"

Toby, clearly embarrassed by Abigail's surprising admonition, addressed the others and said, "I've always been able to get along, contribute even, and if I may speak for Harriet and Sydney, I think you'll find that we can be civil. We all belong to the same club, don't you know, and that should hold some water."

Sydney followed, "Yes, good thinking, Toby. We do have that much in common. You must know by now that we've all come to Bloodstone Island, on different missions. I think it is, as you suggest, a good time to understand that if any one of us fails, there's a likely chance the rest of us will too. So I'll be the first to apologize and trust you'll forgive my poor manners." This was not easy for Sydney to say, since he thought of himself as one possessing impeccable manners. Indeed, it was he who had set the bar for manners and protocol at Brookside. "And, if I may paraphrase you, Abigail, we'd all do well to be playing with the same deck of cards. My chips are all in, so to speak."

Surprised to hear Sydney apologize, Harriet surmised that it must have been a "first" for him. No doubt, she thought, it was Sydney's attempt to placate his new paramour. Turning to look at Abigail, she said, "I don't know what all the fuss is about. I'm just as ready as anyone to go along. After all, I'm the reason we're all here. So if it makes everyone feel better, I'm just sorry for being myself. And where are you off to, Toby dear? Wouldn't you like to say something?"

"Yes, Harriet, but I'm going below now, and I wish to hell you hadn't ordered a rasher bacon for me at the hotel this morning." Toby had hoped that his digestive system would be as tranquil as this morning's sea. Excusing himself, he feebly felt his way down the ship's ladder with the aid of his 7-iron as a cane.

Harriet noticed Toby's pallid complexion and said, "Don't pay any attention to Toby. If I know him, he'll be right as rain in a few minutes."

Harriet's assessment of Toby did not sit well with Sydney who noticed that Toby's ruddy cheeks were suddenly void of color, a definite sign of seasickness. Afflicted, he became helpless and virtually useless. Sydney followed him down below to the head where he knew Toby would be retching in total misery. When Toby stopped to catch his breath, Sydney doctored Toby with a shot of Johnnie Walker. "Here, take this pill with another shot." Sydney also took a long drag from his flask and explained, "Preventative medicine, Toby. Buck up, old man. We'll be ashore before you know it. Take a few deep breaths and come up topside when you're ready. I'll leave the scotch here, in case you need another dose."

Toby, sitting on the floor, did not respond other than groan like a dying water buffalo.

Reluctantly, Sydney left Toby and joined Abigail and Harriet up on the bridge.

"Now that you're back, Sydney," said Harriet, "both of you take a look, way up. Can you see it? There's a small octagonal building perched just above Burning Tree."

"Yes," said Sydney, "reminds me of a folly."

"There you go again," said Harriet. "Well, it isn't a folly or whatever you call it. I think it looks like a short lighthouse, don't you? It overlooks the sea in every direction. Up there, Duckie spent many of his evening hours, alone, listening to his short-wave radio or so he said. He told me how much he loved watching storms gather on the horizon, storms of his own making, I'd say. I still believe his real motivation was to draw up new lists of weekend guests for next year's season, people more in his own image." She went on to explain how Burning Tree got its name. It seemed that during construction of the summerhouse, there was a severe thunder and lightning storm and gale speed winds. Lightning struck the tallest tree, a magnificent pine on the promontory, setting it on fire. It burned for hours until the rains squelched the flames. She pointed out the pine and said that even though it was split apart, its blackened trunk still stood tall, hence the name Burning Tree.

Harriet, swimming in a sea of recollections, had moved her subject matter away from describing the summerhouse to focus more on her number 2 husband, Terrance "Duckie" Hadley. "He seemed ready for someone compassionate like me, to nurse him in his waning years. Before I married him, well, not to be catty or disrespectful of the dead, I found out his first wife died in a 'so-called' swimming accident. They had a son together, Claude. He never was a comfort to his parents. A real creepy kid."

Continuing to digress her thoughts, she rambled, "Duckie hated conversations bearing on the trivial. It's probably why he often excused himself after a lavish dinner party, leaving me to entertain his guests. You can imagine how well that went down with me."

Old memories continued to surface for Harriet, mostly good and some of them not so good. She continued her reminiscences by barking over the idling engines, "Yes, the old place seems to be pretty much as I remembered it. I can't make out the help's cabins though. They must be overgrown."

As they drifted closer to shore, seagulls came out from the island to greet the *Star* and circle low overhead. They cawed incessantly, as if demanding an easy midday meal. It didn't take long for Harriet's sentimental observations to turn bitter.

When Burning Tree's archetypical features came into sharper focus, they did not please Harriet's one wit. Evidently over the last decade or longer, the massive old summerhouse had surrendered to the elements and suffered grievously from lack of maintenance. Bleached wood siding and overgrown stonework revealed that Mother Nature and Father Time had the upper hand and had taken up residence. Before Harriet's husband died, Burning Tree must have already been in a state of falling apart, however slowly.

Although it had only been nine years since Duckie left his mortal coil behind, the summerhouse could not hide its wrinkled face. Nails popped from its twisted siding, adopting the look of a stubble beard. Mortar had washed away between the joints of its limestone walls. Finally, some of the stones had broken loose and cascaded down the banks and out to sea. Even the boarded over windows seemed to weep.

Abigail continued her course for a closer look at Burning Tree, careful to avoid floating seaweed and driftwood. Easing back on the throttle, she held the *Star* against the tide. Harriet now had a much better look at the estate. This time, she welcomed the use of Abigail's high-powered binoculars.

"The place is falling apart. Blast that Pierpont," she grumbled. "I'll see that fraud of a lawyer behind bars. To think Jeffrey trusted him all these years to keep the place up, and that bastard's done nothing. Just wait till I find out what he did with the trust money, sending Jeffrey all those phony repair bills. I bet he lied too about that, that employee embezzling the account." Her anger turned to self-pity; and Toby, who had returned from the head feeling much better than when he left, sensed Harriet's tears welling up. He offered her his last never-to-be used handkerchief.

Still shaken, she wondered if Jeffrey had betrayed her too. *In league with Pierpont? No. Jeffrey must not have cared whether we inherited the island or not. He had plenty of his own money, of course. What's really quirky though is Duckie. He must have taken leave of his senses. He was too smart to trust the likes of a Pierpont.*

"Well, Harriet, if you ask me," said Toby, "I find all these conditions of Duckie's quite disturbing, irrational even. All this falderal for a miserable little island? Pish-posh. You'd think some Caribbean pirate got off course and buried his treasure here. Maybe Pierpont was too smart for Duckie, eh?"

"Nonsense, Toby." Harriet railed on, her voice quavering, "Would you look at the roofs? The slate shingles are falling off." Shouting, she said, "If you can hear me, Percy, you are a doomed man. It's a prison for you, in perpetuity."

"Settle down," said Toby. "Please, come down below with me. Look, you're scaring the seagulls away. We'll get to the bottom of this soon enough. There'll be plenty of time to even the score with Percy."

While the *Star*'s engines idled, Abigail politely but forcefully told Harriet, "Please, I need you off the bridge. If you don't mind, I have to concentrate on what I'm doing." Reluctantly, Harriet retreated below with a hand down from Toby; Sydney joined them.

Abigail gave a sigh of relief. It crossed her mind that she may have gotten in over her head on this expedition. In spite of being rankled, her father instilled in her a stubborn Maine attribute that insisted that she be resolute and patient. As for her passengers, she felt they were fortunate that she had no intention to renege on her promise to Sydney. Besides, she harbored a curiosity about the island and had a duty to find out why it caused a rather unusual interest with the coast guard.

She noticed a dinghy fitted with an outboard "kicker" motor had been beached and poorly concealed only a short distance south from the Burning Tree dock. She wondered, *Why would anyone conceal their boat on the beach rather than tie up to the float? The float's in bad shape, but— Besides, why would somebody familiar with these open waters venture to Bloodstone Island in a boat like that? We're several miles from the coast. Not logical.* She thought, *It's too far for a round trip of day fishing or sight-seeing.* Her thoughts quickly returned to the present, and she focused her attention back to cruising cautiously along the shoreline. Experience reminded her to be aware of submerged rock outcroppings that may not appear on her chart. Floating "deadhead" logs often lurked in quiet backwaters submerged like icebergs. Abigail watched for shore birds that stood on them to rest and feed. Cruising at the speed of a brisk walk, the engines' exhaust churned the trailing sea, making a sound like boiling pea soup. The peril of fouling the propeller occupied the back of her mind.

Alone at the wheel, Abigail's thoughts turned back to when she was a teenager out for a sail with her father. His words came to life as it had many times before,

> *Abby, now that your mother's gone, and I will be soon enough, always remember that you're the captain of your ship. Not an easy*

task, daughter. You have to be ready to do everyone else's job, only better. That way, you might not have to go down with the ship.

She muttered aloud, "So here I am, Dad. It's my ship, and I'm the skipper."

That advice flew over her head many times in the past, but not now. Back then, she was having too much fun winning weekend races in the "Junior's." Her success pleased her father to no end. She recalled, *I can hear him telling me that when I'm older, and whenever I felt boxed in, "Go out for a sail, Abby, and find your peace." Well, Dad, I've got three people with me now, but somehow I feel like I'm sailing solo, just like it used to be in those junior races. I remember,* Abigail thought, *Dad, if you can hear me, I think I know why I feel alone. On this trip, I may have to do everyone else's job. Jesus, Mary, and Joseph, I may have to think for everyone else too.*

Rounding a bend, the posted signs that Harriet told her about came into view. They warned trespassers in no uncertain terms that if they came ashore, they were risking their lives, just like Pierpont reported in his last letter to Jeffrey. Some signs seemed aged; others appeared recently repaired or freshly painted.

She scanned the immediate area for coves and backwaters that would harbor a large cabin cruiser or sailboat. An hour's search turned up nothing. Abigail looked for a landing site other than the dock at Burning Tree, a place where she could anchor-out, launch the *Star*'s dinghy, and safely beach it on the shore. On her chart of the area, she made pencil notes of her progress.

"Damn, look at the time." Abigail grumbled, "I can't possibly circle the island in time." *Oh hell,* she thought, *I have to get back to Burning Tree by 14:00 hours.* Abigail opened the *Star*'s throttle and executed a sharp turn heading for Burning Tree.

Those down below jostled with each other, attempting to gather their sea legs. Sydney cupped his hands and yelled up, "Abigail, Abigail, what in the devil are you trying to do, kill us all?"

"S-o-r-r-y!"

Chapter 20

All Ashore

In the cabin below, Harriet and Toby had changed into their high-end country garb for a stay-over in the summerhouse. Toby hoisted a backpack up and over a handsome new angora sweater he purchased for golfing this fall. He did his best to keep steady while Harriet loaded the backpack with can goods and utensils they would need for a picnic: champagne, condiments, insect spray, band aids, and an assortment of other items for the unexpected.

Sydney, stripped of his luggage when his plane landed in the covered bridge, didn't have a change of clothes with him and had to be content with his newly purchased melon and white sear succor suit. A straw boater hat, black bow tie, and two-tone wing tip shoes completed his ensemble.

Harriet asked Toby, "Where's Sydney off to now?"

"He's running for the head. It must be the heavy dinner from the night before, too rich to retain. As he passed me, I think he mentioned to me that he was going to return a few oysters back to their homeland."

"I suppose that's his idea of being funny."

"Under the circumstances. Quite." Toby laughed.

Harriet asked, "Well now that he'll be gone for a minute or two, I've been waiting to ask you. What do you think of Abigail, as in Abigail and Sydney?"

"I must say I found seeing them together this morning quite shocking. But I don't recall any woman ever took advantage of Sydney."

"Oh, please!" replied Harriet. "You know full well what I mean."

"Of course, Harriet. I found her to be attractive. She's obviously intelligent, has good breeding, and appears to be sturdy fore and aft. I like the cut of her jib, and I think Sydney would agree with me. He and I think pretty much alike, especially when it comes to judging people."

"So," she said, "I guess you don't have any objection to them becoming a serious item?" The expression on Toby's face revealed his annoyance with the conversation and why he was loath to reply. "It's all right if you want to clam up. I think he's doing a little more than sweet-talking Ms. Underwood so he can get off the hook for flying into the town bridge. If I haven't said it before, I wouldn't be surprised if Sydney flew out here just to come between us."

"Harriet, you know full well he flew out here because he heard about the packet going down and us with it. So let's not hear any more about it. We've got a lot to accomplish in a short time, right?"

"I'm sorry, Toby. Please don't be upset with me. I'm just jealous about my time with you. I never could have come this far without you. You're a treasure, and I don't want to let you out of my sight for a minute."

Toby, looking over his shoulder, acknowledged her remark with a nod and began lacing his water-tight walking shoes. Harriet already attired in jodhpurs paced anxiously with a vision of charging up the bank to Burning Tree with all the alacrity of Teddy Roosevelt on San Juan Hill. He looked up and spotted Burning Tree coming into view. He shouted into the galley. "Come on, Sydney. Shake a leg. And don't forget your umbrella."

Abigail maneuvered the *Star Splitter*, slowly turning toward the summerhouse. A weir of rubble and rock had been built to shelter the south side of the Burning Tree cove to break up waves driven by southerly winds. On the north side of the cove, a dock projected out from shore. Abigail estimated it to be about 150 feet long. It was constructed of driven piles and rough-hewn planks over heavy timbers. On the north side of the dock, a float, outfitted with steel slip rings, rode up and down on pilings following the movement of the tide. It also rode up and down with this morning's swells, causing it to heave and move slowly along its length like a Chinese dragon.

Rather than anchoring out, Abigail concluded that her best option was to tie up to the float even if it risked being observed from the summerhouse. Closing in, she saw the float had been severely damaged over time, most likely from severe storms. Parts of the float pontoon had either broken loose or sunk. Treacherous walking, she thought, even for the steady afoot.

Abigail summoned everyone topside with a megaphone and brought the *Star* alongside the float. She approached the float cautiously and summoned Sydney, "Be ready to drop the fenders and cast the lines." Sydney, now on the bow rail, responded admirably.

"Good job. Now jump down and secure the lines to the davits fore and aft." Once the *Star Splitter* had been secured and its engines shut down, she called everyone to gather around. "By the way, you should all know a small boat has been beached nearby and clumsily camouflaged. It seems to me that there's been some activity here quite recently. There could be people here. If the house is occupied, they don't want others to know. And if they don't want it known, it's probably illegal. So let's keep our eyes and ears open." Everyone nodded in agreement.

Abigail knew that disembarking would be difficult even for youngsters with a measure of athletic prowess. Abigail easily convinced everyone into leaving their overnight bedding aboard the *Star*. There would be plenty of time to retrieve their sleeping bags later. Wobbly, one by one, they marched ashore like migrating penguins. After gathering their luggage, they began their trek up a serpentine overgrown trail, zigzagging their way to the summerhouse.

To catch her breath, Harriet had to stop frequently. Her San Juan Hill turned into her Mt. Everest. Summer temperatures at sea were mild, but on shore, the midday sun was hot. Sitting on a rock outcropping, she opened her blouse, removed her floppy straw hat, and fanned her face. Sydney was happy to stop and rest with the others, his feet tortured by his new street shoes. Abigail, who had sprinted ahead, waited.

To impress Abigail, Sydney said weakly, "Let's move on," hoping of course to be ignored. After some grousing, they struggled upward until they arrived at a small circular courtyard. At its center, a toppled over birdbath pointed like a compass to the front entrance.

Harriet caught her breath and spoke first and, to everyone's surprise, announced, "This is all my doing. I'll take the lead and go inside." She headed for the front door and said, turning to the others,

"If it's dark inside and I think it's OK to come in, I'll give you a signal with my flashlight." When she discovered the partially open front door creaking back and forth from a light onshore breeze, Harriet tossed her house keys back in her purse, muttering, *So this is what the door to hell looks like. Easy to get in, no way out.* She steadied the door with one hand and then slowly pushed it open with the other.

She took one step inside and became disoriented by the inky darkness. Slippery underfoot, she lost her balance and took another step in an attempt to recover. She slipped even further, this time becoming virtually airborne. Landing on her back knocked the breath out or her and sent her flashlight rolling and spinning across the floor. Its beam of light shot out in every direction. Toby interpreted the flashing light to be Harriet's sign for the others to follow her.

Once inside, all three slipped with their arms and legs flailing to catch their balance. Each yelled every epithet from their personal vocabulary as they joined Harriet sprawled out on the floor.

"Mother of Mercy, what is this crap?" Sydney moaned. "My suit's ruined. I swear to heaven someone's going to pay dearly for this!"

No sooner had everyone come to rest squatting, kneeling, or sitting in this caldron of miserable reeking gunk than two loud gunshots rang out. Obviously fired inside, they reverberated throughout the summerhouse. Instinctively, all four spread out again on the floor, this time face down. Clouds of screaming bats took flight with the "crack-crack" of the gun and fled outside.

A loud voice like one coming from a megaphone echoed through the darkness. "Welcome. Don't mind the shooting. That's just Claude. He likes to shoot rats in the attic. Hobby of his. As you might have guessed by now, you're swimming around in fresh bat guano. That's why we don't come through the front door anymore. You should have come in the servants' entrance. But then what would you know about the servants? That is you, Harriet, isn't it? We've been expecting you today, but not quite so many of you. You'll be our guests. At least for a while."

More furious than frightened, Harriet rose to her knees and shouted, "You must be Pierpont. You and Claude, that misfit stepson of mine, are trespassing. By tomorrow morning, this'll be my island. And I'll see to it you're not going to be my guests. Tell him so, Toby."

Before Toby could clear his throat, Pierpont said, "I have the say as to who owns and controls this island. And you, Harriet, you were warned not to come here with or without your friends. Now all of you can expect to spend the rest of your lives here, however short that may be. For now why don't you all go outside, use the garden hose to tidy up, and come back in later."

Indignantly, Harriet shouted into the dark, "Oh, we'll be back, all right."

Abigail and Sydney, who had remained speechless, wasted no time crawling their way back through the front door. Harriet and Toby followed suit.

* * *

Stunned, they assembled around the birdbath, choking on their own odor. The onshore breeze exacerbated the disaster by drying the wet bat guano on their hands, faces, and hair. Toby tried and failed in a veiled attempt at humor to mitigate their plight. "You know, Harriet, you have looked better."

Dripping in guano, Abigail grumbled, "I must look like some zombie. Will somebody find the damned hose, please? I can't see with all this muck on me. By the way, Sydney, is this what you meant by encountering a *spot of trouble*?" Up an octave, her voice rang out, "I didn't bargain for getting killed!"

"None of us did, and Pierpont clearly intends to kill us." Sydney's face crumpled up like a wet paper towel. "Well, that's not going to happen. I don't know how, but we're going to turn the table on that demented creep."

"I'm with you, Sydney," said Toby. "Harrumph. Ironic, isn't it? I never in a million years dreamed I could die a married man." Harriet sighed. Toby saw her reaction and redacted, "No offense intended, old dear."

While Abigail hosed herself off, Sydney called Toby to his side and whispered, "I must say, Toby, for a pig-headed old trout, Harriet's got bullocks. I just wanted you to know I find her spunk admirable."

Toby nodded, smiled, and said, "If it can be to our advantage, I want you and Abigail to know that Harriet has a concealed gun, above the waist. I've got my old service pistol. Now we need a plan of action. First, I vote to get out of these wretched clothes." Everyone began pawing through their luggage, which fortunately sat right where they had left it in the courtyard.

Sydney was particularly pleased to discover his umbrella, April, had not been disturbed. However, not having a change of clothes with him proved unsettling when, as a last resort, he had to contemplate changing into Toby's doublewide lederhosen or whatever Harriet had packed for tomorrow. Rejecting both, he reluctantly accepted Abigail's offer to wear her white bell bottoms and loose-fitting pink blouse, extras she'd thoughtfully brought from her boat. Awkward as the fit revealed, he thought that being the butt of everyone's giggles was a small price to pay for dry clothing. Each in turn hosed down and changed clothes behind the courtyard stonewall.

Back together again, Toby opined, "I suppose if Harriet is going to get title to Bloodstone Island, we have to go back inside and outwit a sociopath. Obviously, he's had about nine years developing a plan to own it and keep on doing what he's been doing."

Abigail shook her head as if to unplug her ears. "Toby, I'm not sure that I follow what you just said or that you understand the consequences we may be letting ourselves in for. Let's be clear. You may be, but I'm not here to lay down my life for Harriet's title to this island. I'm here to find out what is legal or illegal going on here, no more, no less."

"Clear enough," said Toby. "I'd understand if you went back to the *Star* right now and go for help. Before you decide, let's hear what Sydney has in mind."

Sydney said, "I suppose we could all make a run for it. Maybe we make it back to the *Star*, maybe not. It's hard to outrun a bullet. Frankly, I'm for going in, and I think the best plan is to have no plan. We should react intuitively to the situation at hand and strike when there's an opening. In the meantime, let's stall, flatter his ego about how clever he is, and don't be confrontational. Sympathizing with his motives may reveal a weakness that we can capitalize on. Oh, and out of fairness to Abigail, she can leave if she chooses. It's not her hunt."

Abigail said, "All right, if Sydney's staying, so am I. I'm your best chance to get us off this crazy island."

"The 'no-plan plan' sounds reasonable to me," said Harriet. "Unless there's some objection, follow me." She took the lead, once again circling around the front entrance to the service door in the back. It also was ajar. The disquieting sound of a motor distracted her.

Noticing it too, Abigail said, "Don't be concerned. It's probably a diesel engine to generate electricity. With the windows boarded up, Percy must use it for lighting and keeping the water tank filled on top of the bluff. Otherwise, the hose wouldn't be working."

Harriet cautiously stepped inside; the others followed close behind in single file. Indoors, flickering electric bulbs lit a passageway leading between larders and pantries. Kerosene lamps hung from the walls, which Abigail presumed they provided light in the house when the generator was shut down. "Well," Harriet observed, "at least the odor of kerosene disguises the stink wafting from the entry hall." She pocketed her flashlight and followed the corridors, she recalled, that lead to the Great Room with its cathedral ceiling, which linked a stage at one and a walk-in fireplace at the other. It was the centerpiece of the summerhouse and large enough to accommodate any event Duckie and his guests had in mind for an evening's amusement. Harriet's mind flitted back to years ago when nights erupted in debauchery. Back then, the decadence seemed foreboding but exciting. Entering the ballroom now, those memories erupted, and they disgusted her.

* * *

Carefully, Harriet tiptoed across the Great Room. A tall man she judged to be in his early sixties stood at the end of a long teak-planked table designed to resemble a ship's deck. He wore an ill-fitting suit reminiscent of the twenties. Two candelabras framed his image. A crystal chandelier blinked on and off overhead.

One by one, the entourage gathered around Harriet. Sydney brought up the rear. Upon entering, he could not resist commenting on the surrounds, "Shades of San Simeon, I'd say." Turning away, he dropped back for a moment to hang his umbrella on a wall rack. Harriet approached the table at the opposite end of Pierpont and stood stoically in anticipation of being greeted.

"Good afternoon, Mrs. Bartholomew. I'm sorry about your reception earlier today, but we've been very busy, and you've come here at an awkward time. We couldn't do much about the reception the bats gave you. Some time ago, I decided to live with them instead of the mosquitoes."

"You're not sorry, and you know quite well there aren't any differences to settle between us concerning the ownership of Bloodstone Island. It will be mine by tomorrow morning and that should be that."

"We'll see. In the meantime, let's be civil please. Won't you introduce me to your party? I hadn't been expecting such a large group?" Percy walked over to Harriet and extended his hand, which is considered poor form both at Brookside and polite society. His craggy smile collapsed at her rejection; turning away, he deftly reached into his vest pocket for his cigarette case.

"As you must know by now, Mr. Pierpont, I am newly married, and this is my husband Tobias Worthington." Neither man offered to shake hands. "On my left is Judge Abigail Underwood, and she is here on official business. This island happens falls under her jurisdiction."

"Judge Underwood is it? What a surprise. I had no idea you might be accompanying Harriet. But I regret you chose to. In truth, I wasn't even sure Harriet would show up, that is, until Claude informed me."

Abigail, lost for words, did not have a ready reply. "Actually, Mr. Pierpont, it was I who invited her and the others to join me on my boat. But I have a problem that only you seem to be able to solve for me. You see, I think we could get along a lot better if we could understand what your business is here?"

"Later, Judge. All in good time."

Percy turned his attention from Abigail to Harriet. "Tell me, Mrs. Bartholomew, I'm curious. Is there a mustachioed lady in your group or is the light bad?"

Before Harriet could summon a reply, Sydney stepped out of the shadows to confront Percy, nose to nose. Startled, Percy took a step back. Irate, Sydney, against his better judgment and advice to everyone else, said, "I, sir, am Sydney Worthington, and I happen to be a member of the New York State Bar. I'm told you are an attorney, and I find your demeanor shocking."

"Likewise," replied Percy, "I'm surprised to find you, an attorney, running around in ladies garments."

Gritting his teeth, Sydney replied, "Amuse yourself, if you must, and laugh yourself to death. And incidentally, I didn't appreciate your crappy welcome to Burning Tree. I assume you meant to intimidate us and send us packing. Yes? But I think for I speak for everyone. We're not moving from here."

"I thought I was clear. I have no intention of letting any of you leave here, ever."

Harriet shivered. "Percy, that can't be your last word. There must be another way to solve whatever problem we caused you. At least I think you owe all of us an explanation."

"I suppose I do."

With a tinge of sarcasm, she said, "To start with, why don't you ask Claude and the rest of your associates show themselves? I haven't seen my son-in-law since he was a boy blowing up chickens with firecrackers."

"Why not indeed." Percy stopped to reflect. "Claude did that? No-o-o. Well, except for him, the rest of my staff is busy right now. They're preparing to greet a very important visitor tonight, and I have a great deal of business to transact. I could say you're arrival comes at an extremely inconvenient time." He turned and began a gimpy retreat when he stopped to say, "Ironic, isn't it? The date that resolves the ownership of Bloodstone Island coincides with my visitor. Claude, come in here please."

Chapter 21

Grave Consequences

Claude, who'd been eavesdropping, entered the Great Room and slammed the door behind him. He strode with a cocky gate toward Harriet, brandishing a shotgun. No longer the mischievous little child Duckie told her about, Claude appeared to have graduated into the criminal element of society. Bearded, tall, and lanky of frame, Harriet could barely make him out in the dim light as he walked toward her. Harriet had every reason to suspect him of being cunning and devious, and his rumpled appearance spoke of someone who had been on lean times or on the run from the law.

"Hello, Mother. I thought you'd show up. I foller'd you long enough to know'd you'd find a way. Too bad for you, I think." Grinding on a worn-out toothpick, he grinned and looked over at Percy.

"Mr. Pierpont, were they down here when I kill't a rat in the attic? I don't like rats." "Quiet, Claude," Percy scolded him for his bad manners.

Claude's smile vanished, and his attention turned back to Harriet. He mocked her with a childlike voice, "Hello, Mommy. Is this our first meeting?"

"I don't think so, but I hope it's our last," replied Harriet.

"Perhaps I'll be the one to see your wish come true."

"Don't threaten me you poor excuse for a nincompoop. You've been following me, haven't you?"

"Good at it too. You didn't make tracking you easy. Tried to give me the slip, didn't ya'? Mr. Pierpont needed to be sure you were coming. You know for a proper greetin'."

"Well, you could start now by not waving that gun around."

Claude did not take the suggestion well. As humorless as his conduct was, he laughed aloud when he ran his eyes over Sydney. "Who's the faggot? Must be Worthington. No matter."

Sydney, although angered, decided not to respond to Claude's crude observation or provoke him to act irrationally, especially when Claude opened the breach of the double-barrel shotgun to be sure it was fully loaded.

Claude continued his smart-mouth interrogation by turning on Harriet, "So, Mommy, is this my new Daddy? He's the fourth, isn't he?"

"Yes, and Toby is my husband. To you, it's Mr. Wadsworth."

"Harrumph. And your lady friend over there, was she invited too?"

Abigail responded in her own defense, "I invited them on my boat. Doesn't really matter, does it? I came here on business."

Claude shot back, "Don't make me laugh. What business?"

Percy heaved a sigh. "Enough, p-l-e-a-s-e. I think it's time we stop all this palaver and settle the issue of why we're all here." He cracked a cynical smile and said, "I sense an air of antagonism in the room. Would you agree, Harriet?"

Harriet said, "I certainly would."

Percy approached Claude and took the shotgun from him. "Claude, under these hostile circumstances, I think we should find out if Harriet and her friends brought any weapons with them. One never knows. So everyone please line up, and if you have any, hand them over to Claude. Don't disappoint him or he'll delight in undertaking a complete hands-on search."

Harriet said, "How dare you humiliate us like this. What's next?"

"I'm afraid it's not what you had in mind when you landed here." Percy retired to the large table in the ballroom and sat down. From there he watched Claude take delight in ruffling through everyone's apparel.

Claude soon had his hands on Toby pistol. "Look here, everyone, an antique pistol, and it's loaded too."

"It's not an antique," growled Toby. "It's my service revolver, you stoop. Now can we get this nonsense over with?"

Percy said, "I'm deeply disappointed in you, Mr. Worthington." He told Claude to carry on and bring Toby's pistol with him after he had finished searching the others. Rising slowly from a high-back baroque chair, he invited everyone to be seated at the table.

Toby excused himself from Harriet and dropped back to chat with Sydney. "If we get out of here alive, I think I'm going to write a book about this misadventure."

"Don't be ridiculous, Toby. The only thing you every wrote was your name on a check. And keep your voice down."

"Obviously, I would need a ghost writer, like Amy. You know, my caddy's girlfriend. She's a reporter on the local paper."

"Yes, I know. But first we've got to deal with Percy. I'm sure he's a psychopath and plans to murder us."

"So we're not dead yet. You've still got your umbrella, and Abigail's flare gun's hidden outside in the bushes, yes?"

"Right. And Harriet has a gun hidden someplace on her, or so you said, well where?"

"That's just for me to know, Sydney." He smiled. "I remind you I am her husband."

"Of course, I had no right to ask." Sydney smiled back and whispered, "I don't think our situation has fully sunk in with the ladies yet. It's all too bizarre for me, let alone the women." He elbowed Toby. "We'd better join them back at the table."

Harriet took a chair on Percy's left. Abigail sat opposite. Sydney joined Abigail, and that left Toby to slide in alongside Harriet. Percy instructed Claude to take a folding chair and sit behind him.

Claude slouched and rocked back on the chair legs. Evidently bored, he hummed and seemed to take pleasure in waving the shotgun around, no doubt imagining targets to aim at around the room.

Harriet broke the silence, "Well, Percy, this is your meeting. If you don't have an agenda, why don't we start with who owns Bloodstone Island in the morning? According to Hadley's will, the island belongs to me. I'm married, as a condition of his will. And I will spend a night here with my husband, Toby, also a condition. So here we are with the marriage license in my purse. What don't I understand?"

Unmoved, Percy folded his hands and leaned forward. "When I contacted your last husband, Jeffrey, I had the distinct impression that you and Jeffrey had no interest in claiming the island. I never received any correspondence to the contrary."

"Of course not. You threatened our lives and managed to scare Jeffrey off. He didn't give a damn about this island. But I do."

Percy interrupted her, "I'm sorry to learn that Jeffrey is no longer with us and up until a few days ago, there was not so much as a whisper from you. The clock was running out for you to make a claim." Pausing, he lit a cigarette, inhaled deeply, and, like a storybook dragon, blew it out through his nose and mouth. "Sometime back, I got in touch with Claude. Surely you knew that after you, he was next in line to inherit.

"Several times he'd expressed a strong interest in owning Bloodstone Island, and he's been coming here recently to help me with, shall we say, the chores. So you see, I think Claude earned title to Bloodstone Island, and I'm afraid you have, by default, forfeited your place in the queue, a distant third behind the state of Maine." Percy paused to grind his cigarette out on the floor as if he was crushing an adversary. "Claude will be selling me the island in return for a generous salary. Isn't that right, Claude?"

"That's right, Mr. Pierpont, you and me, jes' like we're partners."

Percy continued, "Yes, Claude, and I didn't need you, Harriet, or the state of Maine sticking a nose into my business. See my dilemma?"

"Oh, I certainly can," said Harriet. "You're boxed in. You have to kill us. And just how do you plan to, as they say, bump us off?"

"You and your party? I have several options, but I haven't made a final decision on which one. Perhaps you or someone else here can come up with a better idea than I have." Percy registered a self-satisfying grin as if no other plan could possibly better than his own.

"You really are a bastard. I should have known the warning we got in Port Henry came from you. It was delivered no doubt by your messenger boy, Claude."

Claude snickered. "My old lady is pretty smart."

Percy told Claude to stop interrupting when he's talking and turned his attention back to Harriet. "If you were, as Claude says, a smart old lady, you'd have abandoned the idea of showing up. And, for God's sake, what do you need an island for? Romance? A place to revive old memories playing some piddling parlor games?"

Sydney came to his feet. "She doesn't have to answer that. It's evident you need this island for some reprehensible purpose beyond your personal greed, and I'm going to see that you're answerable for it." Sydney couldn't believe that he would ever rise in defense of Harriet, but in this case, his retort went above and beyond his chivalrous nature. When provoked, Sydney and Don Quixote seemed to be cut from the same gallant cloth. "Now I have a question for you, Percy. What are you doing here? Are you so shamed you can't tell us?" Aggravated, Percy's eyes narrowed. His brow furrowed. If there was an ounce of charity left for his captives, it wasn't evident.

Abigail tugged Sydney back down into his chair and slowly rose to her feet. "I have to agree with Sydney. Everyone wants to know, so it's not just him. Since you're not going to let us leave here, I assume, like Harriet said, you intend to 'bump us off.' What could possibly drive you to do such a dastardly deed?"

She leaned in closer to Percy, searching his eyes for some hint of humanity. "This isn't the first time you've resorted to murder, is it?" Even in the dim light, Percy's face blanched. He had been dressed down first by Sydney and now by Abigail. Still he did not reply. But Abigail struck a chord when she suggested, "Percy, I put it to you, if we are to die for some noble cause of yours, perhaps you'd like to share what it is. Our graves will keep your secret, and we can rest in peace knowing we didn't die for nothing." She paused to collect her thoughts, "I've a feeling that it has a great deal to do with your visitor. And that'll be soon, yes?"

Percy cleared his throat. "You're very perceptive, Ms. Underwood. I guess you and the others deserve an answer. Perhaps then you'll understand why I cannot allow any of you to leave here alive. It pained me to come to this decision. After all, I'm not a completely heartless creature without feelings, but I can't stand your carping any longer." Abigail returned to her chair and slumped back. Percy looked over at Claude.

Claude smiled and said, "Now?"

"Not now, Claude. I'll let you know when I make my decision."

After an unbearable period of silence, Toby stammered, "Well, this is a fine 'how-do-you-do.' Not to hurt your feelings, Harriet, but I told Sydney I never thought I'd go to my grave a married man."

Harriet trembled as reality set in; all the air had been let out of her bravado like a dart striking a balloon. "Toby, will you forgive me? I never dreamt this trip would come to an end like this."

"Neither did I, Harriet. But don't blame yourself. I did choose to come along."

"We could have had a grand time, Toby."

Sydney stared at Percy then looked at Harriet. "Chin up, old girl. We're not dead yet."

"Percy," said Sydney, "I'm parched. The least our host could do is offer us a scotch and water. Not too much to ask, don't you know? Since you and I are gentlemen, let's not forget tradition, a drink to go with a last smoke?"

Percy seemed pleased to be reminded. The wrinkles in his brow receded like an outgoing tide. "Your right, of course." He rose and ambled over to an armoire next to the fireplace.

"I hope 'Tilting Man' scotch suits your taste. It's all we have, but to its credit, it is a single malt. I discovered cases of it hidden behind a poorly disguised secret closet in the master bedroom. I believe Hadley must have smuggled it in under his private label. No matter, it will have to do."

Harriet's face fell. "See, Toby, at least I was right about the scotch."

Percy returned to the table with a tray of dusty glassware and a liter of scotch. Situated comfortably in his high-back chair, he poured himself a liberal glass. "Forgive my manners." He waved at Claude and said, "Bring us some water from the bathroom and keep your shotgun handy." Claude stomped off disgruntled at being spoken to more like a lackey than a partner.

Meanwhile, Abigail mused about Percy's past and thought perhaps in another time and place, he might have been a respected peer in the legal profession. She leaned closer to Percy and approached him, cautiously sliding her hands across the table. "I find you an intriguing man, Percy," she said with a trace of flattery. "I must admit you've aroused my curiosity to the breaking point."

She picked up the glasses in front of Percy and distributed them around the table. Impressed with her pluck, Percy gave her a "thank you nod" for lending a hand. She probed gently and deeper, hoping that Percy would reveal a weakness they could exploit. "I'm curious, what college did you get your law degree from? Here in Maine?"

"What difference does it make? That was a long time ago."

"Well, I'd like to know, and since we have time on our hands, well, we're not planning on going anywhere."

Chapter 22

A Tetchy Discussion

"OK, Abigail. If you must know, my degree is from Rochester, magna cum laude."

"Rochester?" said Sydney. "If you mean the University of Rochester in New Hampshire, why it's one of the country's top schools for contract law." Sydney picked up on Abigail's ploy. "I attended lectures there myself. I believe it was in '23."

"Is that so? In '23, I was traveling in Europe on a fellowship. Most of my time, I spent studying in Munich. I even managed to get by with my clumsy first year German. Of course, my mother insisted on coaching me." He sat back and folded his hands like a contemplative professor in his study, sharing his experiences with his grad students.

Abigail interrupted, "So your mother was from the old country?"

"Oh yes, with a name like Bertha Mueller? She was a émigré, luckily before the 'War to end all wars.' Not long after my father met her, they married and settled on Portland. When America joined the Allies, my parents had to face a deep angst against all Germans, even if they were citizens. And the stigma lasted long after the war."

Sydney said, "It must have been difficult on you growing up. I had my share of being bullied. Just my name invited a scrape."

Percy slid the bottle of scotch down the table to Sydney. "My childhood was miserable, no siblings. I was bullied for being a *krout.* I ran the gauntlet every day going to school because of that and my sissy name. Would you believe Percy wasn't a contraction of Perceval but Persevere? Perhaps my parents thought I would need the quality of perseverance." Toby noticed how his mood became pensive as he reflected on the past. "I didn't know it at the time, but that summer I lived in Munich would change my life forever."

"Because?" said Abigail.

"That's where I discovered my bride. She was the daughter of a prominent industrialist. and I was lodging with her family in their guesthouse. Frieda and I intoxicated each other. That was the good part. When I approached her parents for permission to marry, you'd think I was trying to steal the family jewels. In a way, perhaps I was. Funny, at home, I was despised for being German. Now I was despised for not being German enough. Being half did not satisfy their criteria for a son-in-law. After the shock wore off, Frieda and I prevailed upon her parents and mine. In time, we married." He sighed and sat back, sipping his scotch. "With all the family animosity between Germany and America, we're still together."

"Well, congratulations," said Harriet, her words dripping with cynicism. "Perhaps I would have been more successful finding a husband in Germany."

"Never in Germany, Harriet. You're a flippant, foolish, shallow woman. That's such a stupid remark." Stunned, Harriet could not speak.

Sydney responded for her, "Percy, I believe you think of yourself as a gentleman. But as one, I think you should address Harriet with more respect."

"Then she should be a lady and earn my respect." Percy calmed down and said. "It's true, Sydney, in many ways, I still think I'm a gentleman, at least in Portland. Since you're all waiting for your imminent demise, you may wish to take exception."

Harriet, partially recovered, leaned forward as if to challenge his assumption of being a gentleman. Toby squeezed her knee to draw her attention. He shushed her by putting a finger to her lips.

Percy's railing on Harriet prompted Abigail to say. "It seems that Harriet's touched a nerve with you. Something about Germany? Connected no doubt to the visitor your expecting?"

"Of course. Guess I didn't, I say. I've been helping German war refugees come to the States since the twenties. I take a measure of pride in what I've accomplished."

"So, Percy, you're a Nazi sympathizer?" said Toby. "I guess the war is never over for those of your ilk."

"I'm not a Nazi." Unnerved, he lit a cigarette and said, "I'm not the only American that sympathized with Hitler. It may shock you that a number of influential Americans did. To be fair, most of them hated Roosevelt more than they loved Hitler. I, on the other hand, decided to play a more active role than just having a political opinion. If it turned a profit, all the better." He inhaled deeply and looked around the table, expecting to see shock and revulsion. A silence born of incredulity permeated the room.

After what seemed like an hour, Sydney said, "Do your business partners know what you're doing? Perhaps they wouldn't think of you as a gentleman?"

Percy smiled. "By partners, you mean Wimbley and Baseheart, of course?" Percy's smile turned into a chuckle. "As a lawyer, you of all people should know the practice of keeping partners' names on the door. Wimbley died several years ago in the thirty-eight or thirty-nine. Baseheart left about a year later to become a junior partner in a large Cincinnati firm. Never heard of him since. The wife and I could easily handle what little practice I had at the time."

"All right then," Harriet blurted out, "but what happened to Kathater, the one who scammed the trust funds?"

Percy's chuckle erupted into a full-blown laugh. "There's no such person. It was an easy way to deceive you. I simply took the expense money to finance my enterprise. I don't think I'd do very well getting a bank loan, do you?" He took another hard swallow of scotch. "I've managed to do well for myself and Frieda, especially the last couple of years."

"Speaking of Frieda," said Harriet, "how does she fit into the scheme of things?"

"I might as well tell everyone. I couldn't do it without her." He paused to light another cigarette with the one he was smoking. "Are you all surprised? She is really skilled at producing false documents for our, shall we say, clients. She takes all their physical features and provides them with a complete change of wardrobe, the works. American goods throughout, from toothbrushes to shoelaces. And she's in charge of relocating them where they can fade into the neighborhood. It's a big job."

He stopped to reflect. "It hasn't always been smooth sailing. You see, I've been bringing German refugees here for a number of years now, mainly through Spain. I settled a few in the States, even before the shooting started in WWII." He stared at the ceiling in a moment of reflection. "I find it ironic my sister-in-law was my first client. Frieda was lonesome for her sister Wilhelmina and worried about another war in Europe. I got started by engaging the captain of a tramp steamer I met in Portland. His homeport was Barcelona. Captain, ha. He looked more like a greasy boson mate in the engine room than a skipper. He didn't ask a lot of questions about his cargo. And he didn't have any problem accepting cash for Wilhelmina's passage, half on delivery. I arranged to have her embark in Spain and dropped off in Boston. It was the captain's job to spirit her on and off his ship, the *Rosarita*, even hide her if he had too. His ship was ideal, a real rust bucket that worked up and down the east coast of North America. Wilhelmina, to her credit, traveled well, like we say, a good wine. That was 1938. As for the captain and me, it was the beginning of a risky but very profitable venture."

Percy stopped abruptly in the middle of his revealing soliloquy, staring into the bottom of his glass. "Why am I telling you all this?" he said. Sydney seized the moment to retrieve the bottle of scotch and refill Percy's glass before he had a chance to refuse. Perhaps a long shot, but Sydney thought a generous application of scotch might further loosen Percy's heretofore restrained tongue. Percy seemed pleased for the attention and respite.

Toby's stomach growled. It was well past picnic time when he said, "I don't know about the rest of you, but I'm for breaking out the grub."

"How can you be hungry at a time like this?" Harriet asked.

"Well, it's times like this, old girl, I find I would rather be eating than dealing with problems, especially those I don't have a ready answer for."

"I'd appreciate it if you'd stop with the 'old girl' stuff. And I'm not eating in here if I have to starve to death."

"She does have a point," said Sydney, glancing in Percy's direction. Mockingly, he said, "The ambiance in here is hardly conducive to fine dining. Perhaps the courtyard would serve better, and you might like to join us in a repast. Escape is hardly a question. I don't think anyone here capable of outrunning a blast from Claude's shotgun."

Claude shouted across the room, "You got that right, Mr. Wadsworth, who or whatever you are."

Percy took a long drag of libation from his glass and looked over at Claude. "Well said. Just stay on your toes. And the rest of you stay put. As for you, Sydney, we can do without your silver tongue palaver."

"Sorry, Percy. Actually, I am far more interested the twists and turns in your life than I am in picnic fare."

"I imagine you are. As you now know, I've had challenges to overcome. My success getting Wilhelmina stateside inspired me to pursue a profitable business. I repeated the same tactics, of course. I not only brought people over here, but the booty of war. Fortunes in missing artwork from family estates and museums. Stashes of diamonds, precious gems, jewelry, and gold, treasures just waiting to find a new home. So I said to myself, why not here right in Portland?"

Sydney recognized the rhetorical question. "I certainly see the attraction."

"I saw it right away. But if I was going to siphon off a share of the loot, I needed a way- station like Bloodstone Island to land my 'expatriates' and their possessions. To my delight and surprise, Bloodstone Island fell right in my lap." His signature crocodile grin returned. "Once on the island, I could prepare them for a new life in the States, less my modest fee, of course."

He glanced at Harriet. "Thanks to your last two husbands, I've had nine years of free reign to transport through here what you would consider an evil enemy. I did it proudly too. If Germany had won the war, these same émigrés would be the elite."

Abruptly, Percy stopped speaking like a filibustering politician that's run out breath. He rose slowly to stretch his arms straight out like a scarecrow. Showing signs of being tired, he combed his thin gray hair with both hands. He groped for the reading glasses in his shirt pocket and looked at his pocket watch, not once, but twice. Everyone at the table followed suit, checking their own timepieces. No one spoke, including Claude who appeared bored. Percy returned to his chair and slouched as one both physically and mentally exhausted with the day's events. The electrically charged atmosphere in the room earlier evolved into one of gloom.

Chapter 23

A Visitor Turns Up

A *thump, thump, thump* on the service door reverberated down the hallway to the Great Room. Everyone sat up wide-eyed and faced the door. The noise surprised everyone, including Percy, who flinched at the loud knocking. Annoyed, his reaction revealed that he didn't expect his visitor to arrive this early. Late in the afternoon now, Percy checked his watch again.

"Claude, give me the shotgun and see who's out there. Don't go to the door. Go outside around back and be careful." He cursed through his pursed lips, "Dammit all, who else is going to show up?"

Minutes later, Claude returned out of breath. "It must be the guy you're expecting. He's sure foreign looking, and he's got a lot of crates and stuff sitting down at the dock."

Thump, thump, thump. The pounding on the door resumed, only more vigorous this time.

"Stay here, Claude. It can't be anyone else. Watch our guests." Percy walked slowly to the door, drawing a Luger from his holster. He asked, "Is that you, Günter, Günter Meir?"

"Ya, ya. You are Herr Percy Pierpont?"

"Good, please come in, Herr Meier," Percy replied in broken German. "My apologies, but we must be careful." His greeting brought a chuckle from Günter when they shook hands.

Günter removed his Panama hat and said. "Perhaps, Percy, we should converse in English. I think my broken English might be better than your broken German. Ya?"

"Thank you, of course, as you wish. I hope your voyage was not too unpleasant. Concealing your identity had to take precedence over creature comfort." Holstering his pistol, Percy led the way to the Great Room.

Günter rubbed his eyes. Two men, two women seated at gunpoint. "Vas is this?"

"Do not be concerned, Herr Meier. They represent a minor inconvenience." He sighed. "They have to be eliminated before we leave for Portland."

"Are they Jewish?" Günter asked.

"It really doesn't matter."

Günter raised an eyebrow. "In any case, I can't help you, hardly my department. I was not SS, you understand, just Mien Furher's humble *kunstoffiizer* for antiquities and art." Pleased to recuse himself, Günter chuckled softly.

Percy continued to fawn over his client, "Of course, with your background as an art historian before the war, you must have been a perfect candidate for managing the Reichstad's acquisitions."

"Yes, I took great pride in my position. Of course, a few of my colleagues and I had the added responsibility of finding shelters to hide works of art, especially after the war took a turn. Ha, the English museums gutted most of the world's *kunstschätze*. Why should Hitler and Marshall Goering be any different? I was, as the English say, inundated with every type of acquisition." He paused to reflect and with braggadocio claimed, "Naturally, I took a modest commission for my hard work. I carefully culled out my share and shipped it out of Germany. And here it is. But enough. Who is your friend with the shotgun?"

"Forgive me again, Herr Meir. Let me introduce you to my associate, Claude Hadley." Günter and Claude exchanged polite but cautious nods. Percy interjected, "Perhaps you would like a drink to celebrate your arrival on American soil."

"Of course, *danke*." Günter paraded around Percy's captives like a peacock.

Arrogance oozed through every spoken word. His crude demeanor was just as offensive as his manner of speech. Sydney wondered if Günter had more than one personality. Perhaps the war morphed him into this eccentric persona, the antithesis of a learned academic.

From across the Great Hall, Günter bellowed, "I was thirsty, but I think I'm hungry too, after the swill they serve on the *Rosarita.* Incidentally, everything I brought with me is sitting on the end of the float." He took another liberal swallow of scotch. "Those two *dummkopfs* who unloaded it, they jumped on the launch going back to the *Rosarita,* mumbled something about wanting to go to sea. Was that your idea, Herr Percy?"

Percy struggled to find words that would belie the ripples of anxiety on his forehead.

"No, but do not concern yourself, Günter. It only alters my plans a little." Adopting a nonchalant smile. "You know how impetuous youth can be."

Sydney stood up and took a step toward the lunch basket when Claude raised his gun and shouted, "Where do you think you're going, girlie?"

"I was going to bring some food for your guest, Günter, said he was hungry."

"It's all right, Claude," said Percy. "I changed my mind. We could all use a bite."

All eyes were trained on Sydney's as he scurried across the Great Hall to retrieve the picnic basket. He picked it up and deftly retrieved his umbrella hanging from the coat rack directly above the basket.

Anticipating refreshments, Günter looked almost as pleased as Toby. Claude used his shotgun to wave Sydney back to the table. Once the picnic basket reached the table, its contents were quickly consumed. Herr Meir opened Toby's bottle of Pinot Noir. Percy brought three wine glasses he discovered in the armoire. Percy, Günter, and Claude raised their glasses in a toast to success. Claude spit it out and returned to his chair, munching on a handful of mixed nuts. At the sight, Günter tried but failed to contain a chuckle.

Percy pointed to a leather suitcase against the wall. "Everything you'll need from here on out is in it, your clothes and shoes, all sized to the measurements you provided. Of course, there's your passport, bus tickets, even a driver's license and a shaving kit. The folder will tell you who to get in touch with when you arrive. If you need to contact me, use our code then destroy your instructions. Did I mention your new address is Cincinnati?"

"Ya, ya, Herr Percy, I've heard of it."

"In our communiqués, you didn't mention family. No Frau Meir? No children?"

"Nein. Tragically, I have reason to believe my wife died in the fire-bombing of Dresden. She was visiting relatives. Children, we did not have."

"I'm sorry, Günter. Let's go have a chat out of earshot. I want to fill you in on our exit strategy from here."

Cupping a hand to one ear, Günter asked, "Earshot, exit?"

Percy grinned and apologized for using jargon. They walked a few steps away. Percy spoke again, this time in a measured low tone. "Forgive me, Heir Meir, for dragging you into this mess with these uninvited guests. Of course, I hope you appreciate I have to eliminate them, as a matter of self-preservation for both of us. Yes?"

"Ya."

"Good. I thought you'd agree.

"Your plan is?" Günter's thoughts were a continent away. Impatient and seemingly on the verge of being disinterested, he stared at a broken fingernail. "As I mentioned, executions are outside my expertise. But in the meantime, I suggest tying them up."

"Yes, of course. And I have devised a plan, one that leaves no trail the authorities to follow." Percy needed Günter to help accomplish his plan now that his two *grunts* had abandoned his employ for a life at sea. "My plan is to put our four guests aboard their own boat, lock them in the cabin, tow them a few miles out to sea, and scuttle the boat. Simple and foolproof, don't you think? From there, we'll sail to Portland."

Günter nodded. "As I said, I don't know about such things."

"We'll leave after dusk tonight, in two or three hours. Just lend a hand if we need one." Walking back to the table, Percy turned to Claude and held his hand out for the shotgun. "Go find some rope, enough to tie our guest up tight. If you have to, go down to my boat. Günter and I will watch our guests while you're gone."

* * *

Meanwhile, Sydney surmised the situation grew more desperate by the minute. He felt time running out and decided to pick up "April," the umbrella, he'd tucked under his chair, the best weapon he had. Beneath his breath, he whispered to April, *It may be up to you, old girl, to save our asses. You've got one ten-gauge shell to stand up against the three of them. I hope it'll be enough. It has to be.*

Chapter 24

The Brawl

Claude returned, out of breath, displaying a broad grin. He dropped the coil of rope from his shoulder with a thud that sent a cloud of dust rising from the floor. Percy remarked, "Good work, Claude. We should have done this sooner. Here, take the shotgun."

Claude sat down to wipe his brow. Percy hadn't finished thanking him when Harriet let out a banshee shriek.

"E E e e e eya a a a a a a a a h h h! s-s-s-sp-spi-spi-DER! My leg! My leg!"

The shrill scream startled Claude out of his chair, slipping out from under him. Sprawling on the floor, he lost his grip on the shotgun. It slithered away from him like a fleeing garden snake.

Percy said, Shut up, Harriet. DON'T ANYBODY MOVE!

Sydney shouted, "NOW'S OUR CHANCE. TOBY, TAKE PERCY! I'VE GOT CLAUDE."

Toby grabbed Harriet and thrust his hand down her cleavage to grab the Derringer she had hidden.

Percy tried clumsily to draw his Luger. "For God's sake, Claude . . . will you SHOOT SOMEBODY!"

Claude said, "I CAN'T . . . I dropped my friggin' gun."

Toby leaped on Percy and put the Derringer flush against his temple, shouting, "Don't try anything, Claude! Or I'll blow Percy's brains out to sea."

Percy said, "DO AS HE SAYS!"

Harriet grabbed the shotgun off the floor before Claude could.

Sydney yelled at Harriet, "Shoot Claude if you have to."

Claude screamed at Harriet, “Hey, bitch, I’m your SON!”

Günter, shocked at the unraveling events, bent over and fumbled for a concealed pistol strapped to his leg.

Abigail joined the brawl. She landed a crippling kick to Günter’s groin, which sent him bent over, writhing in pain while hurling obscenities in his native tongue.

Sydney swung his umbrella around, cocked it, and pointed it at Günter.

Abigail, continuing her assault on Günter, grabbed him by the ears and lifted her knee flush into his face. He hit the floor like a sack of cement. “Gutenacht, Herr Mier. Too bad I didn’t kill you.”

Claude rushed Harriet and wrested the gun away from her. He raised it up to shoot Toby.

Sydney reacted quickly by bracing his umbrella against his hip. He aimed at Claude and pulled the hair trigger. KABOOM! The recoil knocked Sydney back off his feet and onto the floor. The acrid odor of gunpowder filled the hall.

Claude screamed, “YOU SHOT ME . . . YOU BASTARD!”

Sydney said, “You’ll live.” Bluffing, he exclaimed, “But if you move, the next one will cut you in half.”

Percy twisted and ducked away from Toby who was distracted in the mêlée.

Toby shot in Percy’s general direction, hitting a lantern on the opposite wall. The second shot hit Percy in the buttocks, dropping him face down on the floor, writhing and groaning in pain right next to Günther.

Sydney said, “Good work, Toby. I’ll cover them. Claude, get over here and lie down on the floor with Percy and Günther. Abigail, can you find your flare gun outside? Go fire it.” Sydney glared at the grumbling trio. “You all deserve to be finished off.” Abigail said, “Don’t worry, Sydney. I know right where the flare gun is. God, I hope my knee doesn’t give out. I must have left a piece of it in Günter’s face.”

Harriet stood traumatized. Blood from Claude’s hand had spattered on her clothes.

Toby scurried to comfort her. Glassy-eyed, she seemed to be looking for something.

"Harriet, that was brilliant, screaming about a spider on your leg. It made a perfect diversion. It certainly turned the tables on those Nazis lovers."

Harriet said, "I'm sorry, Toby, but I'm afraid my scream was genuine. I can't stand spiders."

Toby put his arm around her. "Arachnophobia, eh? Still, in all, a good thing for us. Come on, let's give Sydney a hand. Did you see the way Abigail leveled that krout?"

Harriet managed to smile weakly. "Now I know why they call her *Iron Pants*."

Outside, Abigail found the hidden flare gun. An initiate to flares, she was reading the instructions when the gun accidentally discharged; and the distress flare slammed into the second floor of Burning Tree, leaving a smoldering hole in the wood siding. Cursing, as only her father knew how, she reloaded and sent the second smoke signal directly overhead. She counted three shots left in the gun. Scanning the horizon for watercraft, she instinctively gazed westward toward Port Henry but found the sea as empty as an unrequited love.

Chapter 25

Burning Tree Burns

The smoke rising from a hole in the siding warned of a pending doom for Burning Tree. Abigail swallowed hard. The horrible image of a conflagration came to mind. She started to run down to the *Star Splitter* and radio for help, but turned on her heel, sensing that it was far more important to get everyone out of Burning Tree first. Entering the Great Hall, she shouted over and over, "Fire, fire, everyone out! Now!"

She sensed what would happen, and her fears were confirmed as wisps of white smoke crept out of the building through fissures in the siding. Flickering flames raced up the outside walls, exacerbated by an onshore breeze.

Abigail, already hobbling on a painful knee, realized that getting down the path would be a daunting time-consuming task. But the alternative of ending up in a funeral pyre should motivate everyone.

Sydney prodded the threesome with his umbrella. "On your feet, you miserable excuse for humanity, all of you! You can stay here if you'd like and be barbequed. Ha, I like that scenario!"

Percy moaned through his clenched teeth, "What's going to happen to us?"

"When we get back to Port Henry? Toby and I are going to see to it that you three get the chair."

Percy groaned again. "Why did you have to come here?" With no alternative in sight, he squealed, "Damn I've been shot. I may be finished, Sydney. Suppose it's too late to make a deal?"

"I'm afraid so, Percy. I don't know how you could think you'd get away with murder. Eventually, the law would catch you up."

"Well, I managed pretty well up to now. This was going to be my last run, close up shop, retire." Groaning as he spoke, his voice dry and gravely, "If that bitch, Harriet, hadn't shown up, I would have owned this island after I got rid of Claude."

Claude moaned, "I heard that, Percy."

Sydney ignored Claude and said, "Percy, I don't understand you. You're an educated man, a lawyer, and a professional man with some standing in your community. How could you stoop so low as to betray God and country? Heavens, man, to think you're supposed to be a community leader, a gentleman."

"I admit I've made my share of mistakes, but I'm not as evil as you think I am. And I didn't want to kill any of you, but it was your fault, coming here with Harriet. I had no alternative."

"I have a belated suggestion for you. If you were a gentleman, in my day, you'd make an effort to blow your brains out. It would spare your family and profession from the shame and embarrassment you've caused them. You should fall on your sword, if you take my meaning."

"Sydney, stop. Enough. You really are a sanctimonious snob and judgmental bastard. By your leave, I'll have to take your proposal under advisement. But I hardly share your idea of justice."

"I supposed as much, and there's no time to debate the nuances of justice with you. I think you're beyond any possibility of redemption, you bag of slime."

Claude rose to his knees, holding his bleeding right hand wrapped in a piece of torn cloth. He sneered at Percy, "I may be as good as dead, but I'm not going to die for you, Percy, or your krout friend either. All I wanted was the island. You'd kill me or cheat me out of that too." Struggling to stand, he said, "When I get out of here, I'm going to rat on you big time."

Sydney ignored Claude and said, "Come on, Herr Meir, on your feet. It's time for you to start goose stepping. As for you, Claude, Shut up and get a move on."

Toby shouted, "Sydney, I've got my pistol back, so lead on."

"Right. And I've got Claude's shotgun. Abigail's gone on ahead to radio for help."

Günter mumbled through his cut tongue and loose front teeth, "You fools, I'm an American."

Sydney, initially surprised, replied, "Of course, you are. Well, Mr. Sweet Talker, you're not tiptoeing your way out of Percy's scheme, and neither is he."

"Right," said Toby. "He can't get off acting like some double agent in a cheap spy novel. Bullocks. I saw Günter reaching for his leg iron."

Günter pleaded, "I did, but believe me I was trying to take your side. That's when this Amazon of yours blindsided me." He looked up and said, "My God, what's that sound?"

Sydney, leading the group, emerged first from Burning Tree. He looked up and said, "There's your answer, Günter. Thousands of bats emptying their bladders and screeching their brains out."

Leaving the summerhouse in search of shelter, the bats passed close overhead like a dark rain cloud. They darted, massed together across the sky like a kite trying to chase its tail. The summerhouse expressed its pain too as the fire rapidly turned into an inferno. The sound of breaking glass came from every quarter, exploding from their burning frames. Outside walls collapsed and crashed to the ground. Norway rats trapped in the upper floor attics screeched in desperation. Squeezing through cracks in the roofs, those still alive fell to the ground below.

Sydney, startled, exclaimed, "Will you look at all the dead rats? Dozens of them." One fell on Sydney and scampered off into the brush. "Jesus, Mary, and Joseph, it's raining rats!"

Toby yelled to Sydney, "Let's spare all the gibberish and move out. It's getting toasty in here."

"All right, but watch your step and cover your head. Toby, keep your pistol trained on these fine gentlemen. Outside, they may have a mind to make a run for it. In their present condition, I doubt if they'd get far."

Harriet turned around and looked at Toby. "You'll just have to wait a minute. I've lost a shoe, and I need to find my purse."

"For God's sake, Harriet, wake up. Everyone else is outside and gone. Jeeez-zus, woman. Forget the damn shoe. I've got your purse. It's heavy. I put Günter's pistol and your Derringer in it."

"Thanks, Toby. I just wish you wouldn't swear like a sailor. It's very unbecoming of you."

"Harriet, this is no time to discuss etiquette."

Percy agreed, "Will you please hurry up and get us out of here?" Consumed with their own injuries, the three international smugglers had no appetite to resist, run, or fight. They were able however to repeatedly expressed a genuine fear for their lives. The fire posed a much greater risk to their bodily harm than anything Harriet and her friends might have in mind.

The perilous pathway to the dock became more so as smoke and flying embers hindered their progress and clouded their vision. The inferno created updrafts carrying ash and embers high above the summerhouse where upper winds scattered the remains out to sea.

Toby was the first victim where the path steepened. He tumbled off the path rolling down a precipitous bank covered with patches of gravel, indigenous shrubs, and grasses.

Harriet yelled, "Oh, Toby, are you all right? I'll help you up."

Gasping for air, Toby implored Harriet, "I'm all right." Reaching up, he said, "Here, take my pistol and carry on. I need a moment or two to collect myself. Go on now and no arguing. I'll catch you up."

"Oh, Toby, Are you sure?"

"Yes, yes, yes. Off with you!"

Chapter 26

Rescue

Abigail, in amazement, watched the cutter, *Leslie*, eased into a position where she could safely stand off shore. *It's a worn-out wreck,* she thought, *even headed for the bone yard, but right now she looks like the* Queen Mary. She pondered, *How on earth did the* Leslie *get here so fast? It seemed it was only moments earlier that she radioed them for help. In a scow that slow, it must have been treading water on the east side of the island.*

Looking at the cutter, a wave of relief swept over her when she witnessed the skipper's gig heading toward her along with a lifeboat manned by a contingent of the *Leslie*'s crew.

Abigail's thoughts flashed back for a moment to the skipper's recent visit to the Port Henry courthouse. She reckoned, *He must have been expecting some sort of trouble on Bloodstone Island. That may explain his reticence to discuss the information he asked for at the courthouse. Can't think about that now. I'm on a mission of my own.* To help save her companions, she had to locate them first. *Why aren't they here yet? The coast guard may not have time to look or even risk waiting for them. Good God, what's going to happen to my boat? I can't bear to leave it here. I put too damn much into it.*

Unexpectedly, Abigail shivered when suddenly she thought of losing not only her boat but also everything, including her life. As the fire approached and intensified, she was forced to think in terms of her own preservation. It crossed her mind how easy it would be to jump on the *Star Splitter,* grab the hidden spare key, and race safely out to sea. But in the end, that was not the cut of her cloth, and the idea had no chance of winning.

Looking at the cutter, a wave of relief swept over her when she saw two small boats being launched. As they drew closer, experience told her that one must be the captain's gig and the other a lifeboat. She stayed on the far end of the float, jumping up and down on one foot to flag the approaching boats to make sure they noticed her. She thought, *The men aboard the two boats wouldn't be anxious to race into this inferno. I hope they realize the sooner they get here, the sooner they'll be safe back on their ship.* The fire seemed determined to beat the rescue boats to the float. Her "burning" question was, *Where in the devil is everyone?"*

* * *

Sydney and Harriet arrived at the float, ducking a shower of glowing embers overhead. Sydney led the way with Percy, Claude, and Günter stumbling along behind him. Harriet brought up the rear wielding Toby's pistol. When Sydney saw the launch and lifeboat, he shouted to Harriet trailing behind, "Hey, it looks like we might survive after all. Trial by fire, don't to know?" At the ramp and the end of the float, they stumbled into a collection of wooden boxes and crates blocking their path.

The precious cargo in the boxes took a backseat in the minds of Harriet and Sydney. They focused totally on their survival. The party of captors and prisoners wriggled through serpentine fashion. The overloaded float rocked up and down and side to side as they tried to keep their balance. They stumbled but managed to lurch ever forward. Incredibly, everyone avoided being spilled into the sea where an uncertain future waited.

When the group emerged from the warren of boxes, Abigail spotted them staggering toward her. She hobbled toward Sydney. He sprinted ahead and left Harriet behind to fend for herself. Relieved to see him, she collapsed in his arms, limp as a dishrag. She had never allowed a show or display of emotion, but suddenly, a wealth of tears streamed down her cheeks. She dried her eyes on the blouse she'd given Sydney to wear. Slightly embarrassed, she recovered quickly while Sydney choked on words designed to comfort her.

"Where's Toby?" said Abigail.

Harriet replied, "I don't know. I thought he would be right behind me. Oh God, he must still be up on the path! I'm going back. Sydney, take Toby's pistol and do what you want with Percy."

"You can't go. It's too dangerous," Abigail yelled. "You'll get killed."

Harriet didn't look back. She ignored Abigail and headed headlong up the pathway to the summerhouse. Exhausted and gasping, she stopped every few steps, "Toby, Toby, where in the devil are you? Say something."

The intense heat grew more intolerable, enough to drive back all but the most courageous. Half crawling, half walking, she labored to breathe through a handkerchief she'd confiscated from Toby earlier. Swirling smoke smarted her eyes and clogged her lungs. By chance, she stumbled over Toby's crumpled frame, rolled up in a fetal position.

Unconscious and covered in brambles, Toby had suffered a fall of serious proportions. Harriet realized he might have been more injured than she first thought when she left him behind. She fell to the ground and knelt beside him. "Oh, Toby, you can't die on me, not now. You silly, I really do need you. Tell me you're breathing. Well, are you?" She picked at the gravel imbedded in his cheeks. With her fingers, she scraped the dirt away from his nose and mouth. "Come on, Toby, wake up. You're not getting out of our marriage this easily."

Toby's lips barely parted. "Harriet, is that you?"

"Who else? You and I are going down to the boat, so open your bloody eyes!"

'No, Harriet, too late. I'm a dying man. Let's just say our goodbyes. Save yourself."

"You're not dying!"

"I am too. God, woman, a man knows when he's dying. Can't you do anything but argue, argue, argue? I only wish I weren't dying here." Toby choked, struggling to clear his throat. "I've always wanted to have Sydney spread my ashes, don't you know, on the Fifth Green at Brookside."

"If we stay here another minute, we'll both be turned to ashes. Now, husband, open your goddamn eyes. We're getting down from here."

"It's no use, Harriet. I think my leg's broken, so's my pipe."

"I'll buy you a new pipe, and I'll break your other leg if you don't get off your ass."

"Cripes, Harriet, you're the most impossible woman I've ever known." He struggled to his knees.

They heard a voice coming toward them, faint at first then louder, repeating, "Toby, Harriet. Answer me. Where in hell are you?"

Over the roar of the fire, Harriet yelled back, "Up here. Is that you, Sydney?"

"Of course, it is. Is Toby all right?"

"Sort of." Harriet reached out to grip Sydney's hand. "Oh, thank God you came."

"You must have known I would. We're the only two that can get him down from here."

"Well, Sydney, I never thought I'd be glad to see you!"

"Don't get sentimental on me. If we latch on to each side of Toby, we can haul him down to the float."

"Sydney," whispered Toby. "I'm a goner. Really, just say a few words over me on the Fifth hole at Brookside, and I'll be happy."

"Toby, get a grip, old fellow. We can almost fall down to the float."

"I tried that already."

Harriet's voice demanded, "Well, let's try a little harder this time. I've lost three husbands so far, and I'm not about to lose another."

"Well, I guess we can't have that," replied Toby. "Come on, give me a hand."

Harriet, coughing, said, "Let's step on it. I can hardly breathe, and Abigail's alone on the dock with Percy and company."

"Right," said Sydney. He grasped Toby by the arm to put over his shoulder. "And don't worry about Abigail. I left her with the shotgun, and she's pretty trigger-happy right now. I'm pleased to report our three adversaries are laid out on the dock, just like tuna in a wholesale fish market." Sydney flashed a wry smile at the thought. "No time to waste."

* * *

Toby, croaked, "Thanks for fetching me. I'll be glad to get out of here." Toby took a stab at making light of their ominous position on the path. "I believe there's a fire chasing us.

"Ha, all of a sudden, you're interested in living," said Sydney. "I remember you sang a different tune a couple of minutes ago."

Toby replied, "Curse you, Sydney. You know I was only thinking of Harriet?"

Approaching sea level, they breathed easier and heavier. Sydney and Harriet both made small talk on the way down to the ramp. Toby, however, uttered nothing except for an occasional restrained groan from his injuries. The wooden crates still posed an obstacle; but Sydney, having negotiated them moments before, knew the best way through.

Abigail, relieved to see them appear out of the din, yelled, "HELLO . . . glad you folks could make the party! I've been a touch worried. And for heaven's sake, get your tails down here. The coast guard is almost here."

When they arrived at the end of the float, Sydney picked up the shotgun at Abigail's feet. After he paused to assess the condition of Percy, Claude, and Günter, he heaved the shotgun into the sea. Toby thought it an impulsive gesture, perhaps a show of disgust for the violence everyone's endured.

Behind Sydney, a seaman in the captain's gig tossed a line on the float and jumped up to secure a line around a davit. The skipper of the *Leslie* jumped out of the gig and shouted, "Who's in charge?"

"I guess I am. I'm Abigail Underwood. You must be Lieutenant Commander Sinclair."

"Yes, right, it's Willis Sinclair."

"Am I glad to see you! Thank heavens you got my message. We're about done in."

The commander quickly sized up the situation. He asked, Abigail, "What's going on with these three people lying here?"

Before Abigail could summon a reply, Percy raised his head and gurgled, "We need a doctor. These people shot two of us and pummeled my guest half to death."

"My corpsman will patch you up on board. We'll transport you to a doctor in Port Henry soon enough."

"Commander," said Abigail, "be careful. These rather contemptible bastards belong in your brig."

He smiled at Abigail. "I know. We intercepted two longboats returning to the *Rosarita,* two crewmembers and two runaway teenagers from Portland. The kids spilled the beans first. We located the *Rosarita* just east of the island, and we commandeered it. I relieved the captain of his duties and left my junior officer in charge. You can imagine the *Rosarita*'s captain didn't appreciate being arrested on his own bridge. My men are busy right now taking the *Rosarita* to Portland. I left a small complement of my men on board for security. I needn't tell you I'm really shorthanded right now. My chief boson is in charge of the *Leslie* right now."

Three of the sailors arriving in the lifeboat climbed onto the float. The fourth seaman kept the outboard engine idling in case a hasty departure was required. "Boson mate," barked Sinclair, "take two men and pull all, and I mean all, those crates up here. They're coming back to ship with us. Look smart now. Their contents are priceless."

"Yes, sir." The sailor hesitated for a moment and said, "Sir, it might take two trips by the look of it. And that fire is closing fast."

"All the more reason to get on with it!"

Sinclair turned to address Abigail again. "You're the justice of peace in Port Henry, right? And that's your boat the *Star Splitter*?"

"You guessed right again."

"Your passengers look like they've been through a food blender. Are they able to board your boat? I can give you a hand if you need me."

Overheard, Sydney shouted above the din to Sinclair, "Abigail's injured too. I can handle the boarding. Besides, Commander, we don't wish to be beholden when you have duties to attend to."

"All right, and you are?"

"I'm Sydney Wadsworth, an old navy man myself. I'm not injured and quite capable of assisting Ms. Underwood and the others get aboard. We'll follow your orders, of course."

Sinclair turned to Abigail, moved out of Sydney's earshot, and asked, "Is he real?" His brow furrowed, as he looked Sydney up and down, "If he's navy, he's seriously out of uniform."

"Oh, that's not a problem, Commander. He's wearing my clothes."

"I s-e-e," he said as he walked away, having no wish to pursue the conversation further.

Once again, Sydney's officious nature surfaced as he gave orders directed to a slack-jawed commander. "Feel free to direct your men and get these three louts on your ship. I'll handle the lines on the *Star Splitter* when Abigail tells me to cast off."

In disbelief, Sinclair turned to Abigail and said, "Don't shove off just yet. I may need your help. By the looks of it, I won't be able to fit all the crates on my launch and lifeboat. I'd be grateful if we could put a few of the crates on your open deck."

Abigail nodded her approval. "Of course. I'll clear the aft deck for you, including my passengers."

Sinclair said, "Thanks. I'll load the *Star Splitter* first so you can be on your way."

It pleased Abigail to be in charge of her boat again. The twin diesels responded on cue with a key she had hidden for unexpected events. "Sydney, climb back on board. I need you more up here on the bridge with the others. Please man the fire extinguisher in case we catch a flying ember or two."

"Right, Abigail, good thinking."

"OK, everybody, to help the coast guard, we're taking on a load of Nazi loot. Oh, and when they've finished lashing it down, the crew of the *Leslie* will cast us off."

Chapter 27

Looking Backward and Forward

At a safe distance from shore, Abigail turned the *Star Splitter* around to look back and say farewell to Burning Tree. The foursome on the bridge watched the *Leslie* get under way, heading through a veil of smoke and steam for Port Henry. Against a sky colored by fire, the *Leslie*'s eerie silhouette emerged like the *Flying Dutchman* ghost ship.

Abigail's voice crackled, breaking the silence. "I'm sorry, Harriet. I accidentally started the fire with the flare gun."

Harriet replied, "It helped us, didn't it? Please, don't apologize. I'm responsible for this whole miserable, cockamamie mess." No one had enough strength or inclination to level blame or quarrel about his or her traumatic sojourn. Her hands shook as she reached to steady herself on the bridge railing. "Sorry if I'm a little shaky. I guess I need to thank all of you for saving my life."

Toby remarked, "No need to say a word. You saved mine." By some act of providence, Toby managed to salvage his 7-iron. Now it served as a cane to support a badly injured leg. Taking inventory, he lamented that his disheveled never-to-be-used handkerchief suffered the indignities of being subjected to the renowned blood, sweat, and tears, along with a few smudges from Harriet's mascara.

The aftermath of what happened over the last few hours took hold. The evidence of their encounter with Percy Pierpont and his confederates appeared in the form of bruises, scratches, bloody clothing, and a sundry of more serious injuries.

Sydney said in a moment of reflection, "Toby's right, Harriet. If thanks are due anyone, it's Abigail. Remember, we were all quite occupied with saving our own skins." He took a deep breath and proceeded to grumble over the condition of his totally inappropriate attire. "I've got to get out of your clothes, Abigail. I feel ridiculous, and I don't mind saying"—he drew in another long breath—"that all of us still smell like we just had a bat guano bath."

"Sydney, don't take this wrong," said Abigail. "You're wearing my clothes so just try to live with it for couple of more hours, all right?" Sydney, unapologetic, sulked in silence.

Harriet sighed. "Sydney, if I can endure a little stinky poo until we land, you can too." She looked again at the summerhouse being dismembered piece by piece into rubble and ash. She opined, "I think Burning Tree deserved to die by fire. Good riddance, I say. Only God knows why I insisted on owning such a forlorn place. I guess I must have thought Bloodstone Island would look good in my portfolio."

Startled by Harriet's musing, Toby stopped attending to the gash on his leg. "I would remind you, Harriet, that I went to great lengths and sacrifice only to find out now you don't want Bloodstone Island? This was quite an overnighter you planned for the two of us. Humph. If I didn't know better, I would say you duped me."

"I'm really sorry, Toby. You know that I'll find some way to make it up to you."

"Well, when we get back, you can start by giving me the divorce we agreed to."

"Oh, come now, Toby. There'll be time to sort things out, won't there?" Toby, silent, returned to examine his throbbing leg.

Abigail and Sydney feigned not to hear the altercation between Toby and Harriet. But Abigail grimaced when she recalled admonishing the pair not to mock her court with a marriage of convenience. Dismissing her displeasure, Abigail's thoughts turned to fixate on the fire. It mesmerized her, creating a vision of a gigantic pyrotechnic display on the fourth. Her hand remained steady on the throttle and did not move for a long time. "Feast your eyes on this!" she exclaimed. "What irony, the fire's reached Burning Tree's, Burning Tree. The lightning only disfigured it, but it looks like the fire will finally destroy it."

"Holy mother of smithereens," said Sydney. "The water tank's collapsed on the fire." He watched spellbound with the others as thousands of gallons of water spewed from the ruptured tank down over the summerhouse. The fire protested and sent clouds of steam billowing high above the island. Stone sections of the ramparts and parapets broke away from the timber summerhouse and rolled down the steep bank into the sea. “Pompeii must have looked like this when Vesuvius erupted,” he observed. “I think we escaped just in time.”

“So did the *Leslie*,” Abigail echoed. “We’ve seen enough, haven’t we?” She increased the throttle slowly and gingerly turned the *Star Splitter* toward Port Henry. The *Leslie* closed in, cruising on the same course. She knew what would be waiting for them in Port Henry, far more than her ship mates imagined.

* * *

Engines at full throttle, the *Star Splitter* danced over the waves to Port Henry. Approaching the town’s breakwater, Abigail eased back on the throttle and took a brief glance over her shoulder toward Bloodstone Island, a last look at the fire still ablaze on the horizon. It gave her pause to recall how Bloodstone Island always seemed like an innocent little isle, not the sinister one she discovered and just left behind. She murmured, “I wonder how long I’ll remember this trip to the archipelago? I guess an arthritic knee and sore foot will remind me.”

After an extended period of silence, Harriet said, “On the way in, I’ve been thinking about Bloodstone Island and something Abigail told me.”

“Which is?” Toby asked out of politeness.

“I’ve thought about everything that’s just happened. Bloodstone Island wouldn’t fetch a dime at a yard sale. Sure as hellfire and damnation, I’ll be saddled with this property forever, like an albatross around my neck. That made me think this island’s ‘for the birds.’ Well, why not? Abigail said Bloodstone Island was in the path of migratory sea birds. This island would make an ideal bird sanctuary? Yes?” She turned to look at Sydney. “Dear, and you too Abigail, you’ll help me give it to the state of Maine, won’t you?”

Sydney replied with a touch of both surprise and reluctance in his voice, “I’ll certainly try.” Abigail nodded her approval. He said, “That’s very generous of you, Harriet, and I hope the state will recognize the worth of the gift is greater than the property taxes they would lose.”

"All right, everyone," said Abigail, "Quiet. We're going in. Stay inside and keep out of sight."

A small crowd gathered on the docks, waiting to greet them, including Chief McDonald and Officer Peabody. However, she purposely trailed the *Star Splitter* behind the cutter coming in to Port Henry. She radioed the *Leslie* her intention to let the *Leslie* dock first.

Instinctively, she thought the activity surrounding the cutter would attract the locals' interest away from the *Star Splitter.* The strategy worked. Everyone's eyes on shore focused on the cutter, due in part because its size overshadowed that of the *Portland Packet.*

Once inside the breakwater, Abigail headed toward her slip in the marina. At least for the moment, the police, reporters, and curiosity seekers had been given the slip. Although relieved to arrive safely back home, she thought, *Sooner or later, I and the rest of this motley crew will be swarmed with a barrage of uncomfortable questions.* A wave of uncertainty and questions about the immediate future swept over her like, *What am I supposed to do with all this stolen art treasure on my boat?*

Sydney, silent for the most part on the final leg of the trip from Burning Tree, said, "Abigail, you must be aware, as I am, that the one and only town ambulance will be overtaxed getting the cutter's wounded to the town's only doctor, let alone us."

"Believe it or not, I'm well aware of the situation. Right now I need to concentrate without interruption."

Considering her options, she thought her best chance for help would come from the marina superintendent. She radioed his office and mobile number, thinking, *God. I hope you're not out on rounds.* "Cliff, this is Abigail Underwood on the *Star Splitter.* Are you there?" No answer. "If you get this message, I'm on my way in. Ten minutes out. I really could use your help. I've got four people, including myself, that require medical attention. We need transport to the clinic. Over." No answer. "Damn!"

With the engines on idle, Abigail's guided her boat down past the slips. The sea was flat and calm inside the breakwater. Occasionally, she gave a short push on the throttle. Following orders, no one spoke. She hoped today's maelstrom may finally be coming to a close, but questioned, *Would there be another one right behind it?*

As she jockeyed the *Star Splitter* into its home slip, one look by her at the beleaguered Brookside passengers told her that if Cliff didn't show up, she was on her own docking the *Star Splitter.* She saw on everyone's face that they starved for something positive to happen, big or otherwise.

The sight of Cliff jogging down the dock satisfied that hunger. Cliff hailed, "Got your message. Toss me a line. I'll get you tied up."

* * *

Once on solid ground, the future looked up for the beleaguered foursome. To their good fortune, Cliff's swing shift watchman, Frank, had checked in at the marina and joined them at the dock.

"I need another favor, Cliff," said Abigail, "We need someone to guard the crates on my aft deck. It's quite valuable, stolen merchandise. We're helping the coast guard. You don't suppose—"

"Yes, I suppose I could ask Frank to watch this stuff. I'll call the cops so he doesn't have to stand around here all night."

Sydney broke in, "Thanks, Cliff, and let the police know this is going to be a job for the feds."

"True," said Abigail, adding, "Bless your heart, Cliff. You're a prince! And thanks for offering to take us to the clinic?"

"I did? Well, I must have. I couldn't leave you here to fend for yourselves. I assume one or some of you got here in that 'Mother Tucker' delivery truck." Toby and Harriet stared into the distance.

The trip to the clinic was short, but crowded in the marina station wagon. At the clinic, Toby required the most attention from the nurse on duty. His swollen leg wasn't broken but required a doctor's visit for X-rays and possibly a splint for Toby. Until then, a hatful of pain medication had to be a substitute.

The clinic nurse squirmed at the sight of Sydney again. She immediately recalled that he was the least popular patient of hers since she became licensed to practice. Tossing him a hospital gown, she said, "You get out of those clothes and clean up. I'll tend to you last."

Sydney asked her, "I don't suppose you have a cigar." The nurse scowled. Sydney observed, "No, I guess not."

Abigail overheard, "Don't worry, Sydney. I think you left your cigar case on my boat."

Harriet required the least attention. The few scratches on her face and hands were superficial, but the rest of her body suffered the indignities of several bruises large and small.

Fortunately, Abigail's knee, although painful, did not appear to be serious. An application of ice reduced the swelling. She signed for a pair of crutches the clinic had available for such injuries. Alone and armed with a substantial quantity of aspirin and liniment, she limped back to the station wagon where Cliff had waited patiently.

"Can I take you home, Abigail?" he asked, "If anyone's looking for lodging tonight, I can drop them off."

Toby said, "We are already in your debt. Still, Harriet and I would appreciate a lift to the Lighthouse Inn. We're known there, and we've been offered a complimentary stay over or two. In fact, our luggage is there. I'll wager that Abigail and Sydney would be comfortable there too. Shower, good hot meal. Harriet would be happy to lend Abigail some fresh clothes, wouldn't you, dear?" Silence.

Abigail said, "How kind of you all. I really don't want to be home alone after what we've just been through. I think I'd appreciate spending the night in town."

Sydney, barefoot, stood by in his hospital gown, holding a bag of his soiled underwear and Abigail's now ready-for-the-dump clothing. Indignantly, he said, "And just what am I supposed to do?"

Abigail looked at him then turned to ask Cliff, "Could you possibly lend Sydney some clothes?"

"Yeah, I think so. We've got some work clothes and boots in our janitor's closet."

"Perfect!"

* * *

At the Lighthouse Inn, the manager recognized the Worthingtons' arrival and recalled their disruptive, if not prurient, behavior vividly. "I have your room ready, and may I ask if your companions will be staying with us?"

Toby replied, "Yes. I believe you know Ms. Underwood, your justice of peace. She will be staying in town tonight as my guest."

"Of course, we will be honored. I'm sure we can accommodate her on the same floor with you. It's a comfortable room with an outdoor balcony. Is there anyone else in your party?"

"One more," said Toby. "Sydney Wadsworth, a prominent retired New York attorney. Please excuse his attire. We're all a bit out of uniform. It's been a very harrowing day."

"Say, isn't he the fellow that flew a plane into our covered bridge?"

"No, no. You see, he was the passenger, not the pilot."

The manager looked perplexed but agreed to provide him with a room. "I suppose he'll be your guest too?"

"Yes, of course. You needn't worry about payment. We're all members of the Brookside Country Club in New York, except Abigail, of course."

Before they could pick up their keys and retire for the evening, the familiar sound of a police car's siren closed in on the Lighthouse Inn. The manager prayed under his breath, *Please, Lord, not here.*

His prayer went unanswered. The late-model car drew up in the portico and stopped abruptly. With its lights left flashing, out stepped Chief Milo McDonald. Popping into the lobby, he said, "Relax, everyone. I'm not here to make an arrest." He smiled. "Abigail, it seems that you and your passengers are heroes."

"Us?" Abigail pointed at herself.

"Yes, the skipper of the *Leslie* filled me in. He was writing a report of the coast guard's role in the rescue. Preliminary, of course. But you and your passengers need to get down to the station and file a report too. Lucky, I knew where I could find you."

"How?"

"Cliff stopped by the town pier and told me."

"The traitor," she said, smiling. "Chief, we're exhausted and a little beat up. Couldn't this wait until morning?"

"I guess it wouldn't hurt since we already have the coast guard's account."

Speaking for the others, Abigail said, "Thank you, Milo. Best news today."

"You're celebrities now if you don't know it. It wouldn't surprise me if you all get some kind of presidential medal." Milo shook everyone's hand and congratulated each of them for their part in capturing the smugglers. "Recovering bootlegged art stolen by the Nazis is no small achievement. That makes you international celebrities too."

"That's all very nice," said Toby. "I can't speak for the others, but I could do with a little less falderal."

"Sorry, Mr. Worthington, but this is just the beginning," said Milo. "You realize that the feds will also be able to track down the war criminals that entered the country not just their loot. Once their new identities are known, well, it's just a matter of time before they're caught."

Harriet poked Toby and said, "I think we could all use a new identity."

Milo continued speaking to an attentive audience, "You know what else you've done? Surprise! You've put us on the map. The hotels and restaurants will be filled up with tourists!" Applause followed Milo as he paced around the lobby. "Port Henry owes you a humongous thank you! I'll be asking the mayor to put on a 'crackerjack' reception for your bravery." Followed by more applause, led by the exuberant manager of the Lighthouse, Milo took his leave and drove away, lights flashing and siren blaring.

A glum Toby said, "Just what we need, isn't it, Sydney? A reception. I'd forgo the whole bloody thing for a splash of scotch and a good night's sleep."

"No argument there," replied Sydney. "What in blazes am I going to wear in the morning? I've got to get out of these gawd awful bib overalls? I can't afford to be seen in public like this."

In spite of her aching ribs, Harriet laughed. "You're right, Sydney, you can't."

* * *

The foursome retired early, and for a change, the night passed quietly. Morning arrived much too early in everyone's opinion. Eyes still closed, Toby reached for his medication on the night table. Although he and Harriet shared the same bed, they both knew there was no risk of hanky-panky. Abigail woke frequently during the night to refill the ice pack on her knee; and Sydney, who had been slighted with a cramped room, slept fitfully, consumed with facing the press and their less-than-flattering cameras.

Abigail showed up first for breakfast in the Lighthouse dining room. A few minutes thereafter, Harriet and Toby arrived together, wearing a presentable change of clothes retrieved from their luggage. Seated together, Harriet inquired, "Anyone seen Sydney?"

Toby said, "I don't think Sydney wants to be seen. I don't blame him either. He might not show at all."

"That's too bad," said Abigail. "He still has to file a report. I suppose we'll have to slide the forms for his report under the door."

Harriet chimed in, "Let's give him a half hour anyway. We can have our coffee and read the papers."

The local morning paper had spread their story all over the front page. *WWII Art Smugglers Foiled by Port Henry's Justice of Peace.* Last evening, the skipper of the *Leslie* evidently pointed out to a gaggle of reporters that the captain of the *Star Splitter* and her passengers were the real heroes of the day. The waitress arrived with another round of coffee and a note from Chief Milo addressed to Abigail. It read, *You and your passengers are requested to attend a news conference at two o'clock today regarding your activities on Bloodstone Island. Please make yourselves available.*

"Rather formal for Milo, isn't it?" said Toby. "Sounds like we're invited to a cocktail party. Oh well, no matter."

Harriet glanced up from the paper and peeked out the window. "Well, well, will you look whose coming? It's Sydney at his 'best,' a three-piece suit, vest, and bow tie, strutting down the sidewalk like a peacock."

Abigail took umbrage at Harriet's remark. "Let him be. He knows who he is and how he should present himself. I respect that." No one spoke and returned to their reading.

When Sydney sat down to join the others at breakfast, Toby was the first to ask, "Sydney, your suit, we want to know how you pulled it off?"

"Not as difficult as you might think," he said haughtily. "I simply got up early, filled out my report, and walked down to the tailor shop. My credit's good with the owner, so I bought everything I needed off the rack, and here I am. The pant cuffs are a little long, but I can get them tailored back in Livermore Falls."

* * *

Waiting for the press conference to start, Sydney, Toby, and Harriet were relegated to "stand by" and listen to the media event from an adjoining lounge. The hotel manager dropped by to pour them a complimentary tea, which ostensibly was designed to show that he had forgiven Toby and Harriet over their earlier hubbub vis-à-vis their stay in the honeymoon suite. An ongoing account of their escapades filled the Portland Papers. Sydney and Toby devoured them. They both cracked a smile when they read how the coast guard had successfully impounded the *Rosarita.* Its captain was under arrest, waiting to be indicted. The list of charges certainly would send him to prison for life.

When the mayor of Port Henry arrived at the Lighthouse Inn, journalists packed the lobby like sardines in a can. The reporters grumbled anxiously for the press conference to begin. Like many others, one had driven most of the night representing the *Boston Herald.* The mayor weaved his way to a microphone where Chief Milo asked for order. Standing on a footstool, the mayor introduced Abigail and Lieutenant Commander Willis, who provided further details about their exploits and dramatic rescue. After a lifetime avoiding the limelight, Abigail fielded questions by the press and replied to them with her usual self-deprecating modesty. The spotlight made her uncomfortable. As justice of peace, she usually asked the questions.

It shocked the press and everyone, except Sydney, when those at the news conference heard that sometime during the *Leslie*'s crossing to Port Henry, Percy Pierpont had slipped out of the dispensary and jumped overboard. The skipper recalled, "After a brief search, I decided to abandon the effort and proceed on to Port Henry. A more intense search is ongoing today, but so far, to no avail."

Neither Abigail nor Willis could adequately answer a barrage of queries regarding the contents of the crates except that it was considered to be of great value. Willis said, "Their worth would have to be determined by an investigation of experts in the field of art and antiquities. Of course, another aspect is that they will need to identify the rightful owners. I anticipate this will take quite some time."

The mayor could not be restrained and seized the mike, "Remember, these people are heroes. Their actions will lead to the capture of Nazi war criminals hiding out in the United States and an opportunity to recover some of the world's greatest art treasures. Put that in print." The reporters applauded then raced to the phones to get the story into their paper.

The end of the news conference signaled to the "heroes of Bloodstone Island" to slip out the back way and beat a hasty retreat. For Abigail, it meant going home; and for the members of Brookside CC, it meant leaving scenic Port Henry behind for Livermore Falls, New York.

* * *

Outside, there were hugs and a hasty exchange of goodbyes with Abigail. Sydney lingered to embrace her and whisper words of affection that he hoped would be of comfort. Then they promised to meet again soon with the caveat that she needed time and space to think things through.

Toby, impatient, said, "Shake a leg, Sydney. We need to get a move on."

Indeed, they did. Chucking their belongings into the Mother Tucker Chocolate panel truck, they headed west, backtracking over the Port Henry Covered Bridge, taking the same path that Toby and Harriet had taken earlier. Without a seat, it was a rough ride in the back for Sydney, especially with Harriet at the wheel. They stopped in New Hampshire to exchange the truck for Harriet's Lincoln Cabriolet. The rest of the journey passed without incident, and they arrived unscathed the following day in Livermore Falls.

Before settling in at their respective residences, Toby and Sydney agreed to meet the following day at the club.

Chapter 28

The Day Following

At the far end of a broad lawn facing the clubhouse, Toby and Sydney flopped down in a pair of padded Adirondack chairs. The weather was warm and amenable to relaxation. The late afternoon sun spread long shadows across the course, following the golfers back to the nineteenth hole in the clubhouse.

Toby said, "Well, old partner, it's good to be in familiar surroundings again. Great chairs, yes? Trouble is you can't get up and out of them even when you put your nose beyond your toes."

"Right, Toby, they're like a love affair. Easy to get into, but hard as the devil to get out of."

"You're not thinking of breaking off with Abigail, are you? I've never seen you so crackers over a woman."

"I'm not crackers. Perhaps I didn't mention that I invited her to come back here with me. It's just there's quite a list of things she has to do in Port Henry before she can break away, like my court case for flying into the covered bridge. Remember. Damn, come to think of it, I'll probably have to testify in Port Henry, maybe not. Maybe I can just provide depositions. My attorney will advise me. You know him, Horace Bottomly."

"Really? Why do you need him? You are an attorney."

"In the first place, Toby, I'm not the kind of attorney I need. Besides, I'm busy, and I really can't afford myself. The town should jump at the deal I offered them. To put a point on it, they'll be getting off cheap buying Heck a new Piper Cub."

"Strange," said Toby. "I thought you would welcome an opportunity to have a 'cozy' with Abigail."

"Of course, I would. I've done a lot of thinking lately since our incursion into Maine. Abigail weighs heavy on my mind. If you haven't noticed, women like her don't come along every day. If she doesn't recuse herself from my case and come over here in a week or two, I'm damn well going to Port Henry and bring her back. It's really the first time I've had, you know, feelings. If I've got a chance with her, I'm not letting her out of my sight again."

"Sydney, I didn't realize you could be so possessive." Toby chuckled. "I must admit she is a corker."

Sydney squirmed uncomfortably and opted to direct the conversation in Toby's direction. "I'm not getting any younger, and for that matter, neither are you. Now that we're back in civilization, how are you and Harriet getting on? Enlighten me, Toby."

"We're fine. I think. Yesterday afternoon, we chatted and decided to hold off on the divorce for the time being, anyway until things settle out. She's had a pretty rough go of it."

"You're not going soft on her, are you? Before you went to Maine, you referred to her as the old trout." Sydney's dagger dug deeper than a superficial wound.

"You know, Sydney, as well as I do just how obnoxious and demanding she can be when she's in the driver's seat. Then whenever her back's to the wall, she turns on the tears and whimpers as if she's totally helpless. That given, in between those two extremes, I find her to be quite agreeable."

Sydney sat upright. "Well, well, does this mean you'll be moving in with Harriet? You are married?"

Toby leaned over and said, "Really, Sydney, I haven't gone completely daft." He took a deep breath and paused to relight his pipe with the last match in his book. Failing, he mumbled a mild curse and waved at Simone on the clubhouse porch to come over. "She'll have matches on her."

Sydney sunk back in his chair and said, "Toby, why don't you get one of those wind-proof pipe lighters?"

"Because they're more trouble than they're worth. Besides, I wouldn't have the pleasure of watching Simone sashay over here. What I've been trying to say is that my relationship with Harriet is on hold. She's offered to let me live in her connecting guest suite and use her garage in the summer season. That's quite attractive compared with the second floor at the Maple Leaf Inn. You know, convenient to the club and all. However, I have to think of the impression it would have on the membership, being that we'll get divorced before I move in."

"Toby, old dear, the women in the clubhouse already have a clear impression of your relationship with Harriet, which is that you've been seeing each other quite regularly."

"But, but," he stammered, "that's not true."

"Makes no difference, Toby. Just the perception that you're having an affair with Harriet makes it true."

"Ridiculous. How do you know?"

"I'm sorry, Toby. I feel it's my business to know, and I have ears. So you might as well take her up on the offer." Sydney paused. "Provided you're satisfied she didn't murder her first two husbands."

"So you really don't mind if I do? I thought you might since you went to all the trouble to stop our marriage."

"That was then. Think nothing of it, Toby. I'm satisfied that her offer is well intentioned. Another thing that crossed my mind today is that we're damn lucky that Governor Dewey decided not to drop by."

"Indeed," Toby replied. "We don't exactly look like a great reception committee."

Their broad-brimmed white panama hats and dark glasses could hardly disguise the state of their battle-scarred physical disrepair. "Don't worry, Toby. Dewey's a shoe-in for the presidency with or without my endorsement."

"Quite, you know, I don't like being a prig, but I never did like the idea of his hands pawing all over my cannon."

Simone arrived bearing an envelope on a silver tray. "Bon jour, gentlemen." She bent over to deliver a telegram to Sydney. "Oh, Mr. Wadsworth, you poor dear, and you too, Mr. Worthington. What on earth happened to you?"

"Nothing worth mentioning," replied Sydney. "It would take too much time to explain right now, perhaps another day. It should be in the papers anyway." Simone helped Toby light his pipe, while Sydney fussed with the envelope. A telegram fell out onto his lap. Glancing at it, he remarked with a broad grin, "Toby, try not to laugh. It's from the governor of Maine, Horace Hildreth. Let's just guess the contents and give it the old heave ho?"

"Oh, please open it, Mr. Wadsworth," said Simone. "If you don't open it, I might get in trouble, and you wouldn't want that, would you?"

"Certainly not, Simone. Why don't you read it for us?"

Always inquisitive and anxious to improve her English, she snatched up the telegram and began, "**MR SYDNEY WADSWORTH : MISS ABIGAIL UNDERWOOD JP : MR. MRS TOBY WORTHINGTON**." Surprised, she stepped back and said in a whisper, "Ohhh, and who is Mrs. Worthington?"

"Oh, that's Harriet," said Toby, "you know, Widow Bartholomew? But our arrangement is only temporary. The marriage was never consummated."

Simone couldn't resist. "May I ask how temporary?"

"Three days, although it might last a few more."

Sydney interrupted to break off the conversation, "Simone, Toby is starting to prattle on and needs his rest."

Simone said, "I should think so," stepping further back. The nuptial news jarred her usually shockproof persona. "I think I better leave and let you read it."

Sydney continued reading the telegram, "**CONGRATULATIONS: PLEASE ATTEND RECEPTION IN YOUR HONOR: COMMEMORATIVE PLAQUE: HEROISM DEFEATING INTERNATIONAL WAR CRIMINALS: MAINE, U.S. PROUD: FORMAL INVITATION TO FOLLOW: GOV HILDRETH.**"

"What do you say, Toby? I would just as soon go to the movie house and see us on the newsreel. In either case, I'm quite satisfied to stay home."

"Agreed." Toby hailed Simone, "Oh, Simone, when you get back to the clubhouse, have the locker room chap bring us two Singapore slings. Sun's over the yardarm."

The End

Edwards Brothers Malloy
Thorofare, NJ USA
January 12, 2015